Forgotten Memories

by
Jansina

Savannah,
Blessings!
Jansina

*Photography by: Jaymes Grossman, my best friend
who will always be my favorite brother*

Cover photo of: Anthony and Hannah

Thank you!

Forgotten Memories

Rivershore Publishing

ISBN: 1463624352
ISBN-13: 978-1463624354

Acknowledgments

Thank you to all those who have encouraged me in many different ways over the years, and to those who gave their time to read and critique this. Thank you especially to my family, for putting up with my "need" to write and still, somehow, remaining supportive.

Chapter 1

Tuesday, September 8, 1953
Ella Mitchell

"So, um...this is awkward, but...that's my grandma you're sitting on."

I stared at the young man, curious what he could mean. A half smile inched across his face as he motioned to the headstone I was leaning against. I gasped and stood up.

"I am so sorry," I said. "I didn't realize—I mean, I should have realized—I just—I'm sorry."

The man chuckled. "Told you it was awkward," he said, the skin around his deep brown eyes crinkling at the corners as he continued to smile. "I'm Joe."

"Ella," I said, tucking my notebook under my arm and shaking his hand.

"So, Ella...do you often come here and sit on others' graves?" He pushed his dark hair away from his eyes as he waited for my response.

I sighed. "You are not making this any less uncomfortable."

"I'm honestly curious."

"Okay." I hesitated, and glanced at the cemetery, realizing how strange this must seem. "Then yes, I do. I guess I didn't really think of it as...*that*...until today."

"Ah, yes," Joe's eyes shrank as his smile grew, teasing. "Until today you were able to think of headstones as the backs of very uncomfortable benches."

I blushed, and picked some loose twigs and leaves off my skirt.

"Why do you like it here?" Joe looked at the other graves in the cemetery; trying, I assumed, to hide his disgust with the scene.

"It's peaceful," I said. "Most people won't bug you in a place like this."

"Right. Just me."

I smiled; at least he admitted it. My eyes wandered to the gravestone I'd been leaning on as I searched for a new conversation topic. *Margaret Anne Blake.* "Margie was your grandmother?"

Joe nodded.

"She was a sweet lady...we miss her. I'm sorry." Margie's son, though not related by blood to any but his daughter, was an 'uncle' to the entire town. She had been our 'grandma.'

He glanced at me, his smile gone, then turned back to the headstone. "I wish I could have known her."

"You didn't?"

Joe shook his head. "Not well. I met her a couple times, but I was young. My family lived in Afton." He paused, noting my confused look; I didn't recognize the town. "New York," he clarified. "It's hard to visit people often when they're over a thousand miles away."

"Ah," I said, unable to think of a better response. *Joe must be here to visit Margaret and her father.* "So, you're related to Uncle Bruce somehow."

Joe turned to me, a confused look now on *his* face. "He's my uncle," he said, slowly. "I didn't realize I had other relatives here. It's good to meet you, cousin."

I blushed again. "Oh, I'm not related. Everyone here calls him Uncle Bruce," I smiled. "That's just the way his personality is."

Joe nodded. "Yes, I can see him enjoying the title." He pointed to the notebook I had tucked under my arm. "Are you a student?"

I shook my head. "I finished a few years ago." I bit my lip, wondering how much I should share with this strange man. *He's a relative of Margaret, he can't be that bad.* "I'm writing."

"You're writing...for fun?" The concept seemed foreign to him.

"Yeah."

He raised an eyebrow, but seemed interested. "What are you writing about?"

I shifted awkwardly. I wasn't used to or comfortable discussing my writing. "Nothing much." I glanced at my watch; time for work. "Gotta split. Later."

Joe nodded and I started the walk to work. A moment later he caught up to me. "Wait, Ella," he said. "Can I come with you?"

"I'm just going to The Diner."

"What a coincidence; I'm just going there, too. I'd love to accompany you, if you don't mind."

"Um," I glanced in that direction, "sure."

Joe matched my step. "Margaret talks about you a lot. It's great to finally get to meet you."

I shrugged. "I guess she's mentioned a cousin too."

"Good to see I've made such an impression." Joe chuckled.

I glanced at my watch again and quickened my pace.

Apparently unable to walk in silence, Joe said, "Uncle Bruce isn't very creative with names, is he?"

I let out a frustrated breath. "What do you mean?"

"Just that 'The Diner' is pretty much the most boring thing he could call his restaurant."

"It's always been good enough for *us*," I said defensively.

"Oh—I wasn't—" Joe grew quiet as The Diner came into view. "That's it, right?"

I nodded.

"I was here when I was a little boy. Things look so much smaller when you grow up."

Did he have *nothing* good to say about Backus? Well, I didn't, either, but living there my whole life had earned me the right to criticize it.

A good friend of mine, a young man with short, curly brown hair and a hint of a beard, was walking toward us. "Ella!" Nicholas waved to me.

I smiled in response.

"I thought I might catch you," he continued, walking in pace with us now. He turned to Joe. "I'm Nicholas."

"Joe."

"Oh! Margaret said you'd be coming. Nice to meet you."

I glanced at him, confused. Margaret hadn't mentioned anything to *me*.

"Actually, we've met," Joe said. "It's okay; my face is easy to forget. Plus we were only around five at the time." Joe smiled. "I came when I was ten, too, but didn't see you on that trip."

Nicholas laughed. "Well, I don't remember you... but it's good to see you again anyway."

"I'm assuming since you have no memory of me, at least I wasn't your sworn enemy. Or perhaps I

4

was, and you have simply blocked me from your mind." He tilted his head at him, comically.

Nicholas chuckled.

Joe pulled open the door of The Diner.

I glanced at the two of them. "Come inside?" I offered. "It's cold. I'll get you coffee."

"You know I can't stand that stuff." Nicholas scrunched his nose in disgust.

Joe froze in the doorway and stared at him. "You," he paused, as if the information was too much to take in at once, "you don't like coffee?" His mouth fell open in shock.

I giggled. "I love it, and someday I will change his position on it as well."

"Not a chance," Nicholas said with a smirk. "I'd come in though, if I could. I was actually on my way to a job!" He grinned at my surprised expression.

"Really?"

"Hey," Uncle Bruce called from inside, "in or out."

Joe's cheeks turned pink and he let the door of The Diner shut.

Nicholas had been looking for a job for at least three years. He wanted to be a mechanic. In a town as small as Backus, that was not a lucrative career. He could have been successful in a big city, but here most people simply walked and very few owned cars.

"A gig," he repeated. "There's a car that needs fixing." As if I would forget what his dream job was.

"That's wonderful," I said, then hesitantly glanced at The Diner.

"Right. Go. Wish me luck!"

"You got it," I said, and Joe and I went inside.

Uncle Bruce looked up and smiled. "Good; you've met my nephew. Sorry for scolding you before, Joe. It was getting cold in here."

I smiled and walked behind the counter. The rest of The Diner was empty. "Slow day today?"

"A bit." He looked at me sideways, a twinkle in his eye. "I'm sure your Eric will be in at some point."

"I'm sure," I mumbled.

Joe glanced at me, expecting an explanation.

"He's not my—anything," I said quickly. "He just wishes he was. But he's the same with every girl, so I can't even be flattered."

"Ah," Joe said, nodding. "I'm guessing those guys are a bit more prevalent in the city than they are here."

"People here have more self-respect than to act like that," I said, then reconsidered the statement. "Well, except Eric."

"I suppose it is a bit easier to act that way when you're not likely to come across the same people very often," Joe said. "Only a handful of people will know you're a flirtatious twerp. I'm guessing that's not the case here."

I stifled a laugh. "I thought you said you'd been here before."

"Ten-year-old boys don't tend to notice that kind of thing."

Good point. "Well, everyone knows just about anything there is to know about everyone—and they make up what they don't." I rolled my eyes. "What was it the father in *Pride and Prejudice* said? Something about how our whole purpose is to make sport for our neighbors and laugh at them when we will? Yeah. He was describing Backus."

Joe laughed. "It sounds wonderful."

I raised an eyebrow.

"Well, I've always enjoyed Austen's novels."

I sighed. He'd completely missed the point.

The bell over the door jingled, and my thirteen-year-old sister smiled from the doorway. "You forgot your snack," Linda said. "Thought you might want it." She placed a small paper bag on the counter and boosted herself onto one of the chairs, glancing at Joe but not acknowledging him. "Can I have a milkshake?"

"Sure sis." I took the ice cream out of the freezer.

6

Linda hopped off the chair and wandered behind the counter.

"Hey!" I said, shooing her out. "You're a customer. Act like one."

Linda giggled, undeterred. "Can I pour it in?"

I turned to Uncle Bruce.

"Okay, Linda," he agreed. "Anything for my little basketball star."

I poured the milk and flavoring in with the scoops of ice cream.

Linda frowned. "Milkshakes take too long. Next time I'm ordering plain old ice cream."

"Why?" Uncle Bruce asked. "You got somewhere to be?"

Linda shrugged. "Michael said he'd teach me some new basketball tricks when he got home today."

"What a nice older brother," Uncle Bruce commented.

Linda nodded, and turned to Joe again. "Who are you?"

Joe, who had been smiling throughout this entire exchange, reached his hand across the counter to greet her. "I'm Joe."

Linda shook his hand, accepting the gesture as an invitation of friendship. "Hi!"

I handed the pitcher to her. "Here."

Linda began pouring the milkshake into her cup.

The bell rang again. Mother stood in the doorway, hands on her hips.

Uffda.

Linda sipped a little guiltily at her milkshake.

"You left without a word, Linda."

"I came to see Ella."

"You need to tell me when you are leaving and where you are going."

What's going to happen if she doesn't? Afraid the neighbors will invite her in for tea? It's not like she's a little girl anymore.

7

I held my tongue. Mother already disproved of nearly every choice I made, including working in The Diner. A woman's place was in the home; behind the stove; in front of the mirror. Always looking pretty and keeping things nice. No, thank you.

"You must be Mrs. Mitchell," Joe said, again offering his hand. "I'm Bruce's nephew, Joe."

Mother nodded acknowledgment of him but didn't complete the handshake. She turned her attention back to Linda.

Joe stubbornly continued. "Mrs. Mitchell, what is your absolute favorite thing to do around here?"

She looked at him with a slight frown of annoyance.

"I'm going to be staying for a while," he calmly explained, "so I would love to learn what everyone does for fun."

"I see," Mother said. "Well I don't do much that you would enjoy. I'm sure Ella can tell you the things kids your age are doing. I will say, though, you should come to the gala on Friday. That will introduce you to most everyone. And of course you will come to church on Sunday."

"Of course." Joe smiled. "Margaret's mentioned the galas. I've been looking forward to the chance to attend."

Mother nodded and abruptly turned back to Linda.

Linda had been slurping away at her milkshake, grateful for Mother's short distraction. She now turned sheepishly back to Mother, straw still in her mouth.

"Leave that thing and get home right this instant. You know better than to leave without asking, and I'll not have you rewarded for it."

Linda looked on the verge of tears, but set the milkshake on the counter in obedience. If Mother hadn't been standing right there I would have given her a hug and smuggled the treat home with her somehow.

Mother walked out of The Diner and stood by the door, arms crossed, waiting for Linda to follow.

"Don't let her upset you," I said softly. "You're stronger than that. Now go show that basketball how it's done."

Linda smiled a little and hurried out the door.

Uncle Bruce looked at the clock. "Ella, do you think you can show Joe how things work? I'm going to the back room to tinker with some things."

I glanced at Joe. "Um," I said, confused, "Joe will be working here?"

"He didn't tell you that?" Uncle Bruce raised an eyebrow at Joe and chuckled. "Probably too enchanted with the charm of Backus to think of mentioning it."

Joe smiled. "I'm helping out in exchange for room and board."

"At least for now," Uncle Bruce said. "He may find that I'm too stuffy for him to handle working with." He winked. "So you'll teach him the basics?"

"Of course, Uncle Bruce."

Joe walked behind the counter as Uncle Bruce smiled and went to his tinkering room in the back of The Diner.

"Okay..." I said, considering where to start. "What do you know how to do here?"

"Nothing."

Great.

"Oh, wait," he said, "I lied. I do know what *this* thing is." He pointed to the toaster.

"Swell. When someone asks for toast and nothing else, I'll know just who to turn to."

Joe chuckled. "What does this do?" He picked up a contraption Uncle Bruce had discovered.

"It looks pretty and starts conversations," I said. "If you find another use for it, let us know."

Joe put it down.

"I'll show you how to run the cash register." *He can't ruin customers' food if he's only handling their money.*

He stood next to me and I explained how to use it. With only as many keys as there are numbers and a price list taped to the counter, it wasn't difficult.

Once again, the bell over the door rang.

"Good," I said, stepping away from the register to give Joe more room. "You can practice."

Eric leaned his elbows on the counter, smirking at me. "What's good today, baby?"

"Same things that always are," I said, barely resisting the urge to frown and step away. "Joe will help you."

Eric glanced at Joe, clearly curious but unwilling to initiate the conversation.

Joe reached his hand out in greeting. "That's me: the ever-helpful Joe. And you are?"

"Confused."

"At the risk of offending you before giving you a better first impression, I am very sorry your parents weren't more kind in their name choices."

Eric rolled his eyes.

Joe gave a quirky half smile and explained that he was a relative of Uncle Bruce and would be helping out for a while. "So, it's good to meet you, Confused."

"Name's Eric." He pulled out a cigarette and lit it.

Joe glanced at me, his eyebrows slightly raised, then turned back to him. "Well, what can I get you, Eric?"

"Hamburger."

I pointed to the cigarette. "Eric, you know Uncle Bruce's rules."

"Yeah, no smokin' in The Diner, but you can do it right outside."

"Exactly. Put that out, or take it outside," I said, crossing my arms. I didn't mind the smoke, and sometimes I'd light up too, though I only enjoyed the first few puffs. Still, it was disrespectful to do it indoors when Uncle Bruce had made it clear he didn't allow it.

Eric let out a smoke-filled breath and smiled. "Seems to me Uncle Bruce ain't here to stop me."

Joe frowned. "Eric, listen to Ella."

Eric took a long drag of his cigarette, right as Uncle Bruce stepped out of the back room. *Maybe he smelled the smoke.*

Uncle Bruce frowned. "Now Eric, I *know* you know my rule. Put that disgusting thing out, or I will."

Eric snickered. "It ain't disgustin', Uncle Bruce. Never tried it, did ya?"

"I have no interest in filling my body with smoke. If the lot of you had any sense at all, you wouldn't either." He reached across the counter to take the cigarette from Eric, but Eric dodged his grasp.

He took another puff of the cigarette, and started coughing.

With Eric momentarily distracted, Uncle Bruce took possession of the cigarette and brought it to the ashtray outside.

Eric continued to cough, and his eyes began watering. I glanced at Uncle Bruce, who had returned to his position behind the counter. He was holding back laughter. Joe handed Eric a glass of water. Eventually the coughing subsided, but Uncle Bruce's laughter only grew.

"Next time," Uncle Bruce said between chuckles, "maybe you'll listen to my rules."

Eric shrugged, though he was clearly embarrassed. "Still waitin' on that burger," he muttered.

I pulled the meat out of the fridge and put it in a frying pan.

"Would you like coffee with that?" Joe asked.

Eric gave him an annoyed look.

Joe shrugged. "I'll take that as a no. Fries?"

He was clearly miffed. "Said a hamburger," he said, "and meant a hamburger."

11

"So that's a no to any ice cream, too," Joe said. He typed the price for a hamburger into the register like I'd taught him and told Eric the total.

Because Uncle Bruce sometimes stayed late to precook the meat and shorten the customer's wait time, the burger was done quickly. I put the meat in a bun and slid the plate to Eric.

Uncle Bruce shook his head, still very amused by Eric's coughing fit, and returned to his inventions in the back room.

"So Ellie—"

"Ella," I said, annoyed. *Why does Eric insist on calling me names that are not my own?*

Eric ignored the correction. "Let's go to the gala together on Friday."

"I'm going with Nicholas. We always go together; you know that."

"Yeah, but it ain't like the two of you are a couple. You could go with someone else if ya wanted to."

"I happen to enjoy going with a friend."

Eric had hardly touched his burger.

"Are you finished eating? I can get you a 'to go' box if you need it."

"Why? You kicking me out? Want me to tell yer boss what lousy service you're giving?"

Yes, there's the way to a girl's heart. Threaten her. I shrugged. "You didn't seem hungry," I said, forcing a sweet smile.

Eric shrugged. "See ya dolly." He pushed his plate toward me and walked out.

I slid the barely eaten hamburger into the trash. "Now you get to learn how to wash a dish," I said to Joe, unable to keep from giggling.

Joe looked at me warily. I'd been expecting at least a smile.

"Don't tell me you don't know how to wash a dish?"

"I do. Does Eric come in here a lot?"

I shrugged. "Every day."

"And you don't like it."

"Aw, was I that obvious?" I put the plate in the sink and started running water over it.

Joe frowned a little.

"I don't see how anyone *would* like it. But, really," I said quickly, "it's not a big deal."

Joe nodded and took the plate from me. "Believe it or not, I *have* washed a dish or two before."

"Well that's a relief." I grabbed the washrag before he took over the sink, and started wiping the crumbs off the counter.

Joe washed and dried the dish and put it back in the cupboard. "So...are you going to teach me how to cook, or am I just the cashier-and-clean-up guy?"

"Grab an apron and wash your hands."

Joe bowed low, said, "Yes, your majesty," and obeyed.

I giggled.

He learned a few of the dishes we sold, and could use them to figure out others. Fries, for example, were cooked the same way chicken nuggets and cheese curds were. Joe pointed that out, and saved me teaching time.

He was a surprisingly fast learner; much quicker than I had been. Who decided women were the ones meant to stay in and cook, anyway? Uncle Bruce and Joe were both better at it than I was. Mother wasn't a great cook, either, but you had to pretend she was if you didn't want a scolding or, years earlier, a spanking.

I glanced at the clock: closing time. I started the general tasks, commenting every once in a while about what I was doing and why it needed to be done.

Joe started sweeping. "When do you work again?"

"Tomorrow. I work every afternoon, and all day on Saturdays. We're closed on Sundays because nearly everyone is at church and there is no point in being open."

He nodded. "I like working with you."

I backed up. "If you are flirting with me I swear I'll—"

"Hey, don't flatter yourself. I barely know you."

"Exactly." I frowned and looked around The Diner; everything was done.

Joe told Uncle Bruce and brought our coats from the back room. He helped me into mine.

"Um, thanks." I'd never had someone help with my coat, and it was obvious by how I handled it. I somehow managed to miss the second arm, and then missed it again when Joe was trying to maneuver it to a place that would make it easier for me. The experience was embarrassing.

As Joe closed the door of The Diner behind us, my feet found what I'm sure was the town's only patch of ice, and within seconds I was in a seated position.

The little yelp that had escaped during my fall caught not only Joe's attention, but also that of the three other people on the street. *Perfect. I needed a sore bottom and bruised pride on top of everything else today.* It seemed I had no choice but to embarrass myself in front of this guy. The sooner he headed to wherever he would be going next, the better it would be for my ego.

Joe offered a hand to help me back up. "Are you okay?" he asked, though he was clearly holding back laughter.

Jerk. "I'm fine."

"I did the same exact thing earlier today. Except I didn't have witnesses."

"Lucky you," I muttered.

Joe frowned. "I guess that didn't really make you feel any better."

"Not really."

I pointed Joe in the direction off Uncle Bruce's house and went home, glad to be free of him for a while.

Since newcomers were uncommon in Backus (in fact, I had trouble remembering even just one), Joe occupied most of my thoughts on the walk home.

He's probably a good guy, I told myself. *After all, Uncle Bruce clearly approves of him.*

I valued his opinion possibly more than that of anyone else. He was one of the few people who had actually left Backus at one point. Of course, he'd come back, which should tell you how little sanity he had left.

But at least he'd made it out for a time. That was more than most people in Backus had, including my parents.

My pace had slowed to a meandering stroll, so I sped up again, rubbing my hands together for warmth. It was still autumn but it was already cold enough for sweaters, coats, and mittens, as if it had been winter for months—or at least it seemed like it was. If this was spring, and we had just survived six months of winter, this weather would feel like summer had come early.

Shows you how crazy Minnesotans can be.

I reached my house, waved to Michael and Linda as I walked past them playing basketball in the driveway, and went to my room to write...and think. About Joe.

He seemed clingy. By his own admittance I was one of the only people he knew here. That probably meant he would hang on me all during the gala on Friday. I'd just have to find some other young lady to pawn him off on.

That wouldn't be hard. Half the girls in Backus were desperate for a husband. And even I had to admit: Joe was a handsome young man.

Chapter 2

Wednesday, November 12, 2008
Jane Blake

"Oh, this is such a lovely room."

I jumped a little, dropped the pile of notebooks I'd been transferring from the bed to a shelf, and looked in surprise at the intruder. She seemed to be around my age, or a little younger: fifteen or sixteen. She had curly dark hair, and was a complete stranger. *Maybe Grandma Blake knows her?*

"You probably aren't used to having weird people just walk into your house," the girl said, with a smile that revealed dimples in her cheeks. "At least, not ones you've never met." She giggled. "Actually...I'm not used to that, either. I wonder if that's something you *can* get used to." She seemed to ponder that idea, but only for a moment. "Even if it happened a lot, I imagine it would always be just a little unnerving. It doesn't happen a lot here; don't worry. We're friendly here in Backus, but we do respect privacy. Well," she glanced around the room, as if suddenly aware that she had waltzed into it unasked, "usually."

"Um," I shifted uncomfortably. "Hi?"

She took my greeting as an invitation to step farther into my room. "Your sister let me in. I hope that's okay. I heard there was a girl my age here and decided to help you unpack." She motioned to the pile of clothes on my bed. "Looks like we're tackling the closet first." She picked up one of my hangers. "Wanna hand me a shirt?"

"Well," I hesitated. "Uh." *Wow, this is awkward.* "Who are you?"

"Oh!" She laughed. "I'm Rosie; I live next door. You're Jane, right? I think that's what your sister said."

I nodded and picked up the notebooks I'd dropped, glad for the slight distraction.

Rosie lifted a shirt off the pile and put it on a hanger, oblivious to my continued discomfort. "Where did you live before you came here?"

I tried to relax as I rearranged my bookshelf, then turned back to her. "We were in a suburb of Minneapolis."

"Hey!" She spun around to face me, her eyes wide with excitement.

So much for keeping a calm demeanor. *This girl is insane.*

Rosie giggled at my wary expression, then stepped closer and nodded knowingly. "You're related to LeeLee Johnson, aren't you?"

I backed away from her close examination, but told her LeeLee was my great aunt.

Rosie smiled, and tilted her chin up slightly, as if she was proud of herself. "You look like her. Well," she said, stepping closer again. "You look like a younger version of her. You have her lovely blue eyes." She nodded.

"Um, thanks." I used folding a shirt as an excuse to look away.

Rosie, too, picked up a shirt. "LeeLee is wonderful. How many siblings do you have?"

"Three," I said, grateful she no longer felt the need to stare at me. "Two sisters, one brother."

"I met your sister." She paused, and studied the shirt with a focused furrow of her brow. "Maggie, right?"

I nodded.

"What are the others' names?"

"Kathryn—we call her Katty, and Aiden."

"And Aiden you call Doggy."

I looked at her, confused.

She smiled. "Sorry; bad joke." She held a pair of my pants up to her legs. Since I was at least three inches taller, they were too long, but she still grinned. "Cute." She started folding them. "Do you like writing?" She didn't wait for a response. "We have a newspaper here called the *Backus Blab*. I write a fake advice column for fairy tale characters. Sometimes I write about things that happen in the community, but the other authors like that more than I do. You should write with us!"

I smiled. "Maybe."

"Maybe," she mimicked, raising an amused eyebrow. "Can't get more noncommittal than that. Could be that you just don't like writing, though. Is that the case? My twin hates writing with a passion. I know it isn't for everyone. I just happen to really— *really*—enjoy it."

I had to smile at her ramblings. "I like it when it isn't for school."

"Oh good," she said, grinning. "I do love Bev in spite of his dislike of it, but we would get along so much more if he would just *try* writing once in a while."

"Bev?"

"Oh!" Rosie giggled. "Here I go, assuming you know everyone like I do. Bevin is my twin. You must meet him! He's very quiet, though, I must warn you. Hardly talks at all. Probably even less than you do! Ooh, pretty," Rosie held up a shirt, and then started folding it. "I know my talkativeness is part of why you're so silent. Plus, you probably find it weird that a stranger is going through your clothes without so much as permission from yourself." She set the shirt down and looked at me, her brow creasing in concern. "Does this bother you? I only came to help, but please—if you're freaked out and want me to leave, do tell me."

I laughed. "I appreciate the help," I said, putting a final shirt on a hanger and tossing the empty box into the hall.

"Okay." She looked around the room and saw there were still several boxes to unpack. "What's next?"

I shrugged. The bed was put together and the sheets were on it, my bookshelves were set up, with my few treasured books arranged in them, and my bedside table had the lamp sitting on it. Still, the room looked bare. "Knickknacks, I suppose."

"I love knickknacks!" Rosie bounced a little in excitement. "They tell so much about a person. The kind of things people like to have sitting out around their house, the amount of things they keep, compared to what they get rid of," she trailed off, distracted by a small snow globe she'd pulled out of one of the boxes. "So pretty," she said softly, and placed it on the dresser. "Um, what was I saying?"

"Something about knickknacks?"

"Oh yes!" she grinned. "You learn immediately just how sentimental or practical people are, and what they care about. I'm so glad I get to see yours. I want to start getting to know you."

She started lifting out my figurines from the box I'd moved to the bed, and commented on each of them. "I'm just going to lay them out on the bed here, and let you arrange them on your shelves and such however you'd like. Oh, this little doll is so sweet. What's the story with her?"

"Um," I glanced at the doll she was referring to, and raised an eyebrow in puzzlement. "The story?"

"Where did you get her? What was the situation? How long have you had her, and why are you keeping her now?"

"Oh." I had to think about it for a moment. "That was a gift from my grandma. I don't know, I just think it's cute."

Without warning, Rosie changed the subject. "Are you named after that author?"

I looked at her, confused.

"You know," she said. "She shares your name. I haven't read any of her books, yet, but I plan to. I watched the new *Pride & Prejudice* when it first came out. Have you seen that?"

"I've seen both versions," I said, finally realizing which author she was referring to, "as well as all the other books that have been made into movies. I don't think I'm named after her though, and that's fine with me. I read one of her books but just couldn't get into it. Cousins marrying cousins is just a little too weird."

Rosie nodded, her face set in an understanding look. "I'm curious now, though. Why would you watch so many of the movies if you didn't actually enjoy her as an author?"

"Blame Katty. My sister absolutely loves her writing."

"Ah, that makes sense. Austen was always a bit too old fashioned for me. But maybe if I tried reading her again I would actually enjoy it."

I shrugged.

She lifted a small ring from the bottom of the box. "Oh my," she said, her tone growing reverent. "Jane, for this one I *must* learn the story. And if you tell me it's just a ring you found at a garage sale, I will stick my tongue out at you," she said, as if it was a horrible threat.

"I usually prefer thrift stores to garage sales, so I would never tell you that," I said, smirking. "But I don't actually know where this ring is from—or how it got mixed in with my things." I looked at it, curious, and shook my head. "I've never seen it before."

"Ooh!" Rosie said, excited. "It's a mystery ring! Maybe it's magical. Have you read *The Lord of the Rings*?" She paused just long enough for me to nod in response. "It could be like Frodo's ring. Only prettier."

"So, like one of the elves' rings."

Rosie stared at me for a second, then pulled me into a hug. "Jane Blake—I like you."

I laughed a little awkwardly and she released me. I shrugged. "It's probably just one of mom's."

"Well you can think that if you want. I prefer to see it as a beautiful mystery. I mean—would you look at this ring?" She shoved it into my hand. "This isn't the kind of ring people just set aside and forget about. There is a story behind it. There is a meaning to its design, maybe some magic in it," her voice trailed off and she stared into the distance, presumably imagining the great adventures this ring had been on. Suddenly, she turned and put her hands on my shoulders. "Jane, you're going to help me find out what makes it special."

"Okay," I said, but the skeptical look on my face clearly showed how strange I thought her determination was. "I'll ask my mom about it when she gets back from the store."

Rosie shook her head and crossed her arms.

"I *shouldn't* ask my mom?"

"No, go ahead and ask her. But you're going about this entirely wrong."

"Sorry," I said, my voice dripping with sarcasm, "I didn't realize the direct and quick route was wrong."

Rosie smiled. "It's not what you're planning to do that's wrong. It's your whole approach to it. You're looking at it as just a ring and not a big deal."

I set the ring on my bedside table, hinting at my desire to move the conversation to another topic. "It *is* just a ring and not a big deal."

Rosie's lips jutted out in pout-like frustration. "It *isn't* just a ring to the person it belongs to; I guarantee it. If I'm wrong, you can—I don't know—make me do something I don't particularly want to. I just *know* there is a story to this—a whole history filled with emotions."

I shrugged.

"Really?" Rosie groaned and dramatically collapsed on the bed, shifting my knickknacks but surprisingly not landing on them or pushing any off. She tilted her head up to look at me.

"What?" I asked, ignoring her theatrics and switching the order of two cat figurines.

"I have to be even more passionate about this to get you on my side?"

"I'm on your side," I said, rolling my eyes.

"Doesn't seem like it. Look at this ring. Really look at it." Rosie lifted it off my table and handed it to me once more. She pointed at it once it was in my palm. "Tell me that ring doesn't scream 'special' to you."

I raised an eyebrow at her.

She motioned again to the ring in my hand.

I rolled my eyes again but looked at it. I did have to admit that it was pretty. Not the typical large diamond ring everyone seems to want, but it had its own form of beauty. This ring did have jewels: two sapphires—or at least blue stones, since I couldn't tell if they were real—but those were not the focus of it.

Small pearls in clusters of five formed two flowers, using the little blue stones as the centers. The silver along the edges of the ring had designs etched into it: swirling patterns that were only slightly noticeable even when tilted to the right angle. All together, it formed a lovely and unique ring.

Still, I could see nothing magical about it. As intriguing as it was, mom probably had picked it up at some cheap store and had forgotten about it. Thinking about it logically, I became more certain that's what had happened.

The real mystery here was how it had gotten mixed with my things.

Continuing to debate the origin and importance of the ring wasn't worth my time, though. Rosie wasn't going to back down, and I didn't care either way. "So, you write for the local newspaper?"

She nodded energetically. "It's fun. We print it off every other week and pass it out to the people who are interested, but nobody really takes it seriously. I mean could something with 'blab' in the name ever be seen as truthfully portraying Backus?" She tilted her head, and gave a quirky half smile.

I smiled too. "I suppose not."

"Half the 'facts' in it are made up by the authors. And the news is so unreliable," Rosie shook her head, frowning a little. "Really, the only way to learn the truth is to talk directly to the people involved. Aside from a few of the authors, when we hear about something, we just write it; sometimes without even warning the person the article is about."

I made a face.

"Oh dear," Rosie said, "I'm giving you a bad impression of it, aren't I?"

"It just seems like your newspaper is nothing more than gossip in print form."

Rosie was quiet for a moment. "Yeah," she said at last, "I suppose it is kind of like that. See, Jane, this is why we need you on our team."

"To be another gossip?"

"No, silly! To point out when the rest of us are being like that, and to help us change. I've always felt the *Backus Blab* could be great if people would give it more of an effort. Well, and maybe if we changed the name. But everyone else insists that it's just for fun, and says trying to make it better would get rid of that aspect."

"It might, I guess." It seemed to me that reliable news would be more important than momentary enjoyment.

"You should see the number of retractions our editor has to put in each issue. We'd save time if we just researched things and talk to the people involved from the start."

I nodded.

Rosie giggled. "Sometimes our editor even has to include retractions about a previous retraction!"

I smiled a little, which seemed to be the response she wanted. "Why do you think I could change anything?" I asked. "I mean, my own articles would be researched, but that wouldn't affect the rest of you."

"Well a lot of times an outsider's opinion is taken better than the opinion of someone you know. Think about it. If your mom said she didn't like a shirt of yours, what would you do?"

"Depending on her reason, I'd probably still wear it."

"Yup. Me too. I'm stubborn about things like that, and," she tilted her head, as if trying to gauge my reaction, "I kind of think you are too. But what if a stranger said the exact same thing?"

I shrugged. "I'd be curious why the stranger cared enough to comment on it."

Rosie giggled. "Well *I* always listen better when it's a stranger telling me things. I think most people do, and I know for a fact the people in the *Backus Blab* writing team are like that."

"Okay."

Rosie made a face, and then smiled; like she was remembering something that was funny now but wasn't at the time. "Last summer, I told them we needed a logo. They didn't go for it. A couple months later, Tasha, a granddaughter of one of our neighbors, came to a meeting. She said it would look better if we had a logo. Guess what we have now." She giggled. "Anyway, you're not a stranger, exactly, but for the moment you are—to them. Of course that will change quickly, but until it does I think it would be good to get your input in."

"Basically," I said with a smirk, "you want me to sabotage my chances of making friends with the newspaper writers."

Rosie's eyes grew wide, a clear indication she hadn't thought about it like that.

I laughed at her reaction. "I'll do it," I said. "You might be right. In fact, you probably are, since you know these people well. And if it does change, it would be fun to be involved with the paper."

Rosie grinned. "Oh good! I'll put in some happy words about you before you come to our meeting. Even without that, though, I'd like to think they're mature enough to handle a little deserved criticism." Rosie looked around my room. "Well, that's the last of this box. Anything else?"

"I think that's all," I said, putting the final touches on my arrangement of figurines.

"I love it," Rosie said as we stepped back to scrutinize my handiwork.

"Thanks," I said, though I wasn't as convinced. I rearranged a few of them, and decided it would have to be satisfactory.

26

"Jane, can I kidnap you?" Rosie's eyes grew a little wider in excitement and she smiled widely.

"Um," I shifted a little uncomfortably and glanced at the clock on my dresser.

"I would love for you to meet my brothers. I think you and Bev will get along great." She paused and scratched her head. "I think I said that already. Will you come?"

It would be good to meet more of the people here. "Yeah," I said. "Let me tell Dad, and we can go."

"Great! If you wanna bring Kathryn too, she's about the same age as Rymi."

I was surprised she knew Katty's age—or anything about my family that I hadn't told her myself. It was just something I would have to get used to, though. This was a small town, and new neighbors weren't common. "Okay, sure," I said.

Dad said it was fine, introduced himself to Rosie, and very seriously instructed us to have fun.

Katty of course was thrilled with the idea, though at age twelve insisted she still felt all boys were gross, and she doubted this 'rhyming person' would be any different.

Rosie laughed and agreed.

Her house was right next-door, so it hardly seemed worth it to put all our snow clothes on for the short trip over. Rosie pushed open the door and tramped inside, indicating for us to follow. "Bev! Rymi!"

Katty stepped back in surprise at the volume of Rosie's call, then whispered something about the family having weird names. I elbowed her, hoping she'd take the hint and shut up.

"What's your full name, Rosie?" Katty asked, clearly missing the meaning of my nudge. She wanted to know if Rosie had a strange name like her brothers, and went by a nickname instead.

"Rosalia," she said.

"That's pretty," Katty said, and whispered to me, "and almost normal."

"Thanks," Rosie said, distracted by the fact that her brothers had not appeared yet. "Bevin!" she screeched. Still no one came.

She started wandering through the house. Katty and I stayed by the front door.

I glanced at the small house. A staircase greeted us as we first walked in, leading up to what looked like a bedroom. The living room was to the left, and beyond that was a hallway with three closed doors: more bedrooms? As Rosie opened one of the doors to continue her search, I saw a desk with a computer inside. The kitchen, which through the open doorway we could see a corner of, was to the right of the hallway and had pink and white flowery wallpaper.

The house was sparsely decorated, and where other furniture didn't prevent it, the walls were lined with bookcases. There were only one or two picture frames donning the top shelves; the rest were filled with very worn (Rosie later called them 'well-loved') books.

One bookcase was completely filled with books of Christian themes (I noticed *In His Steps* and *The Pilgrim's Progress*, among several devotional books I wasn't familiar with), and another with fiction novels (easily recognized classics, like *Moby Dick* and *Oliver Twist*). One shelf was devoted to books of poetry, and the rest of that bookcase was filled with biographies of various and unrelated people.

Although separated into general topics, there wasn't even a semblance of organization beyond that. Many of the books seemed to have been shoved into place; some even still had bookmarks peeking out the top, as if they had been set there temporarily.

"You guys can come in, you know," Rosie said, moving from the hall to the kitchen.

We nodded but neither of us moved.

"I'll check the basement," Rosie continued. "If they're not down there, we give them up for dead." She disappeared farther into the kitchen; presumably the stairs to the basement were there.

I stepped forward to get a better look at one of the pictures—a family photo. The entire family had curly dark brown hair and dimples in their cheeks when they smiled, and it seemed to me they smiled quite a lot.

The door behind us opened. Katty and I scrambled out of the way.

"Don't look now, but I think we've been infiltrated!" the younger of the two boys said. The other smiled in response, and kept the smile as he turned to Katty and me, trying to put us at ease.

I looked behind us, wondering why Rosie wasn't jumping to explain our existence. *Of course,* I realized, *she's still in the basement.* Either because having to explain to a stranger why I was in their house was, well, awkward, or because my ridiculous heart had decided the older boy was one of the most handsome guys I had ever seen, I could barely speak. "I'm—we're—Rosie, um," my voice trailed off.

Katty remained silent.

Finally Rosie came to our aid. "There you are! Good, you've met. Well, maybe not officially." She grinned. "I'll make it official. Jane, Katty, these are my brothers, Bevin and Ryan Michael—we call them Bev and Rymi." She playfully shoved Rymi's arm. "I hope you were being nice. These girls are our new neighbors and I've already made a bad impression without added help from you."

Rymi made a face.

"It's nice to meet you two," I said, gaining at least a little coherent speech.

Katty nodded but, contrary to her personality, still said nothing. She was probably holding a grudge against them for making her feel uncomfortable.

We stood in unpleasant silence for a moment.

"Good grief," Rosie said. "You all are a bunch of quiet little ninnies today!" She scrunched her nose. "I vote we all play a game together to get past this awkward first meeting stuff."

That sounded like a good plan, and we agreed to it.

"Come on, you weirdos," Rosie said, motioning us to the basement.

We followed obediently.

As I neared the bottom step, a blanket came hurtling through the air and landed on me, covering me completely and rendering my sight useless.

Rosie giggled at the result of her blanket toss. "It gets really cold down here; you're going to want that."

I freed myself from its grasp and joined her on the lumpy couch.

Blankets were thrown in like manner to the other three, and soon we were all bundled and ready to play. We started with Jenga, and played a shortened game of Trivial Pursuit. Since none of us could answer even just one of the questions, we quit keeping score and just read them off for fun. After about an hour of this, I glanced at my watch and realized it was close to dinnertime.

Rosie said she'd come over the next day to help organize and unpack the rest of the house.

Bevin hadn't said a single unnecessary word the entire time we were there, though I also hadn't spoken to him directly. As always happened when I met a boy I liked, I had become shy. I focused my attention on Rosie, and even a little on Rymi, instead.

At least there would be plenty of time to get to know him later on.

Chapter 3

Friday, September 11, 1953
Ella Mitchell

"You going to dance with that new boy today?" Linda held the poodle skirt I had laid on the bed up to her smaller waist and twirled. "He's a big tickle," she giggled at the memory. "Plus, you know, he's a flutter bum." She grinned, pleased at being able to use her favorite terms for 'funny' and 'cute boy.'

I tied a light pink ribbon around my high pony and looked askance at her, frowning slightly. "Neither of those mean he's a good guy." I tucked a stray curl behind my ear and shook my head resolutely. "I'm not going to dance with him if I don't have to."

"He's Uncle Bruce's nephew," Linda said. "Uncle

31

Bruce is cool, so Joe must be too. And he told Mom he's coming to church, so he must be a Christian, right?"

I shook my head. "Going to church isn't the same as being a Christian. You know that. He could be doing it only for the social aspect." *Though if he's anything like Uncle Bruce, he does love God,* I admitted to myself.

Linda shrugged, and turned her attention back to the outfit I'd chosen. "I like your kitty skirt better." She set the black skirt back on the bed, her finger tracing one of the appliquéd music notes. "Can I help you get ready? *Please*?" She had dressed for the gala while I was still at The Diner.

I fingered through the curls in my ponytail, separating them. "I guess."

She grinned, and directed me to a seat in my desk chair so she could help with makeup. "Will you still be walking to the gala with Nicholas?"

My brows came together in confusion. "Why would that change?"

"Well because—" Linda stopped talking and put a hand over her mouth, "didn't you hear?"

I sighed in frustration and tucked some loose curls into a bobby pin so they would stop falling across my eyes as she helped apply lipstick—too thickly.

"You didn't hear." Linda frowned and patted my lips with a tissue. "I'm not going to be the one to tell you." She threw the tissue in the trash and picked up my skirt. "You ever going to get a poodle skirt that actually has a poodle on it?"

I crossed my arms. "No."

She made a face at the skirt, and handed it to me. "When I start wearing poodle skirts mine are *all* going to have poodles on them."

"Or you'll just be handed down mine and will have to deal with the non-cliché designs." I pulled it on.

She shook her head, and, to emphasize her disagreement, stomped her foot.

"Uncalled for," I said, but smiled at her antics.

"Can I walk with you today? Michael's already at the gym." She pulled loose some of the curls I had pinned back.

I shooed her hands away and pinned them up again. "Yeah, you can come. You can keep Joe occupied," I said. "I don't particularly feel like entertaining him."

"Oh, he's walking with us?"

I nodded.

"I guess it wouldn't be very fun for him to walk alone to his first gala," Linda said, again pulling the extra curls out.

I frowned at her.

She giggled. "Your hair is pretty that way."

As we heard a knock at the door, I sighed and glanced at the clock. "One of them is early."

"I'll get it," Linda said. "I'm ready." She shut the door behind her and hurried downstairs.

I changed into a white button up shirt and glanced in the mirror to make sure everything was even. I considered pinning the curls back again, but decided they weren't worth arguing with Linda about anymore.

Nicholas smiled as I came down the stairs. "Hi, Ella."

I smiled back, blushing. He always looked so handsome when he dressed up. Well, and every other time, too.

"You look nice today, Ella."

I blushed a deeper shade of red. "Thank you."

Nicholas started to say something. He closed his mouth and turned away. I looked at him curiously, but he didn't seem to notice.

Linda brought our food for the potluck out of the kitchen, and the three of us stepped outside to wait for Joe. I lit up while we waited and offered Nicholas a smoke, knowing he would refuse. Although he didn't share Uncle Bruce's strange ideas that the sticks were somehow unhealthy, he regarded it the way he did coffee: fine for others but not for him.

A minute later, Joe walked up the driveway.

He looked at us, confused. "Am I late?"

Nicholas glanced at his watch. "Right on time, actually. I was early."

Joe chuckled. "Good. I thought I had left exactly on time." He turned to my sister and grinned. "Linda, it's great to see you again! Well, and the rest of you," he smiled, "but I've only seen Linda once, so naturally she counts more."

Linda giggled.

I dropped my cigarette and put it out as we started walking. I had already taken the first few puffs of it, and smoking it was getting monotonous. Besides, it was difficult to walk, smoke, talk and hold a casserole at the same time,

"You nervous?" Nicholas asked, turning to Joe.

"I'm always nervous," Joe said, with a quirky smile. "But what are you referring to?"

"You'll meet the rest of the town tonight. Most of them, anyway."

Joe smiled. "Ella makes it sound like none of you enjoy letting others into your lives or your town," he frowned a little. "I suppose I'm nervous that's true."

I narrowed my eyes. "You think I would lie?"

Joe looked at me out of the corner of his eye, as if trying to gauge how he should respond. "Yes? No. Maybe, but only on Thursdays?"

I raised an eyebrow. "You are so weird."

Linda giggled. "You are, but I kind of like it." She slipped her arm through his, comfortingly. "You'll get along great with everyone; don't worry."

"Yeah," Nicholas said, winking at me, "Ella just wanted to psych you out. It isn't as though you're a complete stranger. Both Uncle Bruce and Margaret are well loved here."

I shrugged, my sign of disagreement, but kept quiet. Regardless who Joe's relatives were, he was from a bigger town, didn't understand our customs, and wouldn't fit in. It was unfair of Nicholas to pretend he would.

"I guess I should be ready for anything," Joe said, smirking.

"Probably," Nicholas agreed. "Unfortunately, life is kind of like high school even after graduation here."

"Which is why I want out," I muttered.

Nicholas and Linda stopped walking and stared at me, surprised.

I frowned and kept walking, so they resumed their initial pace.

"You want out?" Nicholas asked.

"Well, yeah," I said. "Don't you?"

Joe piped up. "I don't—I just got here!"

Keep out of this, you twit.

"You really don't want to stay here, Ella?" Linda asked, her voice shaking slightly.

I bit my lip; I hadn't meant to upset her. But I shook my head. "How do you *not* want out?" I asked, surprised she wasn't as ready to leave as I was.

Linda shrugged, clearly not wanting to continue the discussion.

"Everyone I've ever been close to is here," Nicholas said. "What you see as an invasion of privacy, I see as people who care about what's going on in each other's lives. I like it."

"Can I say something?" Joe asked.

"Nothing has stopped you before, don't know why it would now," I muttered.

Joe eyeballed me curiously. "Have I done something to offend you?"

"Your mere presence offends her," Nicholas said, chuckling. "Go ahead, Joe."

"Okay," he hesitated, giving me a concerned look.

I shrugged indifference. He took it as encouragement.

"Coming from what the two of you call a big city, I know how it feels to live next to someone and not even know their name." Joe hesitated again, but this time it was like he was ashamed of what he was admitting. "I know how it is to not even care." He frowned. "And how it hurts to have them feel the same about you."

We reached the school and stopped at the bottom of the steps outside.

Joe continued, turning to us. "Coming from that, well," a mischievous half smile came to his face, "I would much rather live in a town of gossips than in one where people are just the creatures you pass by on the street."

"Well," Nicholas shifted a little awkwardly, "now that that's over...are we going inside or what?"

Joe colored a little and nodded.

"Seriously though, Joe," Nicholas said, "don't be nervous. You'll be fine as long as you don't give them all a speech." He smiled, teasing.

Joe chuckled. "Good to know."

"Ella, will you dance with me?" Nicholas asked as we walked in.

"Of course."

Nicholas was right; Joe would fit in fine. I just didn't want that to be true. He should leave as suddenly as he came.

The music and dancing had already started. Margaret curtsied politely to her dance partner, Fred, and twirled toward us, mid-dance. She smiled widely. "Hi guys!" She looked at Linda's and my casserole and Joe's plate of cookies. "You really didn't have to bring anything, Joe. It's one dish per household. But thanks!" She directed him to the food tables.

"I like to do my part," Joe said. "Besides, being the new guy here I didn't want to let people think I was willing to accept things without giving in return." He winked at us. "First impressions are very important, you know."

Margaret giggled, as if she was in on the joke, too.

Joe relinquished his cookies at the food table, and the music ended. Nicholas placed my hand in his and led me to the dance floor as the band began playing again. He expertly twirled me across the gym. I laughed and enjoyed it.

I wasn't very good at swing dancing, but Nicholas was an excellent partner; we danced well together. He ended the dance with a dip and led me back to the sidelines.

"Ella, can we—"

Before he could finish, Eric approached us, stomping his cigarette butt out on the gym floor. "Wanna dance, baby?"

Only because it was impolite to refuse a gentleman's request to dance, I accepted. *Eric can hardly be called a gentleman, though.*

The music started again and he grabbed my hand and pulled me to the center of the gym, where he proceeded to whirl me every direction that suited his fancy. I was sure we were both making a spectacle of ourselves, and I wasn't enjoying it even a tiny bit.

Where is Nicholas? He usually rescued me from Eric's dancing attempts! Of course, regardless of his other faults, Eric wasn't stupid. He had caught on to this ploy, and that only served to make him dance faster—making it next to impossible for anyone to cut in.

And fast we were, and not on the beat. My arms were beginning to ache from being thrown from one side to the other. Expert swing dancers like Nicholas hardly held onto your hands as they danced with you—there was no need. I couldn't have pried my hands away from Eric's grasp if I'd tried.

He stopped suddenly and I nearly fell over.

"Mind if I take over?"

I sighed in relief as my eyesight became accustomed to the stillness, and eventually focused on the speaker. *Joe?*

With a muttered response, Eric released me to Joe's waiting hands. I tried not to groan about the second undesired partner. *He at least has to be better than Eric.*

Joe steadied me. "You all right?"

I nodded.

"We can sit the rest of it out if you'd rather."

I shook my head. He had asked for the last half of the dance, and it was my duty as a lady to give it to him.

He began the basic 1-2-step. I followed along easily.

"You were very good with Nicholas." He smiled down at me.

"Nicholas makes anyone look good," I said, hoping my warming cheeks didn't reveal the awkward embarrassment I was feeling.

Joe chuckled. "Sally is struggling a bit."

I glanced in their direction. *So that's where Nicholas is.* I smiled a little as I watched the two of them. None of the guys enjoyed dancing with Sally; she tried to take on the role of leader, and that didn't work well for either partner. Still, Nicholas always made a point to include her. A Friday night gala hadn't once passed without him claiming her for at least one of the dances. He didn't enjoy it more than any of the other guys, but he wanted her to feel included nonetheless. *He's so thoughtful and kind.*

Joe continued, oblivious of my inner musings. "So my conclusion is that, when in the proper hands, you're a good dancer."

I shrugged.

"Shall we test this theory?"

I looked at him, my attention now fully shifted, and furrowed my brow, confused. "What do you mean?"

Without a word, Joe spun me out, released my hands, spun himself around, and took my hands once more. "That wasn't so bad, was it?"

I stared at him and said nothing.

Joe chuckled at my lack of response and spun me out once more, a regular twirl. As he pulled me in again, he whispered, "Do you trust me?"

I frowned, unsure. "I don't *know* you."

"You've worked with me a week." He winked. "So, do you trust me?"

I shrugged.

He grinned. "That's not a no." With that, he began a move I couldn't repeat if I tried.

Without letting go of either hand, he twisted and tangled our arms. He directed me to the side, back to facing him, and eventually managed to spin me so my back was to him.

He released my hands and I gasped as gravity pulled me forward. Joe took hold of my hands again right before I lost my balance, and spun me around to face him. He grinned and twirled me into a slight dip.

He kept me in that pose, allowing me to catch my breath, and smiled at me. I couldn't help but smile back; a mix of relief and pride. I wasn't a bruised mess on the gym floor, and he'd managed to get me to do something that I imagined looked impressive.

The music ended and he led me back to the edge of the dance floor.

Linda skipped up to us. "That was so cool!"

Joe chuckled. "Well, thank you!"

Linda grinned. "You don't know the people here yet, do you?"

"I know *you*."

She giggled, and began to point at various friends. "That's Mary, my best friend—and her younger sister Cathy is standing by her mom and dad over there— and Laura, dancing with Fred right now, is the girl our brother Michael is sweet on—"

"Linda, hush!"

Joe smiled. "I won't tell a soul, on my honor as a gentleman."

"See, Ella?" Linda said, grinning triumphantly. "Joe won't tell." She continued to point to nearly every person in the room.

Joe kept a smile and a look of genuine interest, though he was likely feeling overwhelmed with all the names and faces.

Margaret linked arms with me and led me to a corner of the room. "Hungry?" She handed me a cookie. "Joe's an amazing cook. Well, you know that from what he makes at The Diner. He lived by himself for a while in New York, so he had to teach himself. Just try this."

I obeyed.

"He's cooked for us every night since he got here." She grinned. "You should come over for supper sometime!"

I put the cookie down and looked at her, frowning at her meddling. "Margaret, what are you doing?"

She looked at me, confused. "What do you mean?"

"Stop it."

"Stop what?" She glanced at the cookie on my plate as she pulled out a pack of cigarettes and offered me one. I shook my head, but she took one for herself. "You don't think it's a good cookie?" she asked, lighting the cigarette.

I stood and walked outside, motioning for her to follow. We went to the back of the church; the woods, and the most private place Backus had to offer.

"Ella?"

I turned to face her. "You *know* I like Nicholas. I don't care if you think Joe is amazing. Do *not* try to set me up with him."

She stared at me and lowered to sit on the steps; I did the same. Had I misread her? I doubted it. I'd known Margaret forever, and she was easy to read.

Finally she spoke up, "I only said he was a good cook. And even you can't deny that."

I couldn't.

"Besides," she said, and then hesitated.

"Besides what?" I crossed my arms; I didn't like her tone.

Margaret frowned, as if unsure how to continue. "You know nothing can happen between you two, right?" Margaret said it gently, but the words stung. She put a hand on my shoulder, as if that would fix it. "You and Nicholas are just too different."

I turned away, frowning, and shoved her hand away.

Margaret continued. "You want different things. You want to work, and write, and be independent," her voice shook a little and she put her cigarette in the outdoor ashtray, "and Nicholas wants someone who will stay home and be nothing more than a wife and mother. They're both okay to want, but they can't mix."

"You don't know that," I snapped. "You have no right, Margaret. You don't know what you're talking about."

"Ella, I'm sorry..."

"You have some nerve."

"I care about you," she sighed. "I don't want you to be disappointed."

"Especially when I could be with someone so much better?" I turned to face her.

Margaret frowned. "I never said a word, Ella. You did. Maybe you see good things in Joe, too."

I shook my head. "You think my feelings for Nicholas, which have lasted for *years*, are going to just disappear in a week?"

"No, of course not."

We sat in silence for a while. Margaret turned away, twisting a piece of hair around her finger. I scowled and shifted my attention to the moon above us, pinching my lips together in anger.

How could she be so cruel under this guise of 'concerned friend'? She's never been supportive of Nicholas and me. I allowed myself a few moments more to revel in hurt feelings, then calmed down. *She does care about me. I can't doubt that.*

"Hey," I turned to her, realizing now that I had overreacted. Margaret only wanted what was best for me, even if she *was* misguided. "I'm sorry I snapped at you."

Margaret hugged me. "And I'm sorry I pried. I know you don't like people butting into your personal life. I should have held my tongue."

"Yes, you should have." I smiled.

She smiled back. "You looked awesome on the dance floor, by the way. Except with Eric...with him you looked miserable."

"Aw, really? I was hoping it wouldn't show."

We giggled, linked arms, and went back inside.

Joe caught my attention as we walked in. "Ella, will you dance with me again?"

I looked at him. *Uff da. He's adorable* and *a good cook. And smart, and since he's so high up in Margaret's estimation I'm sure he loves God, and— stop.*

"You don't have to," Joe said, taking my silence as hesitation. "I feel a little cheated that I only got half a dance, but don't feel obligated. So," he gave a crooked smile, "what do you say?"

I didn't *say* anything; I just nodded dumbly.

That satisfied him, and he grinned and took my hand as we waited for the music of the current dance to end.

Part of me wanted to free my hand, and part of me liked the feel of our fingers so close together. It was just my desire for a guy, I was certain. Right now I wished the fingers holding mine were Nicholas', not Joe's.

The music ended and he led me out. "Sorry," he whispered, "I didn't realize there was so much of the song left when I took your hand."

"Oh—that's—okay—" I stumbled over my words.

Joe smiled a little. "Do you still trust me?" He began the basic step, and I followed his lead.

"I still don't know you," I said, stubborn.

Joe chuckled. "You know, strangers are quite a bit less likely to hurt you than those you're closest to."

"Is that a fact?"

"It really is," he nodded solemnly. "Emotional hurt, I mean. Any stranger can hurt you physically. The people close to you don't hurt you in that way. Or they shouldn't. If they do, you should tell someone. Do they?" He tilted his head at me as he waited for my response.

I raised an eyebrow at him between spins. "What?"

"Yeah, I'm going to guess they don't. No scars, no bruises, and you seem pretty stable. If they do, you know, you can tell me."

I rolled my eyes. "You're ridiculous."

"Right. Well. What was I saying?" Joe pursed his lips together in thought. "Oh yes. So the people close to us might not hit or punch or kick us, literally, but they do it figuratively all the time."

"You sound like you're speaking from experience."

"Do you know a single person who *wouldn't* be speaking from experience?"

I shrugged.

"Well, do you?"

"You're frustrating," I said, seeing no reason to continue the topic.

"So are you." He winked.

"Good."

Joe spun me out again. "Good." He chuckled. "I think we just had our first fight." He pulled me into a low dip, causing my feet to lift slightly off the ground. It was surprisingly comfortable in his firm but gentle hold. "The fight was quite epic, wasn't it?" he asked as he returned me to standing position.

"Was it?"

He spun me out once more. "It was."

I smiled a little. "You are so," I hesitated, unable to think of a proper word, "so, *something*."

"Nah...I'm just Joe. A guy trying to make a girl smile. I guess that's what we do in the big city." He winked.

I giggled.

Joe twirled me out and around behind him, switching hands and bringing me back to the front. He grinned as we returned to the basic 1-2-step. "Turns out you trust me after all."

I colored a little. Maybe I did. That didn't mean anything.

The music ended and he led me back to the sidelines by Linda. Margaret and Nicholas had walked to the dance floor to wait for the music to begin again.

Joe smiled.

"What?"

"Really, Ella, am I not allowed to smile? I feel like every time I do you demand to know why!" He winked.

"Well you always look so," I again searched for the right adjective. As a writer, it shouldn't have been that difficult to find descriptive words for him.

"Dashing?" he grinned.

"Not the word," I stumbled out, trying not to laugh, "I would use."

"Charming?"

I giggled, and finally landed on some words that fit him: "Secretive. Mischievous. Like you know something I don't, but won't tell me unless I ask about it."

"So you ask."

I smiled. "Naturally."

The next song that played was slow music, so Joe offered me a seat beside Linda and sat in a chair next to us.

"Don't you know how to waltz?" Linda asked.

Joe shook his head. "Do you?"

She giggled. "A little. Ella knows it better."

I'm surrounded by matchmakers. I shook my head.

"I wonder," Joe said carefully, looking at Linda, "if you might be willing to teach it to me?"

"Really?" Linda asked. "I don't usually dance here. I'm too short for the older guys and the guys my age—" she nodded toward them, goofing off at the other end of the gym, "would rather run around and play football and soccer than dance."

"I'm sure both groups are missing out by not having you join them."

Linda grinned.

"So, Linda, may I have this dance?" He smiled and held his hand out to her.

She jumped from her chair and gladly accepted it, and soon the two of them were dancing. Very poorly, and with the way Joe was leaning down to adjust to Linda's shorter stature, I was certain he would earn a backache for his trouble, but they were enjoying themselves more than any other couple on the dance floor.

Between them at least seven couples' feet were stepped on, several people were bumped into, and they each nearly lost their balance at least once. But with each fumble came more laughter, and the huge grin never left Linda's face. I smiled at the comical picture they painted.

Nicholas, his dance with Margaret having ended moments earlier, sat beside me and followed my gaze. I quickly turned my attention to him.

"I've been wanting to talk to you, Ella," he said. "Is now an okay time?"

45

Chapter 4

Saturday, November 15, 2008
Jane Blake

I brushed snow off the stone bench and sat down, cupping my travel mug of hot chocolate close to my face and enjoying the deliciously warm scent. Once spring came, this place would be peaceful and beautiful. From the first time we'd come to visit Aunt LeeLee I had wanted to claim this as a favorite reading spot, but never had the chance. I'd always been so busy with cousins, siblings, aunts and uncles that I never could just read. Now we lived next door to it, and I could come whenever I wanted.

I wondered if others would have the same idea. This place would be less conducive to reading if they did.

A glance around assured me that at least for now it was pretty dead. Satisfied, I turned my attention back to Brontë's *Wuthering Heights* for a few more minutes of uninterrupted reading.

"Really, Jane, you pick the strangest of places to spend an afternoon," Rosie cleared more snow and sat on the bench next to me.

I smiled. "I don't usually hang out in cemeteries, but this one always looks so peaceful, and the bench was too inviting."

"You can try to explain it as much as you like, Jane," Rosie said, eyes sparkling in amusement. "It's still weird."

I laughed and gave her a side hug in greeting.

"So today I've decided to drag you all around Backus and show you the sights. All three of them." She hopped up, took my hand, and pulled me to my feet. "It's not very big, but you should know where everything is, so when I say, 'meet you at the school' you'll know where I mean."

I hid a smile. "You mean the only large building here?"

"I do! Now aren't you glad you know that?"

"Oh, of course. I would have wandered for hours otherwise."

She giggled. "Hey, has your little brother Aiden met Danny yet?"

"I'm not sure," I admitted.

"Well, if he hasn't, we'll fix that. The only thing separating them is the cemetery, so all they have to do is go around it—or through, if they're weirdos like you are."

I smirked.

About halfway down the street I heard soft guitar music, accompanied by a clear, beautiful tenor voice. I wanted to pause and just listen, but Rosie kept walking.

"Who is that?" I whispered.

"Oh, um," Rosie looked uncomfortable, "I don't really talk to him much." She glanced behind us, as though she wanted to change course, but continued walking forward.

We turned the corner and I saw a young man, probably in his late teens, sitting on a pile of snow in his front yard. He was strumming his guitar and singing something in a language that my brief study of languages made me guess was Latin.

The bottoms of his jeans were caked with small chunks of snow, and his bare fingers must have been near numb, but he was focused on his music and didn't seem to notice the cold. He didn't seem to notice us, either.

I glanced at Rosie.

She cleared her throat. "Kyle."

He didn't look up.

Rosie crossed her arms and frowned in my direction. She positioned herself directly in front of him and said his name again.

He put a hand on the strings to silence his guitar, frowning. "What?"

With a sigh, she introduced us.

"Hey," he said in a disinterested tone, and started strumming again.

I hopped onto the snow bank next to him, sending a little of the snow downhill. "Did you write that?" I asked.

He glanced warily at Rosie, turned back to me, and shrugged.

"Guess I'll take that as a yes," I said, undeterred. I had discovered a fellow artist, though a different sort than I was, and wasn't going to let pass the opportunity to get to know him.

He shrugged again.

"I'm an author too," I said. "I don't write songs though. And I don't write in," I hesitated, "Latin, was it?"

"Yeah." Kyle bent over his guitar, examining it as he plucked out a melody.

"Since you know Latin, does that make it easier for you to learn other languages?" I asked. "I think someone told me that once, but maybe that's not the case."

"I don't really know Latin," he said, not looking up from his guitar. "At least, not much. Never tried other languages."

Rosie tapped her foot impatiently. "Come *on*, Jane," she said. "There are so many other places I want to show you. You geeks can talk about your love of dead languages some other time, okay?"

I smiled apologetically at Kyle and stepped down. More of the snow came with as I left, but enough was left behind that the loss didn't disturb Kyle's perch.

"It was nice to meet you," I said. "I'll stop by sometime, or you can come see me. I live in the house—"

"He knows where you live. You think we get new neighbors all the time? Everyone here knows where you live."

I frowned a little at Rosie's interruption and attitude, but waved to Kyle and followed her.

When we turned the corner and were safely out of Kyle's sight, I grabbed Rosie's arm and forced her to stop.

"What?" she seemed annoyed, and didn't look at me.

"Don't act innocent," I said. "You were so rude to him! You hardly talked!"

She crossed her arms. "I have my reasons."

I scowled. "I can't think of anything that would make treating someone like that okay."

Rosie narrowed her eyes. "Don't assume you know me, Jane. We met a *week* ago. That doesn't make you an expert on All Things Rosie."

"It doesn't take an expert to see that you're a natural chatterbox and any state other than that means something is off."

"I *said* I have my reasons." Rosie turned away. "I don't need judgment from you. Now come on. Our meeting is today and I want to introduce you to the newspaper staff. If you promise to drop this topic now, I won't be cranky when I do it."

I rolled my eyes at the threat and said without sincerity, "Sorry." I frowned, and added in a gentler tone, "I just don't like seeing people treated badly without reason."

"Believe me, there's a reason," Rosie said. "I told you we don't talk much. In a town this size, that's a conscious choice." Rosie took a deep breath, changed her expression into a smile, and—in usual Rosie fashion—resumed speaking. "You're going to love Kate. I should warn you about Mr. Larsen, though. He's in charge of the newspaper. He can seem like a cranky old man," Rosie turned to me confidentially, "and I won't lie, sometimes he actually is one." Her teeth flashed in a quick smile. "But when you get to know him you'll learn he has a sweet side."

I nodded to show I was listening.

"Kate is younger than us by a couple years, but you wouldn't guess it. She's kind of Mr. Larsen's right-hand helper, and she writes all the articles no one else wants to claim. She's just lovely. Funny thing about Mr. Larsen," Rosie continued, "is that some people say he started working with the newspaper just to spite an ex. The ex despised the newspaper, so he wanted to make it succeed." She scrunched her nose. "I don't believe even at his crankiest Mr. Larsen would do something like that," she shook her head, resolutely, "and I've never been able to confirm the rumor." She abruptly changed the subject. "I wonder what articles they'll give you."

By this point we had reached what was apparently our destination: one of the many houses I hadn't yet visited.

Rosie knocked on the door. "We take turns each week with whose house the meetings are at. This week it's Kate's."

A man with thick gray hair came to the door. He had wrinkles that made him appear to be frowning, and I guessed he was somewhere close to my grandparent's age.

"Late." His tone, though clearly not happy, indicated he was used to her tardiness. I'd only known her a week and already I was used to it.

Rosie smiled penitently.

"And who's this?" His judgmental gaze shifted to me, and his eyes narrowed, seeming to dislike what he saw.

I glanced down self-consciously at my clothes; they seemed fine, though a little snowy from my seat on the snow bank. I subtly brushed some onto the step below us. "I'm Jane," I said, seeing that Rosie wasn't going to jump in for me. I offered a hand.

He didn't respond to either.

"Mr. Larsen, she's a friend of mine," Rosie said, "and a writer. I think you're going to like the ideas she has."

With a final disapproving look and a small grunt, Mr. Larsen said, "We'll see."

He stepped aside and let us in.

I followed Rosie through a long hallway, down the concrete stairs, and into a small, dimly lit and cheaply carpeted room. It was furnished with old recliners and couches. *A better home for this furniture would be the curb on garbage day.* I blinked, surprised at the judgmental thought; Mr. Larsen's crankiness must be getting to me.

There were a few people pretending to be comfortable in these seats, and one of the girls was walking between them, filling their mugs with coffee or tea.

They all turned when I walked in, and looked at me curiously. A couple of them, including the girl with the hot drinks, smiled in welcome. As my eyes grew accustomed to the light and I could more clearly see their faces, I realized some of them were people I had seen and waved to on my walks, but I had never spoken to any of them.

In spite of their smiles, I began wishing Bev had been a part of these meetings. I had spent a little more time around him since our first meeting, and was enjoying, albeit slowly, getting to know him. At least I had Rosie, who took this opportunity to introduce me to the others: Sofia, Justin, Kate, and Sammy. The girl with the drinks was Kate. Rosie was right; I wouldn't have guessed she was any younger than myself.

Kate set the teapot on a coaster in the middle of the coffee table and came to my side, still smiling in welcome. "Rosie's told me so much about you! I'm so glad you could come today." She pulled me into a hug.

Taking the cue, the others stood and gave me similar greetings—Sammy and Justin replacing the hug with a stiff handshake. Kate directed me to one of the unoccupied chairs, and offered me some coffee or tea; I accepted the coffee. Rosie sat next to me, and Mr. Larsen claimed the recliner. Since Rosie and I were the last to arrive, the meeting began.

Mr. Larsen took a swallow of his coffee, and said, "Who has ideas?"

All at once, people began talking.

"Julianne and Rick went on another date last week."

"The Diner is returning to 50's food—hamburgers, milkshakes—nothing modern anymore."

"Kate's got a crush on Bevin."

"I do not!"

"There's going to be auditions at the school for another play in a couple of weeks."

"The Harrisons are going out of town for a few days and are being very secretive about where or why."

"Maybe it has something to do with Marissa Harrison—you know she's pregnant again."

"Speaking of vacations, the Spencers just got back from one."

"I noticed a ring on Sarah's finger when I was at the market the other day."

Unable to keep quiet any longer, I said, "So what?"

Their attention now on me, everyone stared, expecting me to elaborate. *Oops.*

Sofia, who had shared the tidbit about the ring, said, "What do you mean?"

I wished I had kept my mouth shut. In fact I wished I hadn't come at all. Rosie had warned me that these meetings were gossip fests.

But I *had* come, I *had* opened my mouth, and they were waiting for me to explain why.

I sighed and turned to Sofia. "The ring could be an engagement ring—but it could just be a ring."

"That's why we'd research it." She tucked a piece of her brown hair behind her ear with a slightly defiant air.

"By asking Sarah directly?" I knew what the answer would be. To attempt to appear calm as I waited for the response, I sipped at my coffee.

"No," Sammy said, frowning. "Of course not."

I set my cup down and raised an eyebrow. "Why not?"

"Well, because," Kate stepped in. "If people knew we were writing about them, they would tell us not to."

Sofia nodded. "And then we would have no stories, or else they would be angry with us for not listening to them. Either way would mean the end of the paper."

I frowned. "I think they would prefer the real story getting out."

Mr. Larsen turned to me. "And what would you suggest instead? Rosie said I would like your ideas. I'm still waiting for that to happen."

I glanced nervously at Rosie. She nodded encouragingly, and unhelpfully.

"Well," I said slowly, "look at the big city papers. They don't resort to gossiping to get their news."

"Is that what you think we do?" Kate's tone was concerned, and surprisingly not defensive.

"I make a point not to look at the big city papers, because they're *boring*," Sofia said, crossing her arms. "Why would we want to be like that?"

"They're only boring if they have poor authors," I said. "I'm much more interested in reading the kind of stories they print than I would be to read about how Aunt Cassie might be pregnant again— especially when in the next issue we learn she isn't." I looked around, trying to gauge reactions. "Rosie told me you print a lot of retractions. If your stories were right from the beginning—and the only way to know they are is to talk to the people directly involved—well, you wouldn't need to print those."

Everyone turned to Rosie now.

She looked a bit guilty, but shrugged. "Well it's true," she said. "Our retractions section gets bigger with each issue. Kate, how many retractions do we have scheduled to print this month?"

Kate sifted through her folder, and finally came up with the number eight.

"And that's out of ten articles that were published last month," Rosie said.

I hadn't realized it was *that* bad. The silence that followed told me that neither had anyone else.

Mr. Larsen looked thoughtful for a moment. Everyone else was quietly waiting for his response. Finally he spoke up. "You have a point."

I blinked, wondering if I had heard him right. Rosie turned to me and grinned triumphantly, assuring me I had.

"What kind of stories would we print instead?" Justin asked. He was a red-headed boy, at least a couple years younger than myself, who until now had been silently drinking his tea.

When no one answered him, I realized the question was directed at me.

"Oh, well," I bit my lip, "I guess I hadn't thought about it. We could look at a big newspaper and see what they have."

"One thing they have is a historical section," Sofia said. "We should have that." The girl, who looked around the same age as Justin and had light blonde hair in braids on both sides, seemed to accept the idea now that it had Mr. Larsen's approval.

"I'd like to keep writing my advice column," Rosie said.

"No reason you'd have to stop that, I think," Kate agreed.

"I write the more factual articles," Sammy said, shaking his black hair out of his face. "Ones about The Diner, and performances at the school. Those aren't gossip, right?"

We assured him they weren't.

Mr. Larsen folded his hands in his lap. "It's settled then. Sammy and Rosie will continue as they were, the rest of you will do more actual research when writing your articles—and when the subjects don't wish to be written about, you will write about big news that's happening outside of Backus. Jane will be the new historian."

"Wait," I said, "what?"

"Everyone else has their own articles to write. You have none. You do want to write with us, don't you?"

"Um," I hesitated, and glanced at Rosie.

She nodded excitedly.

"Yeah," I said. "Sure."

"Kate, make a note."

Kate nodded, though she had already written it, and much of the rest of what we'd discussed, in her small yellow notebook.

Article assignments for the month were handed out, and the meeting ended. My job was just to start looking around and talking to people. Basically, I was supposed to learn the history of Backus, and let the rest of the town know what it was.

Why did they think giving this job to the newcomer was a good idea?

I asked Mr. Larsen if I could interview him. He refused, saying there were plenty of other people I could talk to. I was sure my Great Aunt LeeLee wouldn't mind telling me some things. If I was lucky I might learn some from my other relatives, too, though they weren't as talkative as LeeLee usually was.

"You know," Rosie said as we walked back to our houses, "you could use your new title as an excuse to find out where that ring came from. Did you ever ask about that?"

"I asked," I said. "Mom didn't recognize it."

"So it's still a mystery," she said, her eyes enthusiastically squinting at the corners. "Exciting!"

"I guess."

I glanced toward Kyle's house on the way back, but he wasn't sitting on the snow bank anymore.

"He's usually indoors," Rosie said, following my gaze.

"Hmm?" I looked at her.

"Kyle. He stays inside and helps his grandma."

"Oh." I shrugged, trying to show indifference.

"Either that or he's at The Diner," Rosie continued, seeing through my act.

"They mentioned The Diner during the meeting," I said, glad for an opening to change the subject. "I haven't been there yet. Is it nice?"

"Oh!" She glanced at her watch. "Man, I've gotta get home. But you should go there!"

"Maybe later," I said. "I have to go home too. I think I'll see if I can get Great Aunt LeeLee to tell me anything I could use for my article."

Rosie grinned.

"What?"

She shrugged. "I just knew you were gonna be great for the paper. You've already got us making changes! And you're dedicated, too."

I blushed. "I don't know. That meeting was awkward."

"It was so good though," she said, continuing to grin. "I told you they needed to hear it from somebody other than me."

I nodded.

We had reached my house, so we hugged goodbye and I went in to start cooking supper.

Mom had already started, so I took over for her at the stove. "Can we have Great Aunt LeeLee over?"

She looked surprised. "We actually already invited her—Great Uncle Frank, too, of course. Why?"

"I'm writing for the Backus newspaper now, as the historian." I stirred the peas. "I thought maybe they could tell me what Backus used to be like—if it's changed at all since they were my age."

Mom nodded. "Good for you for getting involved. I take it that was Rosie's idea?"

"Yeah." I glanced through the window of the oven at the chicken inside.

"I can't decide if I like that girl," Mom said. "I guess I'll have to get to know her better. Let's invite her family over tomorrow. They can taste your homemade cookies."

"They're nothing special."

"You are the only person who thinks that. Everyone else sees them for the amazing treats they are."

I blushed. I loved cooking, but I was no better at it than anyone else. I sometimes experimented with different flavorings, but most things turned out best when I followed the recipe as it was written. That didn't take much skill.

Great Aunt LeeLee and Great Uncle Frank arrived within a half hour, right as the chicken finished cooking. As we ate, I asked if the two of them could tell me anything about Backus' history.

Great Aunt LeeLee, as expected, had plenty. She said The Diner had been a social gathering spot. Almost everyone in Backus would come there to eat, have coffee on cold days and milkshakes or pop on warm days, and just talk. She told me a little about Uncle Bruce, who owned it and enjoyed spending time with the customers and creating often-defective inventions.

She said almost everyone had smoked, since at that time no one realized it was unhealthy. "Well," she amended, "almost nobody. Uncle Bruce—who owned The Diner, as you know if you've seen its current name—always had some suspicions. We never guessed he'd be right." She shook her head slowly, sadly, as if remembering the consequences of their ignorance. My grandpa, who had been good friends with Great Aunt LeeLee, had died of lung cancer. I wondered if others she knew had suffered similar fates.

To soften the mood, Great Uncle Frank brought up the newspaper, at that point called the *Backus Brochure*. He said my Great Aunt Laura had been a part of it for many years.

When they were my age, there had been galas every Friday night. Everyone would bring a dish to share: a town-wide potluck. A band or just a record player would play, and nearly everyone would swing dance or waltz.

Great Aunt LeeLee said a lot of people fell in love at those galas, and it's where she'd started to notice Great Uncle Frank, as he chose playing with the younger children over being part of the dancing couples.

Great Uncle Frank interjected that he hadn't started liking her until months later, as he was watching her interact with people after church one week. "Up until that point," he said, a teasing smile on his face, "I didn't think she knew how to talk to anyone other than the little kids." He winked at her.

Great Aunt LeeLee laughed and elbowed him playfully.

"Why did they stop the galas?" I asked, wishing I had my notebook with me.

They glanced at each other and strange look passed between them, but Great Aunt LeeLee only said, "I guess people just lost interest after a while. Eventually the galas just stopped happening."

After the hesitation and the look, I certainly didn't believe *that*.

Chapter 5

Monday, October 26, 1953
Ella Mitchell

I sat down in the snowy grass and began to write. I loved this spot. The cemetery in Backus might seem like a morbid place to spend time, but it was beautiful and calm, especially in the colder months, and gave me inspiration for my story. The tranquility of it gave me a chance to think, too.

Nicholas had told me, in his gentle way, of course, that he had feelings for someone else; he had asked Uncle Bruce for permission to date Margaret. He wasn't interested in me.

After a crush that lasted years, that was hard to accept. I'm ashamed to admit I cried when I went home that night. Now it was time to move on. I couldn't like him when I knew without question he cared for my friend.

The practical side of me tried to convince the emotional side that things would be better this way, and Margaret had been right: Nicholas and I would not have made a good couple. Finally, more than a month later, my emotional side was beginning to agree.

Besides, my matchmaking spirit had begun to see how cute Nicholas and Margaret would be together, and that cured me of any lingering feelings I had.

Joe sat cross-legged on the ground next to me. *Well, there goes my tranquility.*

"What are you writing?" He offered me a cigarette.

I shook my head at the offered smoke. They just distracted me. I resisted the urge to cover my written words.

Joe motioned to my notebook, though kept his eyes on me. At least he had the decency not to read over my shoulder. "Diary?" He lit his cigarette.

I rolled my eyes. "I've never seen the point of writing my innermost thoughts like that."

Joe chuckled. "You read Austen, don't you?"

"Yes," I said warily.

"Northanger Abbey?" He took a long drag and blew the smoke away from us.

"Naturally." It was my favorite, though I wouldn't admit that to him.

"Yet you don't keep a diary?" Joe tucked the cigarette between his index and middle fingers and gave his crooked half smile.

I raised an eyebrow. "I fail to see the connection."

Joe chuckled again. "There's a conversation between Tilney and Catherine, about whether she keeps a diary. It's always been amusing to me."

"I'm sure it has." I rolled my eyes again and closed the notebook.

"Righto," Joe continued, undeterred. "It's not a diary. What is it, then? Poetry?" He took another puff and looked sidelong at me.

"Do I look like a poet?"

Joe moved so we were face to face, his features curious. "Poets have a 'look'? I didn't know this." He leaned in slightly. "Describe it to me?"

I groaned a little. *What will it take to get him to cop a breeze and get out of here?* Everyone else in town knew I cherished peace and quiet when I was writing.

"I'm still waiting for that description," he said, tapping his foot a little. "I would like to be able to spot the poets in the crowd. I think it would be a wonderful skill to have."

"Poets don't so much have a look as a manner of talking, and being," I said, hoping a general explanation would compel him to leave. "They're romantic fools whose only thoughts dwell on love and broken hearts."

A smile crept across his face, and he snuffed his cigarette on the snow next to him.

I had known Joe over a month already. We worked together in The Diner nearly every day, and in spite of my original intentions, we were quickly becoming friends. He was easy to talk to, though sometimes a bit frustrating in his inquisitiveness, and he genuinely cared about people. More often than I cared to admit, he remembered things about people that I didn't even know.

"So it's not a book of lovesick poetry, and it's not a diary," Joe said, still determined to discover what I was writing. "And I assume it's not a journal either. I'm certain there are differences between diaries and journals, but I've never been able to figure out what they are. Is it the great American novel?"

I spun around so we would no longer be facing each other, and started writing again. Maybe he'd get the hint.

"Ah ha!" Joe sounded proud of himself. "So it *is* the great American novel."

"I'm not talking to you anymore if you're just going to make fun of me," I said.

"Who's making fun of you? I think it's boss you can write. I certainly can't." He still didn't leave.

"Boss?"

"Oh, we say that in Afton. It means," he hesitate, "well I guess it means 'great.' What are you writing about?"

I glanced down at the page. No one ever asked about my stories; they knew not to. My writing was special to me, and up until now, private. I wanted to keep it that way. I wasn't ready for the public to see it yet, and didn't know if I ever would be.

"You don't have to tell me if you'd rather not," he said, too late to truly be respecting my privacy. "I don't know anything about how writers work, but maybe you would like to keep your work quiet until you're ready for the big unveiling on publishing day." He winked.

"My work is never going to be published," I said, hugging my notebook protectively. "I don't want it to be. I just write for fun."

"Do you have any finished pieces?"

"A couple short ones," I said. "No novels." I glanced at my notebook, which, thanks to Joe, contained only a few short lines of dialog. "I guess this one is a script."

"What's the topic?"

"You're just trying several ways of asking the same thing," I said. "You think eventually I'll give in and tell you what I'm writing, don't you?"

Joe gave his mischievous smile. "Maybe."

I raised an eyebrow. "You think that will work?"

Again, "Maybe."

I rolled my eyes, but smiled. "You are silly."

"Come on Ella," Joe tilted his head and pouted slightly. "You have to tell me sometime."

"And why is that?"

"Because I will annoy you until you do."

My smile changed to a teasing frown. "Somehow I doubt the annoyingness will quit just because I've told you what my script is about."

"Annoyingness?" Joe raised an eyebrow at my made up word.

I blushed.

"Anyway, my *annoyingness* will only increase, now." Joe chuckled. It was good to have someone around who didn't take himself seriously. Joe never took offense at the jokes I poked. In fact, he usually managed to make himself look even worse than I had.

I jotted something more down in my notebook.

"You're really going to risk this?"

"You becoming more annoying? I don't believe you can. So yes."

Joe grinned. "You ain't seen nothing yet, El Bell."

I looked at him and raised an eyebrow. "El Bell?"

He seemed incredulous. "Hasn't anyone given you a nickname before?"

I shrugged. "Not really. Linda used to call me E, but that was only because she couldn't say her l's yet."

Joe chuckled. "Well then, I have the honor of giving you your very first nickname. What do you think of it?"

I shrugged. "It's cute, I guess."

"You don't seem convinced."

"Forgive me for not getting excited about a silly name. Besides, I'm trying to concentrate here," I shook my head, teasing but with sincerity laced into the words. "You make it very difficult."

"Did I not promise to be annoying?"

"You had to start right away?"

"Well according to you," Joe said, chuckling, "I never stopped."

I frowned. "I'm going to split if you keep bugging me." I looked at him, mischievously. "I'll sic Eric on you."

Joe laughed. "I must be *really* awful if you would *willingly* bring Eric into this."

I sighed, realizing the only way to get him to leave would be to satiate his interest. "Fine," I said. "My script is a mystery story of a key that was stolen."

Joe grinned, triumphant, and settled in for a longer conversation. "Tell me more?"

I bit my lip. "Well, it's a two-fold mystery, because the reader has to discover not only who stole the key, but also why it's important."

Joe leaned in, showing his interest. "Why was it stolen?" he asked in almost a whisper.

"I don't know yet," I admitted.

"Who stole it?"

"A friend of the detective did the actual stealing," I said, "but the real thief is a guy named Archibald. His friends call him Archie and he hates it, so instead they call him Baldy—which he hates more. He's almost killed a couple of them for that. I mean, literally. He's a bad man."

Joe chuckled. "Baldy! Love it! Is he bald?"

"Not totally. His hair is thinning though, and he's sensitive about it."

"Perfect."

"Catherine is the person he stole from," I continued, encouraged by his enthusiasm.

"Typical annoying rich girl?"

I shook my head. "No, not really. She's on the poorer side, and shy. She tried to solve the case on her own at first. Detective Bingley learned of it and begged to be allowed to help her. It's important to him, too, but I don't know why."

"I do," Joe said.

"I find it unlikely that you know something about my character that *I* don't."

Joe chuckled. "I don't know anything about your character, but I know a little something about people. If you haven't noticed, I am one."

"Really," I said flatly.

"Yes!" he grinned. "I know it's hard to tell sometimes." He winked. "I also like to observe them; learn people's motivations, hopes, joys," he trailed off.

That *was* something I had noticed. When there were customers at The Diner, he would either be interacting with them or watching them as they interacted with each other.

Joe looked intently at me, gaining my attention once more. "Aren't you curious about what I was going to say?"

"Dying like a cat," I muttered. I actually did want to know but, as usual, refused to show it.

Joe raised an eyebrow. "That was weird," he said.

"What?"

"Your choice of wording."

"You know—curiosity killed the—"

"Yeah," he said, "I've heard that before. Just not in that way."

"Just tell me your idea," I said, becoming frustrated once again.

Joe chuckled. "Okay. Think about it. The detective gains nothing from helping this lady. She's not rich. She can't pay him. She didn't even ask him for help, *he* asked to be included." He looked at me to be certain he'd gotten the facts of the situation right.

I nodded.

"Because he's helping her find this key, he's spending a lot of time with her. Right?"

"Right," I said, my brows knitting together at the realization of the mess I'd written.

"Really, that's all he's getting out of this. Right?"

I nodded.

"The answer is clear."

I looked at him, frowning. "It's still fuzzy to me. I'm even more confused about why he would waste time on this. Maybe I'll just take him out completely. She can look for it alone."

"You can't do that!" Joe was vehement.

"And why not? It's my story."

"He's doing it for love! He loves her! Can't you see that?"

I stared at him. "My story is *not* a love story."

Joe chuckled, returning to his usual calm state. "It should be."

"I'm not a romantic, Joe."

"I know, but half your readers are."

I raised an eyebrow at him.

"Since you don't share your writing with anyone," he explained, "but I am going to bother and beg you until you let me see it, you and I are the only people who will be reading this. Therefore, half of your audience—meaning myself—is romantic. And I would like it to be a romance." Joe grinned.

"You are the strangest man I have ever seen," I said, shaking my head. "And there is no way you're going to read this."

"Afraid I will think less of you if I don't happen to enjoy your story?"

"Think I care if you do?" It came out harsher than I had intended, but his grin assured me it didn't bother him.

"Yup, I do."

"You've got a big head."

Joe made a face and patted his hair self-consciously. "Do I? It always seemed normal-sized to me before."

I rolled my eyes and decided to clarify, though he knew what I'd meant. "You're narcissistic."

Joe laughed. We both knew that wasn't even slightly true. Joe was more humble than a lot of people. He knew his faults and wasn't afraid to admit they were there—or to let others see them at their worst. It was a refreshing change from all the masks and flakiness that seemed to come from everywhere else.

I started packing my bag, assuming enough time had passed that we should head to The Diner.

Joe handed me some loose papers that had fallen from my notebook, and continued. "I'm just trying to decipher what works with you—what gets me what I want. So far what I've tried has been working, so I'm thinking I should just keep it up. Actually, I'm thinking if I stopped talking to you, that could get me what I want, too. Should I do it?"

I shrugged, and started to swing the bag over my shoulder.

Joe took it from me and swung it over his own. "You really don't care if I quit talking to you?"

"I would like to see you try."

"I think you're challenging me, Ella," he gave a half smile. "Are you?"

I giggled. "I might be."

Joe laughed.

"Hey you two," Uncle Bruce said with a smile as we walked in. "You're a little bit early today."

I glanced at the clock on the wall, a turquoise one Uncle Bruce had once attempted to modify; it had dents and scrapes left behind as evidence of his failed invention, but still worked swell. By 'a little bit' he meant nearly half an hour. "Oops."

"It's all right! You can leave early tonight to make up for it if you would like."

"Oh, that's okay," I said. "I don't have much else to be doing right now anyway. Joe successfully managed to destroy any inspiration I might have had earlier today."

Uncle Bruce glanced at Joe, amused. "That so?"

Joe smirked and stepped behind the counter.

"He insisted on talking to me when I was trying to write," I said, putting my hands on my hips.

Uncle Bruce looked pseudo appalled. "No!" he said dramatically.

"What is this?" I pointed to a long tube that was running along the edge of the counter.

"Oh," Uncle Bruce said, "that's part of a new invention I've been working on. It's not finished yet but if it works the way I'm hoping, it will make your job much easier."

"What is it supposed to do?" I asked. Most of Uncle Bruce's inventions ended up as flops, but he was always so cranked about them that I couldn't resist asking.

"Well you know how the pop is in the back room, so whenever someone orders one you have to go all the way back there to bring it out to them? It's a real pain, right?"

I nodded. The Diner was small, so getting anything out of the back room wasn't a big deal, but it *would* be nice to have it all by the counter.

"Well it can't be moved out of there, you know that."

"Yeah. That's the only place we have enough room for it."

"Right. So my plan with this tube is to hook it up to the pop back there. And there will be a different tube for each kind of pop—I'll mark them so you'll know which is which—and that will make it easier!"

I scratched my head. "I'm not sure I follow, Uncle Bruce. What do the tubes do?"

"Oh—" he said, lifting up one of the tubes to demonstrate, "the pop gets sucked from the back room, through this tube," he pointed, "and into the customer's glass. You won't have to leave the counter."

"How will the pop get from there to here?" I asked, glancing at Joe. He was being uncharacteristically quiet, and I wondered why. *He isn't really accepting my challenge, is he?*

"Well," Uncle Bruce said, scratching at his graying whiskers, "that's the thing I'm working on now. It needs some sort of a suction to happen, but I'm having difficulty deciding how to do that."

I turned to Joe. "Well? Any ideas?"

He shrugged.

"My, my," Uncle Bruce said. "Not a word. What *have* you done to him, Ella?"

I watched Joe carefully, wondering the same thing.

The bell over the door jingled and we turned our attention to the customer.

Eric grinned at me. I refrained from rolling my eyes and forced a polite smile in return, only because he was Uncle Bruce's customer.

Joe eyed him but said nothing. Eric was the only person in Backus Joe didn't greet with a smile and a genuine inquiry of their health and happiness.

"Get me a hamburger, dolly."

I put the meat in a pan.

"Anything else?" Joe asked, the first words since leaving the cemetery.

Eric narrowed his eyes in annoyance, as he always did when asked that question.

"You done wit' that meat yet?" He sounded impatient.

I glanced at him, confused. He'd been here enough to know the hamburgers took longer to cook.

Eric pounded a fist on The Diner's counter. "Answer me, or so help me—"

Uncle Bruce stood to his full height. "Eric Larsen, have you been drinking?"

I glanced at Joe. He looked back, concern etched in his features.

Eric shrugged. "Nah, Uncle Bruce. Leastways not 'nuff to do nothing to me."

"How many?" Uncle Bruce demanded.

He shrugged again. "Few. Where that hamburger, woman?"

71

I looked toward the stove. It wasn't done, but I didn't want Eric to become even more impatient, so I put it in a bun and slid the plate to him. I backed away once it was in his possession.

"Not your," his voice trailed off like he wasn't sure how to finish the sentence, then he started fresh: "Don't matter if I been drinkin'..." He took a bite of the burger and immediately spit it out; the inside was still frozen. His eyes flashed in my direction. "You!" He stood and advanced as far as the counter between us would allow.

Eric pointed a finger in my direction, angrily. "Murderer!"

I backed away, eyes wide, though if I hadn't been so frightened, I would have found the accusation comical. Uncle Bruce, eyes fixed on Eric, put a protective arm around me.

"Cool it, Eric." Joe stepped in front of us, blocking what the counter failed to. "Stay away from her."

Eric's finger moved to the uneaten burger on his plate. "That there is poison food!"

"Well I can't wait to see its effects," Joe smirked. "Now leave or I will walk you out myself."

"That so?" Eric began walking to the side of the counter: the entrance behind it.

Joe, keeping himself between Eric and me, sidestepped around the counter until he and Eric stood face to face. I couldn't move, and couldn't look away. Uncle Bruce's comforting stance beside me and hand on my shoulder helped, but I still felt myself shaking. Though I was assured of my own safety, I was afraid now for Joe's. Eric might be a coward, but even cowards are capable of causing harm.

Eric seemed to waver a bit, then turned and walked out, stumbling a little.

Joe's tensed shoulders relaxed.

Uncle Bruce turned to me, concerned. "Are you all right?"

72

I nodded. Eric hadn't hurt me; Joe had made sure of that.

Uncle Bruce scowled at the door. "Eric is no longer welcome here. If any of us see him, we are to kick him out."

"No, Uncle Bruce, you can't do that—" I said, surprised at my own words. "Eric is one of your best customers! You can't give that up."

Uncle Bruce shook his head. "The safety and peace-of-mind of my employees is worth much more to me than any money we may get from Eric or any other customer who threatens you."

"Could you give him one last chance?" I mentally winced at the thought of defending that man, but knew I had to. I couldn't let Uncle Bruce give up Eric's business. Not when The Diner was already struggling. "This was the first time he's done this," I continued. "It might not happen again."

"But it's *not* the first time he's harassed you, and I've turned a blind eye to it for far too long. He won't be allowed that freedom any more."

"Regardless whether he's allowed in here or not, the harassment isn't going to simply stop," I shook my head. "If he can't do it here he'll just find other places. And I feel much safer when he does it here." *When I have the two of you to step in and protect me.*

Uncle Bruce frowned. "I'll think about it," he promised. "After that stunt, I doubt he'll be back today."

I nodded, then turned to Joe. "Thank you…so much."

Joe shrugged and pretended the counter needed a good scrubbing.

I scowled at his silence.

He didn't look at me.

I yanked the dishrag out of his hand and glared at him. "Joe. Talk to me."

Joe smirked and shook his head.

"Joseph, so help me—"

Joe chuckled and pointed to my bag.

I rolled my eyes and picked it up.

He opened it and pulled out my notebook.

Uncle Bruce chuckled, fiddling with his invention. "Good luck with that, Joe."

"Oh, good grief. I wasn't serious about it being a challenge for you. And even if I was, I believe you now. Congratulations, now knock it off."

Joe smirked again, and took the garbage out in silence. *This is ridiculous.* Even the peppy songs the radio was blasting out couldn't lighten my mood as long as he was acting like this. Joe returned from the dumpster and started counting the cash drawer, though it hadn't changed since he counted it when he first arrived.

"Joe, this is stupid," I said.

He looked at me but said nothing, and pointed once again to my notebook. He returned to counting the money.

I closed the cash drawer and looked up at him. "Stop it."

Joe looked down at me. For a moment, our faces were as close to each other as they'd ever been. Joe blinked, looked uncomfortable, and stepped away.

"Please, Joe. I miss talking to you." I sighed, trying to ignore my own feelings about our proximity, though my pink cheeks betrayed me. "Fine," I said, "if you're going to be a baby about it, you can read it."

"Oh thank goodness." He grinned. "I was just about to crack. I can't imagine how you can be so stubborn all the time. That is exhausting!"

I playfully whacked him with the dishrag. "You're ridiculous."

"Yes, but it gets me what I want." He winked. "And," Joe chuckled, "I know how to wear you down now. I'll just hold my tongue, and you'll give me the moon."

I shook my head. "Like I have the moon to give," I said, sarcastic.

Joe looked as though he wanted to say something in response, but kept quiet.

"Besides," I continued after a pause, "I don't value your speech *that* much."

He chuckled; I had just proved the opposite was true. I hated that he knew one of my weak points...and hated that my weak point was so dependant on *him*.

Now he had something to use against me. *Can I trust him? Do I?* Images of what had just occurred between Eric and Joe answered those questions. Even in his stubborn state, refusing to acknowledge me, he had stood up and given his protection. *I'd be a fool not to.*

I thanked him again.

Joe shrugged. "All I really did was get in his face. If he'd done anything but stare back at me, well, I don't know what I would have done. Probably run, to be honest." He smiled. "Do you have any idea how intimidating that guy is? I didn't realize how tall he was until I was right next to him."

I giggled. "And here I thought you were being all brave. You just didn't know what you were getting into!"

Joe chuckled. "Yep, that's pretty much it."

Chapter 6

Wednesday, November 19, 2008
Jane Blake

When I asked my great aunt what her favorite part of growing up was, she said without hesitation, the Friday night gala. These galas brought the town together with music, dancing, and of course, food. I would like to tell you stories of people who met at the gala and ended up married, but let's be realistic. This is Backus; the people who went to the galas already knew everyone who was there.

> That isn't to say love stories didn't occur. Both my aunts fell in love while they were at the galas.

I stopped typing, frowned at the words on the screen, and aimed for the delete button.

"Can I read it?"

I shrugged and passed the laptop to Rosie, while she set her own laptop on my bed. "How's yours coming?"

"Pretty good. Cinderella just lost her slipper. You can read it if you'd like."

I picked up her laptop and read the first few sentences as she read mine.

"You know," Rosie said after a moment, "yours isn't bad at all."

"Really." I wasn't convinced.

"You just need an angle. You know, a thread that ties it all together. A specific love story—or not so lovely story—a mystery...something like that."

I nodded.

"You have an idea." Rosie grinned and waited for me to continue.

"I don't think I would be able to get any information on it, though. I mean, the people I would talk to would be my great aunts or Mr. Larsen, and none of them are very willing to talk. Aunt LeeLee would gladly tell me anything, *except* this."

"Jane." Rosie frowned, set my laptop on the bed and crossed her arms. "If you don't explain yourself quickly I'm going to want to harm you."

I smiled at the empty threat. "Well, Great Aunt LeeLee got kind of secretive when she was talking about why the galas stopped. She said they just fizzled, but she hesitated, and would say nothing more."

"Ooh!" Rosie bounced excitedly, raising my concern for the safety of our computers.

"Yeah," I said, putting mine on the relative stability of my lap. "It would be a great story if I could learn what really happened." I frowned. "I don't know how to do that when my sources won't talk."

"You have to think about who *else* you could talk to, silly," she stopped bouncing and closed her laptop. "My Grandma Sally was in Backus during that time, and so were most of her friends. They could tell you what happened."

"Oh, that would be great."

Rosie pointed to the hall.

Aiden stood in the doorway, hands on his hips, and jutted his lip out. "I want to go outside. You said you'd introduce me to singing Kyle."

Ever since I'd mentioned the strange young man who used his front yard as a concert hall, Aiden had been begging me to introduce him. *Why did I tell him about Kyle?*

As much as I would love another artist friend, Kyle had given me the impression *he* didn't. Plus, Rosie couldn't stand the guy; I trusted Rosie's opinion on everything else, and couldn't ignore it in this case.

Still, once I gave Aiden what he wanted, he'd quit annoying me with the same request over and over.

"Fine," I agreed, glancing at Rosie. "I'll take you there, and if he's home I'll introduce you to him. But Aiden, we have to make a deal here."

"Okay," he grinned. "What?"

"If Kyle *isn't* home, you need to drop this fascination with him. He's just a guy who sings. If he's not there today, you quit asking me to take you to see him." I looked at him cautiously, to assure myself he was listening. "Deal?"

Aiden hesitated a moment, then shook my hand with a grin. "Now let's *go*," he whined.

I looked at Rosie.

She shrugged. "I'll hang out in the creepy cemetery till you come back."

I laughed. "You can stay here if you'd like. We shouldn't be long."

Maybe Kyle will be gone and I can forgo ever having to speak with him again. I laughed to myself at the thought. *In this town?*

Aiden pulled on my hand. "We gonna go or what? You take too long. Can I have another cookie? Please?" he looked up at me with big, pleading eyes.

"No. Supper's soon." I helped him into his coat, and started the walk to Kyle's house. He wasn't outside when we got there, but as Rosie had said, he didn't spend *all* his time on the snow bank. Of course he didn't; not in a Minnesota winter.

Aiden half skipped, half skidded up the icy walk to the front door, and knocked before I had a chance to touch the bell. A lady's voice said, "Kyle! Get that, will you?"

He was home. *Uff da.*

Aiden realized this fact as well, and began bouncing in place.

In a moment, Kyle opened the door. To my shock, he smiled when he realized who it was. "Jane, right? Thought you'd ditched me." He chuckled. "Not that there's much of anywhere you could go to avoid people here."

I smiled a little.

Aiden stepped resolutely forward. "You're Kyle? I'm Aiden."

"This is my brother," I explained. "He, um," I colored. "Well he wants you to sing for him—if it's okay."

Kyle extended his hand. "Good to meet you, Aiden." He looked at me, then back at Aiden. "Clearly," he said, bending to Aiden's level confidentially, "*you* are the older sibling here. Am I right?"

Aiden squealed in happy amusement.

"I think I shall take that as a yes," Kyle said, winking at me.

I giggled.

"So, I guess I can sing a little. Come on in," he opened the door farther. "I'd love for you to meet my grandma."

Aiden looked up at me for permission.

"Um," I bit my lip, "I kind of left Rosie at my house, so we should get back," I said.

Aiden's lower lip made a swift return.

I sighed. "Okay, we can come in for a very little bit."

Kyle nodded, and closed the door behind us. "Grandma?" he called out in warning. "I have some friends I'd like you to meet."

We're friends already?

He led us to the living room, where an elderly lady with long gray hair was lounging on the sofa. "Well hello there, children," she said, a pleasant smile on her face.

"Grandma, this is Jane and her brother Aiden. They're the new neighbors. Jane and Aiden, this is my Grandma Carol."

"Yes," she said with the same welcoming smile, "call me Grandma Carol. Don't like none of that Mrs. or Ma'am stuff."

I returned her smile and shifted a little awkwardly, but Aiden marched right up to her. "Guess what, Grandma Carol," he said excitedly.

She closed her eyes tightly and seemed to be thinking.

"You'll never guess," Aiden said, grinning.

"Then why did you tell me to? Now I most decidedly have to venture at least one idea. Now let me see," she tilted her head, and nodded assuredly. "I am going to guess that you have just discovered an amazing new cure for the winter sniffles. Yes?"

Aiden shook his head, pleased that he had stumped her. "Not even close."

"Well in that case, I am sure I haven't the slightest idea what you might be referring to. But I would love for you to tell me."

Aiden grinned at the open invitation. "I'm losing one of my teeth!" He wiggled it for her, in case she doubted the truth of his statement. "Jane says a new one will come back and I don't have to worry that I'll be toothless forever like some old people are—"

"Aiden!" I scolded, embarrassed.

Grandma Carol started laughing. "Oh Kyle, do bring your friends around more often...they rather amuse this 'old person.'"

Aiden grinned up at me.

"Now, Kyle, go get these two some warm drinks. And you, sir," she turned to Aiden, "sit on the couch by me and just see what this old lady looked like once upon a time." She patted the couch next to her and Aiden enthusiastically hopped up.

I followed Kyle into the kitchen. "We really can't stay," I said.

"Yeah," he said, but still took mugs out of the cupboard. "Just sip a little of the tea or coffee or whatever and Grandma Carol will be satisfied. I'll sing something quick and you can be on your way."

"Okay."

Kyle prepared a mug of hot chocolate for Aiden and I accepted some peppermint tea.

Aiden peered up from the photo album he and Grandma Carol were flipping through. "Look Jane," he said, "she was my age once!" He seemed shocked at the discovery.

I smiled and sat beside them, sipping the tea.

Kyle put a frozen marshmallow in Aiden's hot chocolate and instructed him not to try drinking it until the marshmallow had melted at least a little.

Grandma Carol turned to Kyle. "Your friend is not very talkative. Her little brother makes up for her lack of chatter, though. I rather like this little guy."

Aiden looked up at her. "I'm not little," he said indignantly. "I used to be but I grew."

Grandma Carol was very amused by this.

I sipped my tea, shifting uncomfortably and glancing at the antique clock on the end table.

"Grandma," Kyle said, "I'm going to head outside with Jane and Aiden and sing a little. They'll have to head home after."

Grandma Carol frowned. "So soon."

"We'll come again sometime," I promised.

Aiden frowned. "I haven't finished my chocolate yet." He resolutely gripped the mug.

"Aiden." I pried it out of his chubby fingers and handed it to Kyle. "Don't you want to hear Kyle sing?"

"I want my hot chocolate!" He stomped his foot. Thankfully he was still much smaller than I was, and I picked him up. He was kicking and squirming but I managed to get a good grip on him.

"Thank you for the tea and the hot chocolate," I said to Kyle. "Looks like we'll have to hear you sing some other time. Sorry."

Kyle nodded and walked us outside.

I looked at him curiously, unable to resist a chance to learn more about him, in spite of Aiden's tantrum. "You haven't mentioned your parents," I said, shifting Aiden's now quiet but still squirming form to my other side. "Are they at work?"

"No."

"Where are they?" I asked.

Kyle frowned. "You know, Jane, I really don't know you all that well."

"Dad always says strangers are the people that logically you should trust the most, since you haven't given them power to hurt you yet," I smiled.

Kyle didn't return my smile. "Can we just not talk about it?" he snapped.

I stepped back, surprised.

"Sorry," he said. "Well, um, I'll see you." He went back inside.

Confused, and frustrated with Aiden for making a scene, I returned to the house.

Rosie looked up. "Just about finished here," she said, "and I have some thoughts for yours. I thought of some other story ideas, too. Want to hear them?"

"Of course." I sent Aiden to his room until he calmed down enough to be reasonable.

"What happened to him?"

I shrugged. "He didn't get what he wanted, that's all."

"Kyle wouldn't sing for him?" Rosie frowned, and sarcasm painted her tone. "Big surprise there."

I looked at her, perplexed once again by her uncharacteristically judgmental attitude, especially after the warm reception we'd just been given. "Kyle was very willing to sing. It just didn't work out tonight."

"Oh." Rosie turned back to her computer.

I frowned. "Someday you're going to tell me what this is about," I said. "For a town where everybody supposedly knows everything, there are way too many secrets here."

Rosie shrugged. "I have to get home for dinner now, but meet me tomorrow and I'll tell you my story ideas. Let's go to The Diner. You haven't been there yet, have you?"

Aiden emerged from his room after Rosie had left. "Jane," he said pleadingly, "can I have hot chocolate please?"

I smiled a little. Only a five-year-old would throw a tantrum and still expect to be given what he wanted.

"Is that a yes?" he asked, grinning, clearly taking my smile as a good sign.

Oops. I shook my head. "It's too close to supper," I said, "and you know Mom never rewards tantrums."

Tears came to his eyes. "I'm sorry," he wailed.

"I forgive you," I said, gently.

"So I can have some?" he looked hopeful once again.

I sighed. "No."

He started crying more and trudged to the couch.

Mom and Dad walked in, back from visiting a neighbor. Dad looked at Aiden, who was sitting, arms folded, and whimpering pitifully.

"What's his problem?"

I opened my mouth to explain, but Aiden answered for himself. "I want hot chocolate."

"And you can't have it because...?"

"It's too close to food time," he said, wiping his snotty nose on his sleeve.

"Well that seems reasonable to me," Dad said. "Doesn't it seem reasonable to you?"

Aiden frowned, seeing he would get no sympathy using his current tactic. He turned to try Mom. "I didn't drink other hot chocolate and I wanted to."

Her eyebrows went up. "You've already had some today? Then I think you definitely don't need any more."

"Please?"

"No, and do not ask again."

Aiden cried a little more but kept silent about it the rest of the night. In a short while he was once again smiling and laughing.

Everyone but me knows how to handle him.

The next day, Rosie and I headed to The Diner. It was decorated 50s style, with various shades of faded turquoise and pink decorating the walls, counters, and tables. It wasn't very big; there were only two booths in the entire place. The rest of the seats were high round stools arranged along the edge of the counter.

Rosie slid onto one of those stools and ordered a burger and coke; I did the same.

I noticed the menu called the place 'Uncle Bruce's Diner,' so mentioned that my great aunts had told me a little about him.

Rosie nodded. "He owned this place when he was alive. It was supposed to be left to his daughter, but Margaret died young. When Uncle Bruce died, it passed to Margaret's husband. But he doesn't even live here, so Kyle manages it instead."

I looked around; I had forgotten Kyle worked here.

"He doesn't work today," Rosie said, and then seemed embarrassed that she knew.

I gave her a curious look, which she returned with a smile but no explanation.

Our food arrived and we started to eat.

"So, you said you had some ideas?"

"Yes. First—and this only sort of relates to your article, it's mostly just something I've been thinking. I want to hold a gala. Maybe a lot of them, if it's a success."

"But if there's a reason the other galas stopped wouldn't that—" I began.

"Bring it out into the open? Yes. Yes it will." She grinned. "Plus, we can always use an excuse for a dance party! And the boys in this town could stand to take some dancing lessons. I bet Mr. Larsen would teach them. And I hear your Aunt LeeLee used to be a great dancer—she could teach us girls."

"It does sound fun," I said.

"Good. We'll start planning it then."

I nodded.

"Now for my article ideas. Well," she said, looking around, "I was thinking you should write about this place. Uncle Bruce and Margaret were well liked here. I'm sure people would love to see an article about them." She glanced at the ring on my finger, the one we had found. "You should learn where that ring came from, too. If it's at all connected to Backus, that could be another whole article." She grinned, still excited about the possibility of learning the ring's origin. "And, I don't know, check out some newspaper clippings or awards or something like that," she shrugged. "There are all sorts of trophy cases in the school you could look at."

"Oh?" I asked.

"Sure. I'll come with and show you sometime."

Kyle stepped out from a back room. "Jane! I didn't expect to see you so soon."

Rosie turned an icy glance toward him. He nodded acknowledgment of her.

"Oh, hey!" I said, ignoring the looks passing between them. "I thought you weren't working today."

"Considering I didn't tell you that, I *should* find it creepy you knew." He chuckled.

"You should," I said, also smiling, "but you won't because, you know, this is Backus."

"Are you saying our town is full of stalkers?" He put his hands on his hips and raised an eyebrow.

"That's one thing to call them," I giggled.

"My great uncle always called them caring neighbors. He wasn't from here, so the small-town atmosphere really appealed to him. Great Aunt Ella wanted nothing to do with it, though. They moved as soon as she could convince him to. At least, according to Grandma Carol. Never actually met them myself."

I smiled. "Well, I haven't decided what I think of it yet. I probably fall somewhere between those."

Chapter 7

Tuesday, October 27, 1953
Ella Mitchell

"Ella, Joe's here!" Linda screeched from downstairs.

From my room I could hear mother scolding her poor manners.

What is he doing here? I glanced at the clock, wondering if I was running late and Uncle Bruce had sent him to check on me. *My shift doesn't start for another ten minutes,* I noted with continued puzzlement. I still had time.

I quickly pulled my hair into a clip and went to the door. "Hey Joe," I bit my lip, concerned. "Is something wrong?"

He shook his head, smiling. "I decided that since we were both headed to the same place anyway, we might as well walk together. Well, if that's all right with you." He gave me a questioning glance.

I nodded. "Sure. But," my eyebrows knit together in confusion, "your house is closer to The Diner than mine is. It's out of your way to come here. Why didn't you just meet up with me on the road?"

Joe looked as though he was trying to figure out if I was joking.

"I just don't see the point of you walking here," I tried to explain, "when The Diner is in the opposite direction."

Joe opened his mouth, presumably to give some sort of reasoning for the irrational behavior, but Nicholas' entrance stopped Joe's explanation before it began.

He nodded to Joe, then turned to me. "I came to walk you to The Diner for your shift, but I see Joe beat me to it."

I shifted a little uncomfortably. Although, thankfully, my feelings for him had dissipated, things had been far from normal ever since he'd talked to me at the gala the month before. "Did you need something there?"

"A cup of coffee, perhaps?" Joe teased.

Nicholas shook his head. "A glass of root beer sounds lovely though. Speaking of pop, have you managed to get that invention up and running yet?"

Joe shook his head. "But that won't stop Uncle Bruce from trying until he either makes it work or has tried every possible option, and even some that aren't possible."

Nicholas nodded, smiling.

We started walking in the direction of The Diner. "What's the special today, El Bell?" Joe asked. "I always forget."

"Free pop with a hot dog," I said. "I think Uncle Bruce mentioned possibly adding a milkshake deal on Tuesdays too, but I'm not sure if he's following through on that."

Nicholas looked at us, confused. "Is he in need of more customers?"

I nodded.

Nicholas frowned. "Why not advertise for out-of-town people? Big city folk love this kind of small town vibe."

I glared at Nicholas for the mere suggestion. "No."

Joe raised an eyebrow at me.

I ignored him and kept walking.

Joe shook his head. "You're not going to make me ask it."

I shrugged. "If The Diner became popular with big city folk, there wouldn't *be* a 'small town vibe' anymore. We'll think of something that doesn't involve bringing strangers to our town."

"Any *more* strangers, you mean," Joe said with a chuckle.

We arrived at The Diner. "Hey Uncle Bruce!"

"Hey there! Nicholas—it's great to see you. What have you been up to lately?"

"Well, mostly working," he grinned. "I have a pretty steady gig now, fixing cars a couple towns over."

I headed to the back room to get Nicholas a root beer as they continued their conversation. When I came back out I overheard Uncle Bruce ask in a low tone, "When are you going to ask her?"

I made my presence known and the conversation stopped. I handed Nicholas his pop.

"Thank you, Ella," Nicholas said, and smiled at Uncle Bruce.

I looked around; The Diner was nearly empty. It had been that way for a few weeks now, even with Joe here. His cheerful interest in others had attracted more than the usual customers, at first. Now the rush had flattened out.

Nicholas went home after finishing his root beer.

"Uncle Bruce," Joe said, "have you thought about holding a bash here? People would come, and they'd be reminded of what they love about this place."

Uncle Bruce looked at him, a smile forming. "I like the way you think, Joe."

Joe smiled. "Ella?"

I looked up from sweeping the floor. "Yeah?"

"Will you help me plan it?"

"Oh, sure. I mean, of course," I said, surprised at the request. "It's a good idea."

"Thanks El Bell." Joe smiled.

I smiled back, feeling my cheeks turn pink. I turned away. I had just experienced rejection from Nicholas; I refused to let my stupid heart like yet another boy who would break it.

Okay, that's being dramatic. My heart is still fully intact. Still, I don't want to open myself to another disappointment. Besides, Joe doesn't like me. Every time we got a little bit close he pulled away. The dancing, the cash register...No; he didn't like me.

"Okay kids, I'm heading out for the night. Got some new inventions I'm working on at home and I'd really like to get some headway on them if I can." Uncle Bruce smiled. "Have a good rest of the evening." He winked at Joe and left.

I glanced around The Diner. The few people who had been there when we arrived had already gone. "A party could actually work," I said.

Joe nodded.

I looked at him. He was being strangely quiet now.

He looked back at me. "Hey, um," he shifted a little, and started tracing designs in the soapsuds left in the sink. "Ella?"

I looked at him, confused by his nervousness. He had never had a problem talking with me before. "Yes?"

He stepped closer, wiping his hand on the towel. "Um, I was wondering if," he paused, seeming to reconsider. "Well, could I walk you to the gala tomorrow night?"

"Walk me to the gala?" If that was all he wanted, I didn't see why he'd have such a hard time asking. "Yeah, but Nicholas usually does, so you really don't have to. I mean, you can. But, well, why?"

Joe stepped closer again, took my hand in one of his, brushed the curls away from my face, and, gently, kissed my cheek.

I stared, blinked, and stepped back a little. Had he really just kissed me?

Joe's pink cheeks told me he had. *Why?*

He shifted a little awkwardly and smiled at me. "You can, um, think about it."

"Yes," I said, "I mean—yes—you can walk me—I'd, um...I'd like it." I felt like a bumbling idiot.

Joe grinned. Remembering himself, he released my hand. "So, um, I'll come around six."

I smiled, and cleared my throat to purge myself of the awkwardness the kiss on the cheek had caused. "So..." my voice trailed off.

Joe gave his goofy half smile. "Sorry, didn't mean to mess our friendship up."

"You didn't," I said quickly.

"Good." He picked up the mop and went back to cleaning, as though nothing had happened.

I bit my lip, and slowly began wiping the dishes that had been left to dry. *He must have acted on impulse,* I decided, *and now he wants to forget about it.*

A few more customers came in throughout the day, but the traffic was nowhere near as thick as it had been. Joe initiated small talk with me, but the kiss on the cheek and the gala were never brought up again. I hoped the walk there wouldn't be this awkward.

Joe and I closed up The Diner and he walked me home. I wondered if he planned to make this a tradition. It wasn't likely. The days were getting colder and the snow was on the ground: here to stay for the rest of the winter. The shorter a walk to The Diner could be the better, and stopping at my house made Joe's walk nearly twice as far.

We parted and I retreated to my room, pulled my diary out, and began to write. Joe had been right in believing that many young ladies write in diaries. Where he had been wrong was in assuming I would bring mine out where anyone could see it. That would just be irresponsible.

I touched my hand to my cheek. He'd kissed me. On the cheek, but a kiss is a kiss, right? I scrunched my nose as I realized that wasn't true. Even my own brother could kiss me on the cheek. It was sweet nonetheless. What did it mean? What did any of this mean? I wished I knew.

He would walk me to the gala tomorrow, but that was hardly anything to leap for joy about. Nicholas had gone to the galas with me for as long as I could remember and it never meant anything to us. Well, it hadn't meant anything to *him*.

I was writing in long over-thought sentences again. I scratched out half of it. Then I blotted out the rest. I wrote simply, *I know now I like Joe, and not Nicholas. I don't know when the switch happened. Joe kissed my cheek today and is walking me to the gala tomorrow. I'm trying not to hope for much.* There. That covered all the important parts.

The next day I spent more time getting ready than usual. The gala wouldn't be until after five hours of work, but I wanted to be ready before going to The Diner.

I messed around with my curls until they lay in what could possibly be a proper style around my head, let them down and arranged them again, only to eventually decide to wear my hair loose. I washed up and found some nice smelling lotion I'd never tried before, and wore my favorite poodle skirt: the one with the record and music notes that my mother hated. I felt cute, no matter if Joe noticed.

Joe again came to my door and we walked to work together. "You look nice," he said. "All ready for the gala tonight?"

I nodded. "I figured we could just go right from The Diner," I hesitated, "er—if you're ready. That way we won't be late to it."

Joe nodded, though he looked a little hesitant. "You sure you won't need anything from your house?"

"I'm sure."

"Okay. Hey—did you hear Uncle Bruce finished the pop tube? It's so boss!"

I nodded. "It really is. I thought for sure Uncle Bruce was going to give up on it. But he didn't, and now we don't need to head to the back room anymore! Although I imagine it makes an awful mess."

"It does," Joe said, making a face. "You should feel free to work on it, though. You know Uncle Bruce loves new ways to tweak his inventions."

"Yeah," I agreed, "but I'm not good at doing that."

"That's only because you don't try wholeheartedly," Joe said. "If you did I'm sure you could come up with some really great ideas."

I shrugged. "That's Uncle Bruce's thing, and sometimes your thing. My thing is," I thought about it, "well, writing. And I kind of like math."

Joe made a face. "Math? My brain hurts just trying to figure out customer's change sometimes."

I giggled.

Joe raised an eyebrow. "Are you making fun of me?"

"Did I say anything?"

"You didn't have to; your girlish laughter said enough on its own."

I grinned. "Counting change is basic math, Joe."

"Tell my brain that."

I looked askance at him. "I thought I just did."

Joe shook his head. "You have to direct it up here," he pointed to his forehead. "And talk loud...my brain is a little deaf sometimes."

I rolled my eyes.

"Well clearly you don't care whether my brain hears you."

"You're right," I said, giggling, "I don't. I think your ears can relay the message just fine."

Joe pouted, and I laughed more. He looked ridiculous, a grown man frowning like a little kid.

"You care nothing for my poor incompetent brain cells," he said, crossing his arms indignantly.

"Oh give me a break," I said. Still, I stood on my tiptoes and yelled, "Counting change is basic math!" I leaned back on my heels and looked at him, beginning to feel embarrassed. "Happy now?"

He grinned. "Yes. I'm always happy when I've managed to make you self conscious."

I blushed more.

"And there's my reason why," he said, nodding to my pink cheeks.

"You're mean," I said, crossing my arms and looking away from him.

"Yeah? Well you're pretty."

He winked when I turned to him. I blushed even more, frowning a little.

"What? Guys aren't allowed to give compliments now?" He chuckled.

"I," I hesitated, "I don't know...you just never have before," I said, flustered, "that's all.

Joe nodded. "You're right. I need to get better at it. I find it easy to compliment Margaret...but then, Margaret's my cousin. There's no chance she'll take the compliment as anything more than, well, a compliment."

"Like other girls would," I said, taking the hint. *The kiss on the cheek was out of friendship. He felt comfortable because he knew—well, he* thought—*I wouldn't take it as more than that.*

Joe nodded again. "Yes. Like all those other girls would." He looked like he had more to say, but held his tongue.

We arrived at The Diner and Uncle Bruce greeted us with his customary smile, which brightened my day only a little. He headed out almost immediately, insisting he was close to eureka and wanted to get there before the gala began.

Once again, Joe and I were left alone. Oh my stupid, stupid heart. It never could interpret guys correctly, and it never could pick the proper guy to like. Nothing could happen between Nicholas and I, but I was finding out Joe wasn't a better choice.

I was only 20. My heart hadn't had much experience yet, and maybe age would teach it. But most girls my age were either already married or very close to it. At the very least they had a boyfriend. I had no one.

I stole a glance in Joe's direction. He was cleaning the milkshake blender and whistling a tune; utterly oblivious to the inner battle I was having with myself.

Joe glanced at me. "Something wrong?"

Okay, maybe not *so* oblivious. I shook my head. "Nope."

"Liar," he said with a smile.

I turned my attention to washing out the coffee pot and preparing it for a new batch of coffee.

Joe put a hand on my shoulder. "Hey."

I glanced at his hand and he removed it, taking the hint.

Joe watched me until I had no choice but to look back. His face held pain in it: pain and confusion. "Please talk to me, Ella. Tell me what's wrong. I want you to trust me," his voice trailed off.

And I want to trust you, Joe. But I don't understand you, and I'm not willing to let you in until I know what your plan is. I shoved the coffee filter in the machine and poured far too many coffee beans into it. Frustrated, I slammed the bag of coffee beans on the counter, and felt angry tears come to my eyes.

Joe looked more confused than ever. "Tell me what I did, Ella. I take it back, whatever it was."

I shook my head, turning away to hide the emotion my face betrayed. "You haven't done anything."

Joe took both my hands in his, forcing me to leave the coffee alone and look at him. "Ella Mitchell, we have been good friends ever since I came to town, and by golly I am not going to let anything I have done or failed to do change that."

The unwanted tears escaped, and my hands restrained in Joe's couldn't brush them away. I hated crying in front of anyone, and especially in front of the guy I had fallen for.

Joe's brow creased with concern. "Ella?"

I tried to pull away. "Just leave me alone, Joe." The tears had made matters much worse and I wished I were anywhere but there. "I told you I didn't want to talk about it. Why can't you respect that?"

Joe frowned, knowing that wasn't the reason for my tears. "Ella—what did I do?"

I tried once more to pull away and this time Joe released me. I wiped the tears away and stepped backward, away from him. "Nothing. Nothing at all."

"Don't lie to me, Ella," he said, gently but firmly.

I turned away, and started rearranging the dishes in the cupboard. For once I was glad The Diner had no customers.

"Please, Ella," Joe coaxed, "I want to make this better. Tell me how I can do that."

"You can't," I said. "You don't even know what's wrong."

"You're right," he admitted, "I don't. But I would if you would tell me. I would never want to hurt you. I care about you."

"As a friend," I said flatly.

Joe looked at me. "Yes, as a friend," he said slowly. "As one of my closest friends. And as someone whose friendship I do not want to lose."

I poured water into the coffee pot. "You should have thought about that before you kissed me."

Joe frowned. "You're right," he said, "and I'm sorry. I had no right."

I didn't want to be right. This time, I wanted him to tell me I was wrong. I wanted him to tell me the kiss was more than just an impulse, and that he didn't regret it—would never regret it. *Oh, you stupid tears, why won't you just leave and stay away?* I kept my gaze on the coffee pot. "So that's it then," I said, when my voice was finally stable enough. "It meant nothing."

"No, it didn't mean nothing. I'm sorry I did it only because I should have waited, until we were dating—until I knew if you even *wanted* to date me. I won't make that mistake again, and I wish you would give me a second chance, and a chance to prove that I mean what I say."

I stared at the lifeless coffee machine, unsure how to respond to this new information.

Joe started washing some dishes, having said all he could.

I picked up the towel to dry them.

He glanced at me. "Forgiven?"

I didn't look at him, but nodded and brushed off my wet cheeks with the back of my hand.

"So," he handed me a handkerchief, "we're still going to the gala, right?

"I'll have to go home first, and that will make us late," I said.

Joe grinned, strangely excited by that news. "Fine by me."

He walked me home after work and I fixed my hair and made sure I no longer looked like I'd been crying. Mother would have questioned tearstains if they were noticeable. She didn't, so I figured I was safe.

Joe stayed downstairs, I assumed being entertained by Linda. She had opted not to go to the gala, since she'd woken up with a stuffy nose and a sore throat. It had been more Mother's decision than hers, but in any case, she would be staying home with Mother and Father instead of attending it. She was probably glad of the momentary company Joe offered.

I no longer looked like an emotional wreck, so I went back downstairs. Linda had her ear against Father's office door and held her finger up to shush me when I saw her. She motioned for me to sit beside her and eavesdrop, and mouthed that Joe was inside.

I ordered her away from the door. There was only one reason I could think of that Joe would need to speak to my father alone, and it gave me butterflies to think about. As I considered it more, though, I realized there were several topics they could be discussing. My initial excitement waned. I wanted to ask Linda what she'd overheard, but knew it would be better to let Joe tell me himself, if he had anything to tell.

Linda and I went back to the couch and waited for them to finish. Eventually Joe came out, looking embarrassed but smiling. Father shook his hand and wished us an enjoyable evening. Linda hugged me and made me promise to tell her everything about it when I got home, saying with a dramatic sigh that it would be her one consolation for a disappointing evening, and we left.

The entire walk to the gym, Joe rambled on about meaningless topics. Maybe Father had given him permission but asked him to wait. If that was the case though, I wished he would tell me and not keep me in suspense.

More likely, as I had suspected before, the meeting had been about something completely different. Dad had sometimes talked privately with Nicholas about cars and sports. Although Joe wasn't very interested in either, he did have a thunderbird car. That alone would be food for at least three conversations. Why hadn't I just asked Linda when I had the chance?

Margaret greeted us with a smile and a hug. As expected, the dancing had already begun. Joe put my chicken salad and his fudge on the food tables.

Returning to my side, he took my hand and led me in among the swirling couples. I giggled, shoving my insecurities aside for the moment, and followed his lead. We'd been practicing more complicated dancing steps, some including leaps. He would warn me before attempting one, but even so I always managed to botch them up somehow.

Joe twirled me around, smiled, and pulled me close as the music ended. I sighed happily. I could definitely get used to this, if I was given the chance.

Monday, November 2nd, 1953

An entire weekend had passed since Joe had taken me to the Friday night gala. He hadn't been in The Diner on Saturday or Sunday. My brother Michael advised me to let Joe make the first move, if he was going to make a move at all, and my own sense of practicality said the same. Linda knew what Joe and Father had talked about, but I was stubbornly trying not to resort to that. If it was important, I knew Joe and I were good enough friends that he would tell me himself. If not, I didn't need to be worrying about it. If only that knowledge would calm my nervous heart as I knew it should.

I sighed and glanced at my watch. It didn't look like Joe would be coming to pick me up today. I tried to suppress the disappointment that brought, and glanced in the mirror. I had forced my frustratingly unruly hair into a pony, and my poodle skirt was laying well; I was ready.

I pulled my coat on and started walking to The Diner. It wasn't long before I realized Joe was walking toward me.

"I thought you were going to let me walk you there," he said as we met up.

"I wasn't sure you were coming, and didn't want to be late," I explained.

"I will always come, Ella." Joe smiled, looking gently at me.

I couldn't help but smile at that. Such a cheesy response, but I was starting to enjoy the cheesiness.

Joe offered me his arm and I accepted. We kept walking toward The Diner, but Joe stopped suddenly, startling me. "Ella," he said, "I forgot something. Well, I didn't forget it, but," he hesitated, "can we take a little detour?"

I started to check my watch.

"We'll get there in enough time," he assured me.

"Then I guess it's fine," I said. "Though, maybe I should go on ahead to The Diner while you get it—I mean we're already almost there, so," my voice trailed off as Joe shook his head.

"I really wish that you would come with me."

"Aw," I teased, "scared to go alone?"

"Something like that." He flashed his crooked smile as we turned a corner.

I smiled, but was confused. "Where exactly are you going? Uncle Bruce's house is in the other direction."

"I didn't say it was at my uncle's house," Joe said, mischievously smiling. He led me a little farther and stopped in front of Old Granny Mara's place. Her family from the big city had decided they wanted her closer, so they could take care of her easier. Her home, a small white house with a dormer window I had always admired, had been left empty for months.

"What are we doing here?" I asked.

Joe grinned. "I just thought I'd show you where I'll be living from now on."

I stared. "Really?"

"Went to Minneapolis and signed the papers this weekend," he said, still grinning.

So that's where he was. "That's great," I said, looking again at the house—no longer Old Granny Mara's place, but Joe's.

"I know something that would be even better."

I turned to Joe and waited for him to continue.

"Curious?" he asked.

I nearly hit him.

Joe chuckled. "I'm sort of nervous," he said. "Though not as nervous as I was when I was talking to your father," he smiled a little. "He can be a very intimidating man, you know. I rather like him though. He's quite amusing when he doesn't look like he wants you dead."

"Joe," I said, putting a hand on his arm, "you're rambling, and we're going to be late for work."

"Uncle Bruce said it would be okay if we were a bit late today," he said. "Ella, I," he stopped talking, took my hand in his, and led me to the steps.

I stared dumbly at him. My heart was beating wildly and I could do nothing but follow his lead and wait for him to continue.

We sat down, and he took my other hand in his as well.

I swallowed and waited.

"Ella Mitchell," Joe said, looking directly at me. "You intrigue me. You are beautiful, and spirited, and awfully terribly stubborn, and I like everything about you. Ella, may I court you?"

I grinned.

Joe was waiting for my answer. "I am trying to decide if that grin is because you're happy that I asked you, or because you're laughing at me for having the nerve to." He frowned a little, though his eyes were teasing.

I squeezed his hands. "I would never laugh at you for something like this, Joe," I said. I looked at his eyes; his beautiful brown eyes. "I would love to court you."

Now Joe grinned. He leaned forward and gently kissed my cheek. This time there was no possibility of misinterpreting the kiss' meaning. "We should get to work," he said softly.

I nodded.

Keeping one of my hands in his, we walked to The Diner together. I played the scene over and over in my head, smiling wider each time. *How did I become so blessed? I've done nothing to deserve this.*

Chapter 8

Thursday, November 27, 2008
Jane Blake

Usually Thanksgiving morning was filled with delightful smells of pies and turkey, potatoes and stuffing...the house would have been decorated and Mom would be running from place to place, directing Dad and I in preparations for the company that would arrive sometime around noon.

Today there was none of that. I had started to bake a pumpkin pie, but beyond that our meal was no different than any other day.

Grandma Blake and the rest of our relatives would be spending the weekend with Uncle Davey and his family in Florida. Mom and Dad had decided that since we hadn't lived in Backus for very long, we should stay and learn how they spent their holidays. But Thanksgiving was very much a family-centered holiday; the people in Backus spent it as everyone else did—indoors or visiting family elsewhere.

The doorbell rang. Apparently there was one family who didn't spend Thanksgiving inside.

"Hey," Kyle said, shifting a little awkwardly.

"Hey," I greeted, opening the door a little wider: a silent invitation for him to come out of the snow.

He did, but stayed near the front door even as I closed it.

"What's up?" I asked.

"I, um," he shifted a little, "I was wondering if you and your family could use some food?"

"Who's at the door, honey?" Mom called from the living room.

"Hey—come meet my parents," I said. It had only been about a week since we'd moved to Backus, so there were still a lot of people my parents and I hadn't met.

Kyle looked uncertain, but untied his boots, shoved his hands in his coat pockets, and followed me to the living room.

"Mom, this is our neighbor, Kyle. Kyle, this is my mom."

Kyle removed his hand from his pocket only long enough to shake hers in greeting. "It's nice to meet you, Mrs. Blake," he said, staring at the ground.

"And this is my dad," I said, as he and Aiden walked into the living room. Katty and Maggie, having heard a stranger's voice, followed them out, and introductions were passed around.

Aiden ran and hugged Kyle's legs.

Kyle smiled down at him and awkwardly patted his head. "I, um, just came to see if you would like some of our extra food? We have more than we need." He backed up a little, inching closer to the door. "I'm sure you already have your Thanksgiving meal though."

Mom looked toward Dad.

"We're having spaghetti tonight," Aidan said with a hint of a pout. He remembered last year's Thanksgiving and was longing for a repeat of the same.

Kyle looked surprised. "Well—we have turkey and stuffing and potatoes and some other things—if you guys want. I can bring it over."

Mom looked at Dad again, and he nodded slightly.

"I would love to meet your grandma," Mom said. "Robert, why don't you bring the car around and pick up the food and Kyle's grandma, and we'll all have Thanksgiving together? Would that be all right, Kyle?"

He looked a little wary. "Grandma doesn't get out much," he said hesitantly.

"Well then it's the perfect opportunity for her to. Try and convince her, Robert."

Dad nodded, pulling his keys out. "Okay Kyle, show me where you live," Dad said, walking to the car. "Jane? Will you come help get the food?"

Aiden followed us to the door. "I wanna go too," he said.

Dad shook his head. "You stay here with Mom, Katty and Maggie."

Aiden started crying. "I want to go!"

Mom called Aiden to her and he obeyed. She patted her knee and he climbed up. "Don't you want to keep me company? We haven't spent much time together lately."

Aiden glanced at us, and turned back to Mom, weighing what he felt were his options. "Okay. Can we play Candyland?"

"If you set it up," Mom agreed.

Aiden grinned, forgetting his tears of a moment before, and hopped down to get the game set up. Dad, Kyle and I took the opportunity to escape.

"Why doesn't your grandma go visiting much?" Dad asked as he started up the car.

Kyle shrugged. "Grandma Carol's health isn't the best, and this weather doesn't help. Plus, there isn't really anything she'd need to go to. I do the shopping and such. It's just easier for me."

"Makes sense," Dad said. "But let's just see if we can change her mind and entice her to join us. I think she'd enjoy it if she gave Thanksgiving with us a chance."

"She might," Kyle said. "She's in a pretty good mood today so I think she could have fun."

Dad nodded, and at Kyle's direction, pulled into the driveway. "Let's go in and meet the lovely lady," he said.

Kyle nodded a little and opened the door. "Grandma Carol," he called, "I brought Jane over again, and her dad."

Dad and I followed Kyle into the living room. Grandma Carol smiled. "Hello, Jane dear, so good to see you once again. I did so enjoy our visit last time." She turned to Dad, and gave him a quick inspection. "You must be her Dad, though you look nothing like her, really." She looked past us, as if expecting others. "Where is that little boy who was here last time? He amused me very much. Daniel? Kenneth?"

"Aiden," Kyle reminded her.

"No, that wasn't it," her brow creased and she looked at her hands, trying to think. "Well, maybe, I guess he could be an Aiden. Such a strange name to give a child." She looked up.

Dad and I covered a laugh.

She didn't seem to notice. "Well, what are you all doing here, then?"

"I went over to offer them our extra Thanksgiving food," Kyle said, adding softly, "Like I told you I would."

"Oh did you? That's nice," she nodded. "That's good. We have a lot you know...too much for just us two to eat. You should really give it to these friends of yours. Who are you again dear?"

Dad stepped forward and held out his hand. "I'm—"

"Yes, I know *you*," she said. "You're Aiden. Such a strange name. I was talking about the frightened little girl behind you."

I bit my lip, trying not to feel offended at being called a little girl, but stepped forward. "I'm Jane, ma'am."

"Ma'am. So formal. I'm..." a confused look flashed across her face for a moment, and disappeared just as suddenly. "I'm Grandma Carol." She turned to Dad. "And you're Ryan."

Ryan?

"Actually, Grandma Carol, this is Jane's Dad—Mr. Blake."

"Mr. Blake. So formal! I do not understand this unneeded formality."

"I'm Robert," Dad said quickly. "You can call me Robert."

"Like that better that Ryan do you? Well I don't blame you. I would too."

Dad colored a little. "My name is Robert."

"Why are you here again?"

"We were wondering if you might join us for our Thanksgiving meal."

"Oh no, I couldn't possibly. You see we have far too much food here ourselves and wouldn't want it all to go to waste by leaving to have some of yours. Thank you though for the invitation, and maybe some other Thanksgiving we'll accept. You should really take home some of the food we have though—we certainly cannot eat it all ourselves, can we Kyle?"

Kyle sat next to his grandma and looked at her gently, saying, "Grandma Carol, I've offered them food and they've accepted, and they are wondering if we could come, and bring our food, and have Thanksgiving with them. Doesn't that sound more enjoyable than having it here? You could see Aiden again, and meet Katty, Maggie, and Jane's mom."

"Jane's mom is Maggie then?"

"No, Grandma Carol, Maggie is Jane's younger sister. Jane's mom is," his voice trailed off.

"Kara," Dad said quickly.

"Such strange names you all do have. Okay. Why are we all waiting around here then? Pack up the food and let us be off!"

Kyle stared at her. Not even a struggle.

She stared back at him. "You got a problem?"

Kyle shook his head. "No, Grandma Carol."

"Good."

We packed the food in our car, made sure it wouldn't spill on the way over, helped Grandma Carol into the car, and bundled her up with blankets.

Aiden was standing at the door waiting for us, and grinned widely as we walked up. Dad and Kyle walked on either side of Grandma Carol, helping her up the icy path and steps.

"Hi!" Aiden yelled.

Grandma Carol looked up in surprise. "Oh yes! The little boy I enjoyed so very much! You are back." She smiled at him.

Aiden grinned. "Actually *you* are at my house. Ain't it pretty?"

Dad helped her inside and led her to the couch, next to Mom.

"And who are you then?" Grandma Carol asked.

Mom smiled. "I'm Kara. You must be Kyle's grandma."

"Grandma Carol, you can call me. My, what similar names we have. Maybe we should change yours to something that sounds a bit less like mine."

Mom laughed a little. "Oh, I think both our names are fine as they are. Did you have a nice ride over?"

"Nice as ever. These blankets are too warm though, I do not want them." She began shoving them off of her legs. "Let us eat, then. I am hungry and have been waiting for that boy to hurry and finish cooking and coming home and whatever else he has been up to. I am hungry and would now like to eat."

Mom looked a little surprised, but nodded. She turned to Kyle. "Is everything ready?"

He nodded. "Just have to set it out. Shouldn't take too long. Especially," he said, catching Aiden's attention, "if I have some help. What do you say?"

Aiden nodded vigorously. "Can Jane help too?"

Kyle glanced at me.

"Of course," I said. "And since the pie is all mixed, I'll just put that in and by the time we're done eating it will be ready for us."

"Thank you so much for all of this," Mom said, as she realized just how much food they had brought over.

"Oh it was far too much for us you know, and I wouldn't want it wasted, so I says to Kyle to go find someone to eat the extras, you know. To not waste it."

"Well we certainly appreciate it," Mom said.

"You haven't any food here then? Are you poor?"

Mom blushed a little. "We just haven't had time lately to do much shopping, since we've been unpacking."

Dad helped Carol to her chair, the rest of us sat down, and Dad bowed his head.

"Prayin', huh? We don't much do that, Kyle and I, but whatever you think is best." Grandma Carol shrugged and bowed her head.

Kyle bowed his head as well, and Dad led us in a prayer. Once we'd said the Amen's (I noticed Kyle kept quiet), we began passing the food around and chatting.

Mom managed to get Grandma Carol chatting quite animatedly, and Kyle and Aiden were having a very serious discussion about whether Legos or their competitors were the better brand of toys. Maggie and Dad were commenting on the food around the table and the fact that Grandma Blake would be coming for a visit next month, and Katty was joining into each of these conversations at will.

Having finished his discussion with Aiden, Kyle turned his attention to me, pushing me out of my comfortable silent observer position and into the entertaining hostess role.

"Your family is so fun," he said. "I'm glad Grandma Carol agreed to come today."

"You seemed surprised she did," I said.

"I was," he admitted. "She hasn't wanted to do anything in a very long time. It's good to see her out again. I have to apologize though, for how rude she's being," he frowned. "Sometimes I don't understand her. She didn't used to be like that. She was always a very sweet lady, ask anyone who knows her and they'll back me up on that."

I nodded.

"You don't believe me."

"I do," I said. "I'm just trying to figure out what could have caused that kind of a change in her. Was it sudden?"

Kyle slowly shook his head. "No...and it kind of comes and goes. Tomorrow she'll probably be her normal kind self again. It just doesn't make sense."

"Somehow it will make sense," I said, glancing at Grandma Carol. "We just have to figure out how."

"What are you, a psychologist?" he winked.

"Not yet," I said with a smile.

"Ah," Kyle nodded. "But you want to be. A few years back I studied psychology for my health class. It was interesting, I guess. Not something I'd have any desire to go into though. Why do you like it?"

"I can't think of a reason *not* to like it," I said. "To learn about the human mind, about what motivates people to do the things they do, or not do the things they refrain from doing," I smiled, my eyes shining in excitement, "it just all seems so intriguing. I'm a writer, sort of, so anything I can learn about people is great."

"So is that what you're doing when you're just quiet? Studying us and deciding what next to write about?"

"Something like that," I admitted. "I'm a journalist, though, not an author of fiction. Still, I like seeing how people react in different situations. It's just what I enjoy. What do you enjoy—besides singing?" I asked.

"Oh no," Kyle said, raising his hands up in a defensive manner. "I'm not giving you more story food!"

I laughed. "Story food? Didn't I just finish telling you I'm not a fiction author?"

"All the more reason not to give you details. You actually use real stories in your articles!"

I laughed. "Well, you're probably going to say something boring like 'accounting.' Why would I ever want to use that in an article? Nobody likes to read about accountants unless they're being made fun of."

"Well that's not very fair," Kyle said with a laugh.

"Think about it," I said. "Name one piece of writing that has an accountant in it and *isn't* a comedy."

Kyle thought for a moment. "*Stranger Than Fiction*? Wasn't that guy an accountant?"

"I think he was a tax collector. But in any case, isn't that a comedy?" I grinned, feeling proud of myself.

"I never thought it was very funny," Kyle made a face.

"Still, I'm pretty sure it's a comedy."

"Yeah," Katty piped in, nodding. "It's a comedy. I laughed during it."

"It's depressing!"

"Yeah but it's funny, too," I said. "Comedies can be depressing as long as they make you laugh along the way to the depression."

Kyle raised an eyebrow at me. "You're really not going to alter that in any way?"

"Why should I?" I grinned. "It's the truth!"

Kyle shook his head. "You're ridiculous."

"Haven't you read any Shakespearean comedies?"

"Do I look like the type who would read Shakespearean comedies? Or Shakespearean anything?"

I shrugged. "I act them out for my siblings whenever I have one assigned in school—or if I decide to pick one up just for fun."

"You *would* do that." Kyle chuckled.

"What? Read Shakespeare for fun? He *is* fun when you can get past the odd way of speaking."

"Whatever you say," Kyle said, shrugging.

"Okay," I said resolutely, "you are coming over for my one-man Shakespeare play next time I put one on. And after that, you're going to be part of it."

His eyebrows went up.

I continued, giggling a little. "It'll make the reading go that much faster. And I won't look quite so ridiculous and schizophrenic trying to talk to myself in every other scene."

Kyle chuckled.

"The characters do enough talking to themselves as it is, without being amplified by a lack of actors." I nodded. "You laugh but until you try it yourself you ought not judge," I said with a superior air.

"Who said anything about judging?" Kyle grinned. "I think you would be very amusing and enjoyable to watch. I myself am not an actor, though, so I will gladly watch you, but will decidedly not join in."

"You'll join in if I say you'll join in," I said, frowning in defiance, "and I just said you'd join in. So there." I crossed my arms and turned away to emphasize my point.

Across the table, mom gave me an incredulous look.

I blushed.

Kyle just chuckled again. "Okay then. You're so mature, Jane."

I turned to face him again and grinned. "Just about as mature as you are, Kyle. Refusing to join in a show that will entertain little children," I shook my head, a sarcastic note in my voice, "That's definite maturity right there."

"And agreeing to *watch* a show that is designed to entertain the children isn't showing maturity?"

I shook my head. "Not when the show is Shakespeare. It's only entertaining because of the way I do the different voices. Shakespeare is meant to be an adult's play. Everybody knows that."

Kyle shrugged.

The timer beeped and I jumped up to take my pie out and serve it.

"Oh how wonderful, how perfectly wonderful," Grandma Carol gushed. "You know I used to cook the most delicious of pies and cakes—real pretty ones too. No more cooking for me now, though. That boy over there," she pointed an accusing finger at Kyle, "won't let me into the kitchen. Can you believe that? I mean, really!"

"Tell them why, Grandma Carol," Kyle said. "What happened right before I asked you not to cook anymore? And," he looked at the rest of us, "I *did* ask. I couldn't order Grandma Carol to do or not do anything, and she knows that very well."

Grandma Carol just shrugged.

"If you won't tell them, then I will," Kyle said.

"Oh fie," Grandma Carol said. "He banned me from the kitchen after I started a," she paused, "a *very small* kitchen fire. I handled it fine and it didn't do any permanent damage. That boy is just a worrywart." She turned to Kyle. "And he knows *that* very well."

Kyle chuckled. "Grandma Carol's way of handling it was to calmly call me from the other room and inform me that there was a fire and 'maybe' I should try to do something about it. I might be a worrywart, but she doesn't worry *enough*. I have to do it for the both of us." He smiled.

"Nonsense. You hear the nonsense coming out of this boy's mouth? Sadly I didn't raise the boy myself so I can't be blamed or congratulated for anything that he does or says. That nonsense is in no way my doing."

I glanced at Kyle, remembering what he had said when I asked about his parents. His expression was unreadable, though.

Grandma Carol was talking to me now; she had barely paused, "This is good pie. Jane, you made this?"

I nodded.

"I suppose you use canned everything. Pumpkin pie is easy when you use cans."

I shook my head. "Sometimes I do, but I try to avoid it. Cans are okay but fully homemade is better."

"It really is." She nodded emphatically.

"Grandma Carol, would you like to come over sometime and help me cook? I would love to get your input on my recipes and try some of yours."

Grandma Carol grinned. "I would love that very much, Jane." She turned to Kyle. "Would you *allow* me to cook with Jane dear, or am I banished from any kitchen anywhere?"

Kyle smiled. "Have fun cooking with Jane, Grandma Carol."

We finished the pie and cleaned up the dishes and leftovers. Kyle helped me with the dishes; Aiden showed him where they all belonged, and Maggie and Katty put the leftover food in containers. Mom and Dad kept Carol entertained. We played games after everything was cleaned, and, feeling happy and full, Kyle and his grandma went back to their house.

Chapter 9

Tuesday, November 3, 1953
Ella Mitchell

Uncle Bruce grinned when we walked into The Diner the next day. "When is your first date?" he asked as we washed our hands and prepared to begin our work for the day.

Joe looked at me. "Well," he said, "we sort of hadn't talked about that. What do you say, Ella? Will you go out with me tonight?"

I looked at him in surprise. "Oh, ah, sure." My words had funny spaces between them that I seemed to have no control over.

Uncle Bruce smiled. "I'll let you kids out a little early tonight so you both have a chance to get ready for it. What will you do?"

Joe smiled. "I'd kind of like to surprise Ella with something, Uncle Bruce. So if you don't mind..." he chuckled, letting the sentence hang in the air.

Uncle Bruce chuckled along with him. "All right," he said, "I'll keep my nosy self out of it, for now. But I expect a fully detailed description when you both come in to work tomorrow, do you understand?"

I smiled. "Uncle Bruce, you are such a softie."

"A romantic," he corrected, "just like my kookie nephew."

"Romantic fools, the both of us," Joe agreed.

I giggled a little as I picked up a towel and began wiping the counters down. "Has anyone come in today, Uncle Bruce?"

"You better believe it. You missed the morning rush!"

I glanced at the clock. "Couldn't have. You opened less than ten minutes ago. Our customers would still be in here. They like to enjoy their coffee and chat with you."

Uncle Bruce smiled. "That so?"

"Yes, Uncle Bruce, it is."

"Well you, my dear, missed the memo that the rest of the town got by reading the *Backus Brochure*."

"You know I don't read that garbage." I scrunched my nose at the reminder of the town's pitiful excuse for a newspaper.

"I don't either," he said, frowning, "but," his frown changed into a wide smile, "I figure if they're going to give me free publicity I'd better take it."

"They advertised for you?"

"You bet they did."

"But why?" I was confused. The *Backus Brochure* hadn't advertised for anyone, as far as I could remember. Of course, that may had changed since I had stopped reading it.

"Because it was a breaking news story, that's why!"

"Uncle Bruce," Joe said, smiling with a mischievous glint in his eye, "I am really not following your train of thought here. I think you've taken it completely off the tracks." He shook his head. "Frankly, I have no hope for it ever returning."

Uncle Bruce gave Joe an amused look. "Same to you, kid."

I giggled and said, "Well, I kind of agree with Joe. I don't understand what you're talking about either."

Joe nodded. "Why was The Diner breaking news? I hate to be the one to tell you, but you've been open for quite a while," he chuckled. "Pretty sure everyone in Backus already knows about this place."

Uncle Bruce smiled. "But what they didn't know was that The Diner has broken one of its long-held traditions."

"What's that, Uncle Bruce?" Joe asked, tilting his head.

"The opening time. We open an hour earlier, and we get a whole new crowd!"

"Really? You opened at seven today?" I asked.

Joe looked at the clock. "My goodness we came in late."

"That's okay," Uncle Bruce smiled. "You didn't know about the earlier opening time. I didn't want to make you both come in earlier if there wasn't going to be anyone here. But now we know for certain— people *will* come earlier. So tomorrow, would you mind?"

"Seven it is, Uncle Bruce," I said. "That's great!"

"And the party?" Joe asked. "Are we still on for that?"

"Certainly. I made that silly *Backus Brochure* mention that as well."

"Um," I bit my lip, "I suppose you gave a date for it then?" I asked.

"Naturally."

"And," I moved some dishes from the counter to the sink, "I suppose that's going to be a surprise just like opening early was a surprise?"

Uncle Bruce chuckled and reached under the counter to pull out a copy of this week's *Brochure*. "How 'bout you read the article yourself? I know that breaks your boycott of them, but boycotts are made to be broken."

I shook my head, amused. "I didn't boycott them, Uncle Bruce, I just don't like reading what they put in it. But for you, I will."

"That's my girl."

Joe looked over my shoulder as I read the article.

"*The Backus town Diner*," I read out loud, "*would like to announce some new promotional features they are implementing.*" I turned to Joe. "Let's see how many highfalutin words we can throw into this." I rolled my eyes and continued reading. "*Starting this Monday, they will be open at 7am—a drastic change from the 8am opening time they have had since the moment they were opened...way back before this author can attempt to remember.*"

"Way to call you old, Uncle Bruce," Joe interjected.

Uncle Bruce chuckled and waved a dismissive hand. It didn't matter to him what they said.

I continued. "*The other big news The Diner would like to portray—*that is *not* the proper use of that word—*is that they will be holding a bash. Food is on The Diner, come prepared to enjoy yourself. The party is scheduled for this Wednesday night, and—*Wait, what??" I looked up.

"Wow," Joe said, shaking his head. "I don't blame you for not reading that. Although, I bet if you tried writing for them, you could help them change. Consider it a challenge from me."

I frowned at him, too distracted to respond to his challenge. "Uncle Bruce," I said, setting the paper on the counter. "*This* Wednesday?"

He nodded.

"This Wednesday, as in the Wednesday two days from right now?"

He nodded again. "Is there another?"

"You expect us to be ready for a bash when you give us only two days to prepare for it?" my voice grew in volume, my frustration coming through.

Joe put a hand on my arm. "Hey," he said gently, "there isn't a whole lot of prep that needs to go into it. It just needs a clean up here and a cook up there. We'll be ready in no time."

I glared at him. "Clearly you have never thrown a party for potentially an entire town before."

"And you have?"

I frowned. "No, but I know what goes into one, and it's not 'just a pinch here and a prod there.' It needs planning and preparation! Uncle Bruce, how could you?"

Uncle Bruce's brow creased, and he looked apologetically at me as I continued.

"Margaret helps with the gala each Friday and people bring their own food to that, and that *still* takes more prep time than you've given us!" That was probably an exaggeration, but I was too upset to think about facts.

He nodded understandingly. "I'm sorry, Ella."

I opened my mouth to continue, but a customer entered, and I stopped myself.

Mrs. Randall, an elderly lady who lived down the street from The Diner, walked in. She ordered a cup of coffee and asked me to make it for her. "Men are fine and dandy at some things, you know, but coffee, women are just better at. Do you mind, dear?"

"I would be glad to make some coffee for you," I said, putting some on.

"You boys oughtn't be offended by this, you know," Mrs. Randall said, pointing to Joe and Uncle Bruce. "I have tasted some pretty horrible coffee in my time, and it's all been made by men. Women just seem to have a knack for good coffee. They're better at it, you know."

"I honestly do not doubt it," Joe said, smiling good-naturedly.

"You know I never drink the stuff," she said, though she had just shown she was basically an expert on it. "I figured today was an exception. I often ask myself what I am doing in a town that gets so cold in the winter and even sometimes in the fall and spring." She shook her head. "I really haven't found a decent answer yet. But I will think of one someday, or I will move."

"Where would you move to?" I asked.

"Oh, somewhere warm, naturally. Iowa, perhaps."

I covered a smile, and could hear Joe trying to hide his laughter. Iowa was hardly a southern state.

"I was out walking today, and I remembered reading something about this place in the *Backus Brochure*," she paused. "Why I was reading that thing is beyond me, but so I was."

Joe chuckled.

"You know," Mrs. Randall continued, "I have always wondered why they call it a 'brochure.' It is clearly a newspaper! If they're going to publish something like that they could at least get the term correct."

I nodded; I had wondered the same thing. I handed her a cup of coffee.

She accepted it, and looked around. "You don't look ready for a party here," she commented.

"We're not," I said, trying to keep the frustration out of my voice.

"But we will be when Wednesday comes," Joe said, grinning optimistically. "And we hope to see you there."

She smiled. "So tell me, what is the scoop around here? Are there any new marriages, babies, or scandals? Is there any news at all? You know I can never believe what that brochure paper says. I like to hear it from the source—and then pass it on. Then it's truth."

Well, maybe, but it's still gossip. I glanced at Joe.

Uncle Bruce was grinning with his knowledge, but he would say nothing without Joe's permission. I decided to take that stance as well.

Joe shrugged. "Well, there's nothing new here." He winked at me.

Mrs. Randall's eyebrows went up.

Joe smiled and looked at me for direction. I nodded slightly.

"Actually," he slipped his hand into mine, "Ella and I have some news."

I couldn't keep the smile off my face as I watched him reveal our courtship.

"Oh this is splendid! This is grand! You know it is all we have been talking of! Well—originally we did want Ella to go with that Nicholas fellow, and there were some who said Eric would be the better match for her—but once you came to town, Joe, the general consensus was that you would be perfect together."

I wanted to hide in the back room. Everyone knew the gossips talked about anyone and everything, but I'd had no idea they were secretly matchmakers—and that I was one of their victims! And Eric? Nicholas I could understand, but Eric? Ugh.

"The both of you are simply darling—darling! Joe, you are quite taken with her, aren't you? And Ella, those dear pink cheeks say more than words ever could."

I was certain if they were pink to begin with, they were positively red, now.

She looked at her watch. "Well, I do believe I will be heading home now. It's oh so cold today and I don't want to wait any longer to get back to my cozy house."

A steady stream of customers came in throughout the rest of the day. Advertising in the town's newspaper had been a very good idea. Around five o'clock Uncle Bruce told Joe and me we could head home, so Joe walked me to my door. He promised to be back in an hour to pick me up and bring me to my surprise. He said to dress nicely—then stammered and muttered something about me always dressing nicely so he was sorry he'd said that and wouldn't again.

I giggled at his adorable awkwardness. Glancing through my closet, I decided my blue dress would be best. The skirt flared out just like my poodle skirts did, but it was fancier than those. I pulled a sweater on and attempted to do something decent with my hair. The curls were surprisingly tame today, and in a short while I had a pretty updo, with a few curls left loose at Linda's urging.

I borrowed some of my mother's makeup and after putting it on, washing it off, and putting a very little on again, I felt ready for whatever Joe had planned.

Throughout all this, Linda was hopping around, chatting and excited for me, and Michael was chuckling and muttering 'I told you so' when he thought I wasn't paying attention. Father nodded at me when I came down, dressed for the date—his sign of approval. Mother smiled and said something about how she was hoping this didn't end badly for me.

I sat on the couch, pulled out a cigarette, smoked the first couple puffs and snuffed it out, and then simply fidgeted until Joe knocked on the door. He smiled when he saw me, and offered me his hand. I accepted it.

Dad told Joe to have me home by 10 and Joe agreed. He led me to his car and opened the passenger side door for me.

"I didn't realize we'd be driving," I said as I sat down.

"I know you're in good shape, but it's still pretty far to walk." Joe got in and started the car. "By the way," he blushed a little, "you look beautiful."

I smiled and self-consciously patted down the wrinkles out of my dress. "So I take it we're going out of town?"

"Yeah. First time for you?"

I giggled and playfully shoved him.

"Hey now—no abuse of the driver or you'll put us both in danger."

"You call that abuse? Really?"

Joe chuckled. "The point remains. You value your life; you keep your hands on your side."

I rolled my eyes but obediently folded my hands in my lap.

"You didn't answer my question," Joe said.

I giggled. "Of course I've been out of town. Uncle Bruce used to take Margaret and me to the big cities every weekend. And my father works the next town over, so I've gone with him sometimes, too. In the summers, when Mother was tired of watching us, he'd take us with and we'd play at the park while he was working."

"Well, then you may recognize some things. My only option is to keep you so occupied you don't notice. I must think of ways to exercise this option," his voice trailed off as he presumably began to think of ways.

"Is it a long drive?" I asked, ignoring his ridiculousness.

"If I told you that, you would have even more of an advantage. You must think me very silly, to think I would give away key information." He shook his head.

"I do think you're very silly." I giggled.

"Hmm..." Joe mused. "Apparently silliness is something you admire in fellows, or you would never have agreed to come with me today. Unless you only agreed out of pity...I know it's easy to feel sorry for a guy like me." He glanced at me as he took a right turn. "But from what I know about you, you don't seem the type to go on pity dates. Are you? Tell me truly, Ella dear, is this a pity date?" The corners of his eyes wrinkled, my only clue he was teasing.

"Oh Joe, of all the ridiculous—"

"You need not spare my feelings," Joe said, in a serious tone. "In case you decide to start that, today. Tell me the truth. Did you agree to it because you think I'm funny looking and it might be the only date I'm ever lucky enough to go on?"

"I'm not talking to you anymore, Joseph." I crossed my arms. "You are unbelievable."

"Ella, if you don't talk to me, this date won't be very enjoyable for either of us." He colored a little. "And I was sort of hoping that you would let me take you on another one after this—even if this *is* just a pity date. Sometimes pity dates turn into more, you know," he smiled. "That happened to Uncle Bruce."

I looked at him, surprised. "It did?"

"Okay...no, it didn't. Aunt June was quite smitten with him."

I smiled. "Well, regardless, this isn't a pity date."

He still seemed skeptical.

I shook my head. "I'm not going to boost your ego by saying more than that. If you don't want to believe me, fine."

Joe smiled. "I was teasing, El Bell. Someday you'll get used to that." He winked. "Though to be completely honest, the teasing did hold a little truth to it. You're, well," he kept his eyes on the road and his voice got quiet, "you're amazing. So the fact that you agreed to court me," he turned to me for a second and smiled, "kind of caught me off guard."

I stared at him. *He thinks he is the lucky one? Is he serious? He has to be teasing.*

He seemed serious, though.

I frowned. "I wouldn't have gone on this date with you if I hadn't wanted to with all my heart, and you know me well enough to know that's true." I smiled. "No more insecurities, okay?"

Joe saluted me, and grinned a little.

I looked curiously at him. "What?"

"Well, two things," he said. "First: you're incredibly adorable when you get all worked up. And second: my plan worked. Where are we now?"

I looked around. "I honestly don't know," I said. "I was distracted."

He grinned. "Good. I love it when my plans succeed." Joe pulled into a parking lot. "Do you like theater?"

"I haven't seen much of it," I admitted.

"Well that's why you don't recognize this place. Not that I recognize it, either, but I hear it is quite popular with Minnesotans."

I looked at the name. "The Orpheum." I shrugged. "I think if I had heard it before I would remember."

"It *is* a rather strange name." He smiled, and hopped out of the car. He grabbed hold of the roof, and before I knew what he was doing, he had rolled over the top to my side and opened my door.

I stared at him. "You do this often?"

Joe chuckled. "Only for pretty young ladies," he said with a wink.

I made a face, hiding how impressed I was by the maneuver.

He offered his arm and I accepted it. The parking lot was full, and people of all sorts were walking inside.

The theater itself was gorgeous. Ornate carvings lined the walls, and a large red curtain covered the screen. I felt a little out of place, even in my best dress.

Joe glanced at me. "You okay?"

I nodded. "Just kind of in awe. I mean, it's not like we have anything like this in dinky little Backus."

Joe chuckled. "You're right about that. I do love Backus though."

I knew that about him, but was curious. "Why?"

"Oh that's right," he said, his eyes teasing. "You have decided that Backus is a den of gossips and want nothing to do with the place."

"I'm still living there, aren't I?"

"Yes, but I've always sensed that you live there out of necessity, and begrudgingly at that."

I looked at him out of the corner of my eye as the usher directed us to a row near the front of the stage. I wasn't sure how to respond. He was right, of course. I knew he liked Backus, though, and didn't want him to worry that if things worked out between us I would force him to leave; I wasn't *that* self-centered.

"How did you manage to get seats so close to the front?" I asked, glad for an excuse to change the subject.

"I've had these tickets for a while," Joe said, coloring a little. "I, um," he fumbled with the ticket stubs, "have kind of been planning this for," he hesitated, and shoved the ticket stubs into his pocket, "a while."

"How long is a while?" I asked.

"Well—that's something you're not going to find out," he smiled mischievously, "for a while." He winked.

Chapter 10

Saturday, December 6, 2008
Jane Blake

I sat down with my computer and began to type. It felt good to be writing again. The town paper had taken a week off for Thanksgiving. I was finding it difficult to get back into the routine of researching and writing, even with Rosie's suggestions.

I had no new information. Maggie and Katty were running around our backyard with some neighborhood kids, and Aiden was declaring loudly that he wasn't tired and didn't need sleep. Even without the background noise it was difficult to concentrate.

Plugging headphones into my ears to distract from the chaos bedtime created, I decided to make a list of possible topics.

```
-Diner
-Ring
-Specific love story
   Great Aunt LeeLee and Great Uncle
   Frank?
   Rosie's grandparents--Sally and
   Fred?
-Backus Blab?
-Spotlight a community member? (Maybe
Grandma Carol?)
-Galas
-Fashion
```

I sighed. Those all required more research. Out of habit, I signed into my social network account the moment I went online. *Focus, Jane.* I opened a new tab and did a Google search of Backus history. A couple pages told me how Backus was first created. Interesting, but only good for one article.

I pushed my laptop aside; Google would be useless here. I'd have more success talking to people directly.

That would have to wait, though. I was in the process of moving the majority of my things from my room to the basement, so Grandma Blake could have my room while she stayed with us for Christmas.

By the middle of the next day, my room was ready for her. Grandma Blake hadn't visited since we'd moved here. When we lived in the city, we had been only a couple miles from her. We could visit to talk, cook, or just spend time together. I missed that.

Aiden squealed and ran outside, my sisters and me following closely behind, when we saw her car in the driveway.

Grandma Blake opened her arms wide and hugged us all. "Oh my goodness, you've grown!" she said to Aiden. "And you, my dear Jane, are stunning. There's my Katty's beautiful smile! I've missed that. And Maggie—your hair is getting so long and gorgeous! All of you need to stop growing up so quickly!"

Mom and Dad came out and greeted her. Hugs and compliments distributed, we led grandma inside and showed her to my room.

"I certainly hope I'm not taking this from anybody," she said as we moved her bags inside.

I shrugged. "Don't worry about it."

She glanced around. "You know, I grew up in this house."

"Really?"

She nodded. "It was a whole lot bigger, then."

Aiden giggled. "It shrinked?"

"Must have," she said with a wink.

"Whoa." His eyes grew wide and he glanced around the house.

"Jane," Grandma Blake said, glancing toward the kitchen. "Are those cookies I smell?"

I nodded. "Your favorite." I'd made my special version of chocolate chip cookies—the one recipe I had been able to improve with my additions—in honor of her coming.

"Do you have enough made for a friend of mine to have some as well?"

"Sure," I said. "Someone from here?"

Grandma shook her head. "No, he actually lives by me in the city. You remember Mr. Jensen?"

"Of course. You've been friends for a while, haven't you?" I remembered him spending some holidays with us, and the summer before, after Grandpa Blake had died, he had spent most of his time comforting Grandma. "He's coming?"

"Yes. He'll be staying with Mr. Larsen, but spending Christmas with us."

I looked at her, surprised. "You know Mr. Larsen?"

133

Grandma nodded. "I know just about everybody here. Mr. Larsen—Eric—has been a good friend of mine for many years."

"Really? He seems kind of like a," my voice trailed off as I tried to think of a good word for him.

"An old sourpuss?"

I smiled. "I was going to say loner."

"You're nicer than I am. He can be both, sometimes. So you've met him, then," she said, smiling. "I'm glad."

I nodded. "He's the editor of the local paper—the *Backus Blab*."

The smile left Grandma's face. "You're kidding," she said blandly.

I shook my head. "Why the reaction, Grandma?"

"Well," she said, shaking her head, "when I wrote for the newspaper it was called the *Backus Brochure*. When I finally grew tired of the articles being, basically, gossip, I left in a huff," she smiled a little, "and said that if they were going to continue to print that garbage they might as well let the readers know in advance—so I suggested a name change."

"*You* are the reason it's called the *Backus Blab*?" My eyebrows went up in surprise.

"I never expected them to take me seriously!" Grandma laughed. "I'm surprised Eric got involved in it. He never seemed the type. Are you a part of it at all?"

I nodded. "I started writing for them not long after we moved here."

She raised an eyebrow, her cue for me to continue.

"Rosie—Mr. Larsen's niece—asked if I would. We're trying to make the stories more legitimate."

"So it's still printing gossip."

"Or something bordering on it, yeah. Hopefully we'll be able to change that. It will probably take some time, but I think it's going in a good direction now."

She didn't seem convinced. Naturally she wouldn't, since she had tried the same thing years earlier without success. "What is your job with it?"

"I'm the historian," I said.

"Is that a new position? I don't remember a section for that."

I nodded. "It kind of was created just for me."

"Well, that's a good change," she smiled. "It's easy to get historical facts wrong, but it's less easy to make gossip out of it."

"Yeah," I said. "I still would like my facts to be as truthful and accurate as I can make them, though. Which is why," I sat on the bed and motioned for her to join me, "I was sort of hoping you could help me with some of them?" I bit my lip out of nervous habit. Grandma had never liked talking about her past. It was over and done, she said, and bringing it up again didn't help anyone.

Grandma surprised me by reacting with laughter. "I didn't realize I was old enough already to be classified as historic."

"Well, Backus has only been around about one hundred years," I said quickly, "so anything that's been here longer than about ten years is considered history."

She smiled. "I appreciate you trying to spare my feelings with that obvious fabrication, my dear. I don't believe a word of it."

I opened my mouth to object; Backus hadn't been founded until 1898, and even then it was a lumber mill before it became an actual town.

Grandma continued before I could assure her of this fact, however. "Nevertheless I am very willing to help you in any way I can."

Shocked by this, I could only respond with, "Thank you!"

"Now," Grandma Blake said, glancing again toward the kitchen, "where are those cookies I was promised?"

I smiled and led her to them. As she watched me put a pile of cookies on a serving tray, I noticed her expression change to confusion, and what seemed like a touch of sadness.

"What is it, Grandma?"

"That ring..."

I followed her gaze to the ring I was wearing. The mystery had never been solved, much to Rosie's disappointment. It was lovely though, with the unique pearl flowers and sapphire centers, and I had decided to wear it until the rightful owner was found.

"Do you recognize it?" I asked quickly, excited.

Grandma didn't answer, and instead had a question of her own. "Where did you find it?"

"It was in with my things," I said. "I found it when I was unpacking the boxes in my room. Grandma, do you know who it belongs to? Is it yours? I don't remember seeing it before, and neither do Mom or Dad."

Still avoiding my questions, Grandma held out her hand. "May I see it?"

I slipped it off my finger and into her waiting palm.

A slow, nostalgic smile came to Grandma Blake's face as she sat at the table and looked more closely at the ring. "It makes sense that your parents don't recognize it," she said, "because they never saw me wear it."

"So it *is* yours," I said.

She nodded, and as she kept her eyes on the ring, tears started to form.

I quietly sat beside her at the table. "Grandpa Blake gave you it, didn't he?"

She nodded again. A single tear, released by the movement of her head, slipped down her cheek. She brushed it away quickly.

I got up and handed her a box of tissues.

Mom peered into the kitchen. Taking in the scene before her, she motioned me over. In a low tone, so only she and I could hear, she asked, "What happened?"

Neither of us were used to seeing Grandma Blake emotional. I matched her volume and explained, "The ring I've been wearing was hers, from Grandpa."

Mom nodded understandingly, and ushered me back to Grandma's side. She left the room to give us privacy, but by the time I returned to the table, privacy was no longer needed.

Grandma's smile had returned, leaving only a crumpled Kleenex and slightly blotchy cheeks as evidence that anything at all had been amiss. Grandma Blake had never been one to reveal her emotions, and she wasn't about to start now—even if those emotions were completely acceptable.

After 50 years together, Grandpa Blake had died of lung cancer. Grandma Blake would probably always miss him, but even at the funeral she showed little emotion.

She had walked to the front of the church, and said, "When he asked me to marry him, I made him promise to give me 50 years." She hesitated for a moment, and then actually *smiled*. "He did. It's only now I realize I should have asked for 75."

We all laughed a little, but everyone was wishing she hadn't felt the need to guard us from her true feelings. If anyone is entitled to tears, it's a widow at her husband's funeral.

Grandma handed the ring back to me. "This was my engagement ring," she said. "When we were married, your Grandpa replaced it with this." She held out her hand to display her wedding ring—a beautiful diamond design inlaid in a twisted gold and silver band. I'd always admired it.

"I actually liked this ring a bit better, though," she said, looking again at the ring I'd been keeping as my own. "It's much less pretentious. But your Grandpa declared I could have nothing less than diamonds. He said I would simply have to endure one cliché in my life, and he was certain that eventually the ring and I would become the best of friends. That hasn't happened yet."

I smiled, surprised and delighted with how much Grandma was sharing—and also at the reminder of the unique and amusing way Grandpa would word things.

In the past if I ever dared ask about Grandpa, Grandma gave a quick answer and changed the subject, not wanting to be reminded of memories that must have been painful. Later I would wonder at the reason for this change, but for the moment I was content to set my psychiatric tendencies aside and simply enjoy listening to her recount tales I hadn't yet heard.

I had been thirteen when Grandpa died, so I was old enough to remember bits of his personality and held onto several cherished moments we had shared.

Grandma was describing the first time she had met Uncle Davey. He had been three at the time, and was staying in an orphanage Grandpa had secretly been visiting. Immediately after their wedding, they adopted him—at Grandpa's urging, of course. No bride wants to begin a marriage with a three-year-old child to nurture.

As she finished, I started sharing a memory of Grandpa Blake when I was eight. I had fallen off the monkey bars and skinned my knee. When I insisted that ice cream was "the only thing in the world that could ever make me happy again," Grandpa said he felt sorry for me, because if I kept that resolve, I was destined to be a very sad girl the rest of my life. He refused to buy the ice cream.

"He didn't!" Grandma interjected. "Of the two of us, he was much more softhearted!"

I smiled. "On this particular day he decided I needed to learn not to rely on outside sources to ensure my happiness, more than I needed ice cream. He spent the rest of the day making me giggle in spite of myself, and by the time we were ready to go home I had completely forgotten that I had wanted to remain sad. And when Grandpa saw that was the case, *then* he bought me ice cream."

Grandma smiled. "That sounds more like him."

"I'm glad he did it like that," I said. "That has stuck with me ever since as one of the best days I've had. If he'd simply pacified me with what I asked for, I doubt I would even remember it now."

I heard a noise and glanced toward the kitchen door. I blushed as I realized we had an audience.

"Hello, Jane! It's been a while." Mr. Jensen smiled widely.

I stood and hugged the older man. "It's good to see you again, Mr. Jensen. I hear you'll be spending Christmas with us again this year."

"Yes, well, since my Etty died and we weren't blessed with children of our own, the kids of my friends have been passing me around from house to house each holiday. They just don't know *what* to do with me." He winked.

"Oh, hush," Grandma said, smiling.

Mr. Jensen continued, "So it looks like it's your family's turn to be stuck with me yet again."

Grandma rolled her eyes a little, though her smile remained, and—was that a blush? *How can anyone but Grandpa Blake make her blush?*

Mr. Jensen was handsome, I supposed, in an older gentleman's sort of way, and I knew I liked his personality, but...no. I didn't want another grandpa, and Grandma couldn't have gotten over a love that had lasted more than fifty years, just like that. Hadn't she just been crying over him moments before?

I must have just imagined the blush, I decided.

Mr. Jensen interrupted my disturbing thought process with, "Did you girls happen to save any cookies for a tired old traveler?"

"Watch your language," Grandma said.

139

I looked at her, confused.

Mr. Jensen smiled and apologized, then turned to me. "You see, if I call myself old, that means I'm calling your Grandma old as well—which I would never *dare* to do—so I need to lay off on the personal insults when I'm around her."

After Mr. Jensen left for Mr. Larsen's and Grandma headed to bed, I got cozy with the piles of blankets and pillows on the guest bed in the basement and pulled my laptop out of its case. Grandma had given me plenty to work with. She and Grandpa had spent many years in Backus. They would be my focus for the next few articles: how they met, fell in love, and what happened in the fifty years that followed.

My laptop was now fully booted up, and I began to type.

> My grandparents' love story began, matured, and ended, all here in Backus. They met more than fifty years ago, when...

I stopped writing, stuck already. I would have to do more asking before I could finish that article. I decided instead to write about one of the stories she had told me earlier that night, since it was still fresh in my mind.

> My grandparents are the only people I know who began their marriage with a three-year-old child that belonged to neither of them. Well, only technically. In their hearts, he belonged to both of them.
>
> My grandfather––

I backspaced and replaced the word with 'grandpa.' He would never fit the stern image the word 'grandfather' evoked for me.

My grandpa first met my Uncle Davey during visits to an orphanage outside of town. Without telling anyone where he was headed, he would visit whenever he had some time off, and soon the children began to count his visits among their happiest times. If you knew my Grandpa Blake, you know why. If you didn't have the pleasure of knowing him...I'm sorry, but he simply cannot be reduced to words.

The first time my grandma met the boy she would eventually call her own, my grandpa had secretly planned it. His plan, which eventually worked, was to introduce them to each other and wait as they (inevitably, in his mind) grew to care for one another in the same way he already cared for Davey.

"You going to tell me what this is about yet?" Grandma asked, standing resolutely by the car until he told her.

Grandpa merely grinned. They had been dating for six months away, and by this point Grandpa knew she didn't enjoy surprises, but he couldn't resist them.

Grandma wasn't amused.

"Oh, just stop being a stubborn ninny and come play with me."

Grandma raised an eyebrow at his choice of wording, but allowed herself to be directed away from the car.

A young boy, maybe three-years-old, sped past them on a tricycle, then turned around and smiled widely at Grandpa. "Who's the chick?"

Grandpa smiled at the boy and said gently, "Davey, what is it we call women?"

"Sorry," Davey said. "Who's the lady?"

Grandpa introduced Grandma, and they decided to head to the beach. Davey said he'd have to ask Frank, and ran inside a nearby building.

Grandma turned to Grandpa, expecting an explanation. He gave her none, and simply smiled.

Grandma frowned.

"Uh oh," Grandpa said, noticing her changed expression. "What did I do this time?"

"Who is Davey?" Grandma asked.

Always one to tease, Grandpa responded with, "The boy you just met."

The amused look that followed only made Grandma glare at him further. Eventually Grandpa explained the situation. As soon as they were engaged, they began preparing to adopt the little boy.

My grandparent's marriage lasted more than fifty years. Maybe we all could learn from their example: adopting a precocious three-year-old child is good luck for newlyweds.

But I tend to subscribe to my grandpa's favorite phrase: "Luck has a very small job in life, aside from turning smart people into fools. Instead, life is a series of choices, love, and very special people."

It took two such people to open their hearts to a young boy in need of a family, and it took the same to make a marriage last for fifty years and beyond. Backus should be proud to say it helped to mold these two very special people.

Chapter 11

"About Backus," Joe said, turning my attention away from the ornate theater once again.

So we're back to this. "Yeah?"

"If your friends didn't all live there, and your family didn't live there, and you had the money to move out on your own," he hesitated, "would you?" He offered me a cigarette.

"That's a ridiculous question," I said, declining it. "Of course I would. There wouldn't be anything at all there for me if my friends and family weren't there."

"Okay," Joe said. He took a long drag of his cigarette before he continued. "If your friends and family were still living there but you had the money to move away, would you move?"

I hesitated.

"I think you would—if I can take a guess at my own question."

"And why do you think that?" I tucked a curl behind my ear.

He inhaled the smoke, and let out a small cough away from me. "Because even with your friends and family living there, I almost only hear you say insults about it. I think you would much rather be living somewhere else, but simply don't have the funds to get out."

"You might be right," I admitted. "There are a lot of things about Backus I don't like. I mean—you saw how Mrs. Randall was today. Would you really enjoy that kind of thing all the time?"

"Did I say I would enjoy it?" Joe asked, tilting his head curiously.

"You implied it," I said, squirming a little. "You bought a house there. That means you're staying, at least for long enough to justify doing that."

"You say that like it's a bad thing," Joe said, frowning as he rested his cigarette between his fingers.

"No," I said quickly. "I mean—I'm glad that you've decided to stay." I hesitated. "Backus needs someone like you to show us how the place ought to be run."

Joe raised an eyebrow at me.

"What?"

"It's just," Joe said, "I kind of like Backus the way it is." He shrugged, lifting his cigarette to his lips once more. "It has a small town charm that is often lost, and I wouldn't want to mar that with my big city ways." He glanced around for an ashtray, which was easily found, and excused himself to dispose of the cigarette.

When he returned, I said, "That small town charm is already lost to those of us who have lived there for more than a few months." I was growing more uncomfortable as the conversation continued, but was nevertheless unable to keep my blunt opinion to myself. "And it's been replaced by the reality of gossips and lies."

Joe shook his head.

"You don't see that? Even after what Mrs. Randall said? They've been talking about us, Joe. Like they can just marry us off to whomever they wish. You actually enjoy that kind of thing? You think that's charming?"

"Backus has faults, sure. But so does every town. My hometown certainly had its share of them. We just accept those and also see the good that places have to offer. Don't you think Backus has given you anything at all?"

I shrugged. "Nothing that I can see."

"Well I can tell you what it's given *me*."

"What's that?" I asked.

Joe tucked a stray curl behind my ear and kissed my forehead. He smiled and looked me in the eyes, and said very softly, "I think you can figure it out."

I blushed, smiling.

He folded his hands in his lap, grinning at my reaction.

I sat back in my seat, realizing I had become tense, and stared at my hands. "I don't understand you, Joe," I said. "I really don't understand you at all."

"And why is that?" he asked.

I started picking at a hangnail. "Well, I just don't get, how after everything I do and say you could still, you know," I paused, "like me."

"Well, your prettiness sort of makes up for all your other faults," he said with a wink.

I playfully shoved him.

"Hey—no abuse of the driver, remember?"

"That only applies in the car," I said with a giggle.

"I think since I'm your ride home tonight, it works no matter where we are. Be nice to me or you'll learn how fun living in a theater can be." He winked.

I crossed my arms and turned away. "At least it might be better than living in Backus," I muttered.

"Wouldn't you miss people? Margaret? Wouldn't you miss Margaret?"

"Of course I would. And I would miss Linda, and Michael, and my father, and Uncle Bruce—and you—" I frowned, "and not many others."

"You have a lot more friends than just us," Joe said.

"I know, but those are surface friendships. With anyone else, I don't know if what I tell them is going to end up on the *Backus Brochure*'s front page or if they'll keep it to themselves. With you, I know you would never sell out what I tell you. It's just a deeper friendship, a deeper level of trust. You know."

Joe nodded. "Speaking of the *Backus Brochure*," he started.

I frowned, worried he would repeat his challenge to me, and in my stubbornness I would be forced to become an author for it.

He didn't, though. Instead he asked, "What all needs to happen for this party to be a success?"

I shrugged.

"Come on now—I know you have ideas stored in that pretty little brain of yours."

"Are you calling my brain little? That's a Shakespearean insult, you know." I smiled to show him I was teasing.

Joe blushed. "I wasn't meaning to..."

"I have a few ideas, I guess," I said. "We could decorate." I shrugged.

"What kind of decorations?"

"Streamers? I don't really know. Balloons, I guess." I nodded, deciding that would be a good choice. "Balloons are fun, and they would keep the kids happy."

Joe nodded. "What else? I mean, other than decorations, what is needed?"

"Well, we have to figure out what kind of food to give everyone. I don't think we should let them pick off the menu. That could be chaotic."

Joe nodded.

"Plus, some things are more expensive to make than others, and since the point of this is to raise awareness of The Diner and ultimately get Uncle Bruce more revenue, I don't want him to be losing money."

Joe nodded again. "I fully agree. So what's a cheap food to make that won't leave customers angry?"

"Pop. Uncle Bruce always says the pop is the cheapest thing we buy. People can drink whatever kind of pop they want. And for the actual food," I thought for a moment. "I wonder if we could stop at one of those stock-up stores that Uncle Bruce always shops at and get hot dogs and hot dog buns? Those are pretty cheap when you buy them in bulk."

"Sounds like a boss plan," Joe said. "I'm not sure if those stores will be open after the show but if they're not I can make a trip tomorrow night and get some."

"I can come with if you want," I said.

"I would like that very much," Joe said, grinning.

I blushed a little at his grin. *What is wrong with me?*

"Okay, hot dogs and pop. I think that sounds like a decent meal for them."

"And if they want anything else, they can always feel free to order it," I said. "That would be better for Uncle Bruce anyway."

"So it all works out. Just as Uncle Bruce and I told you it would," Joe winked.

I rolled my eyes at him. "Just because I'm resourceful it doesn't mean the two of you have to take advantage of that. You know this plan could be way better if I had had more time to come up with it."

"Of course it could be. I wouldn't expect anything less from a girl of mine." Joe kissed my forehead again.

I pulled back. "Please don't call me your girl," I said. "I'm not." I shook my head. "I'm not ready to be that yet. I want to get to know you better first."

Joe nodded. "I'm sorry, Ella. I didn't mean to imply that I thought you belonged to me—I know you could never belong to anyone. You're much too strong-willed for that—um—but—I love your stubbornness," Joe hesitated, frowning. "Here I go accidentally insulting you again, I'm so sorry—"

The lights dimmed and the screen lit up, cutting Joe off from any further embarrassment his tongue might have planned for him. The show was wonderful; the actors in the film were, not surprisingly, much more talented than the kids in Backus' community plays. I was entranced.

Though he was clearly enjoying it, Joe wasn't quite as entranced as I was. Every so often I noticed him glancing at me, to see my reactions to the various scenes.

He turned to me as the show ended and the lights came up. "Well?" he said.

"It's amazing," I said. "It's beyond amazing! I love it."

Joe smiled. "I thought you might. I've always loved going to see shows. I have to say though; I sort of prefer live performances. I wanted to take you to one of those, but it's hard to find them nowadays."

I nodded. "I've only ever seen Backus' children plays, and those are pretty awful. These actors were really astounding. I kept forgetting they're actors."

Joe nodded. "I'm sure they'd be thrilled to hear that. Isn't it the goal of every actor to transport you away from real life and convince you they are in fact who they say they are?"

"In other words, an actor's whole purpose in life is to become an extremely good liar."

Joe chuckled. "Yes, I suppose it is. We pay them to do what every child's mother teaches them not to."

I giggled. "Yep. And they do it well."

"Some of them do," Joe chuckled. "It would be fun to do something like this, wouldn't it?"

I thought about it for a moment. "Yeah, I guess it would be pretty fun. I was never interested in the children's plays, but now that I see they could be done this well..."

Joe nodded. "I think the people here make acting look supremely easy, don't you?"

I nodded too. "They do! They make me think I could do it. That's probably not a very good thing."

"How do those children's plays get started?" Joe asked. He looked as though he was coming up with a plan.

I eyed him warily. "What do you mean?"

"Who puts them on?"

"Brave parents," I answered slowly.

"Exactly," Joe said. Realizing everyone was heading out the doors, he helped me maneuver through the crowd and back to his car. We got in and he smiled as he started the car.

"So," I said after we had driven a little in silence, "you didn't finish what you were saying in there."

"Didn't I?"

"You know you didn't," I said, frowning. "I'm going to hit you again if you act like you don't know what I'm talking about."

"Aw," Joe said, "and I thought the moods and abuse had ended for the night. Too much to hope for, I suppose." He shook his head sadly.

I rolled my eyes. "Just finish what you were saying, Joe."

"You're curious, aren't you?"

I frowned. "I won't be any more if you keep dragging it out like this."

Joe chuckled. "Okay. Well I think what I was getting at is that everyday people put on the children's shows—so why couldn't everyday people—like you and me—put on a teen and adult show?"

"Because we don't have time for it, we don't have a script, we don't have actors, I highly doubt there would be any interest in it," I turned to him and smiled sweetly. "Should I go on or are you good?"

Joe shook his head. "Naysayer," he muttered.

"Realist," I corrected. "I just don't see it working."

"I'm going to try it. Are you with me?"

I looked at him. He seemed serious.

"Well?" he asked.

"Okay," I said, giving in far too easily, "I'm with you. I'll help."

Joe grinned. "Good. I have a feeling it would be really hard to gather interest for something that only the new guy started. With your backing at least it's not me trying to change everyone's ways," he chuckled, "it's both of us trying to."

I shrugged. "I guess it's worth a shot."

"I wonder if a Shakespeare in the park would be well received?"

"With Minnesota's snow in the winter and mosquitoes in the summer? You're better off indoors."

"Good point. My house is pretty empty still. We can hold practice in there until we get a place to perform."

"Listen to yourself, Joe. 'A place to perform,' like we have more than one option. The only place suitable for performing is the theater in the school."

"That little school has a theater inside it?"

"Not a big one, but yes, it does."

"Well that will be perfect for it, I'm sure. What play should we do?"

"I don't know," I thought about what they'd done in the past. "I think we always just used our own plays; whoever was in charge of the play would write it, too."

"Backus sure is talented," Joe said. "Directing and writing and being in charge of little ones, each of those on their own is a big job; together, it's monumental."

"Well, don't be too impressed," I said, popping his inflated idea of the parents in Backus. "The scripts have been anything but great." I scrunched my nose and looked at him. "Joe, are you sure you want to do this? The more I think about it the less I think it's a good idea." I frowned. "Whatever we do is going to be pulled apart."

"But behind our backs, not in front of our faces, so we won't even know and can go along in blissful ignorance," Joe said with a grin.

"We'll know. They don't say anything to your face but you can see the insincerity in theirs. And a lot of people just stand around with an idiotic smile and you know very well what they are thinking."

"And what do you do, Ella?"

"Hmm?"

"When you've been to one of their plays, and didn't like it, do you tell them you didn't?"

"Well, no," I shook my head, "that would hurt their feelings."

"So what do you do instead? What do you tell them about it? Or are you one of the people with the idiotic smiles?"

"I tell them the truth," I said. "I tell them I'm impressed that they gathered the children and were able to keep them interested for an entire play. I *am* impressed with that part."

Joe nodded. "So if someone comes up to me after we perform this thing and tells me they're impressed I was able to keep the adult's attention for so long, I should be worried."

"Most definitely."

Joe chuckled. "You know, about the script. We have a very talented author sitting in this car."

I looked at him and shook my head. He knew better than to think I would use my script for this. Well, if he was going to be silly, I would be too. "You write?" I asked, winking.

He laughed. "No way! But if I'm not mistaken, your current project is a script."

"I don't want my writing used, Joe."

"But Ella," he said in a pleading tone, "think of the children..."

"The children?" I raised an eyebrow. "We're putting this on with the adults."

"And who do you think is going to be watching it?" He winked.

I shrugged. "Whatever you say, Joe."

"Now there's something I don't hear every day, and especially not from you." Joe grinned. "Want to repeat it for me?"

"No."

"Aw...pity."

I rolled my eyes.

"So," he smiled charmingly, "we can use your script?"

"Do we have another option?" I asked, sighing.

"No."

I frowned. *What is it about him that makes me give up so easily?* "Fine. You can use my script."

Wednesday, November 4th, 1953

Wednesday morning came. The Diner was as prepared as it could be in the short time we had been given. Joe assured me it was going to be a good day. I was beginning to believe him. The Diner did look very nice, and, as promised, Joe had gotten enough hot dogs and buns to feed the town of Backus.

"You ready for today?" Joe asked.

"Guess so. You?"

"You bet. Are you cranked? I really am excited," he grinned. "I think there are some people here that I still have not met, and I am hoping that the promise of free food will entice them to endure the introduction."

I smiled. "If you really want to meet the rest of Backus I suppose I could go around with you to the different houses. I know which people avoid the town functions."

"If you wouldn't mind doing that, I would love it. I'm starting to feel like a part of this town and I think everyone should be aware of that fact. I'm here to stay now."

I looked at him, surprised. "Here to stay?"

"For a while," he amended. "I really like it here. And there's nothing left for me in New York or anywhere else. I see no reason *not* to stay here."

"What about your family?" I asked. "What about your parents?"

"Did Uncle Bruce tell you about the games he's planning today?"

"No," I said, frowning at the sudden shift in conversation. "I hadn't thought about doing games."

"He mentioned charades," he said. "I think there were some others too but you'll have to ask him what they are. My memory is really bad, you know."

I smiled. "Yes, I know."

Uncle Bruce looked at the clock. "People should start coming any minute now," he said. "I've got hot dogs and coffee and pop all ready for our very first customers." He frowned. "Do you suppose people will be wanting hot dogs and pop this early in the morning? I was just thinking that maybe we should have had a morning option and a lunch or dinner option, instead of just the hot dogs," his voice trailed off in concern.

"If they want something different they're very welcome to order it off the menu," I said. "It would be unfair for them to assume that we will cater to everyone." *Given more time, I would have thought of a breakfast option.*

Uncle Bruce nodded. "I think it's wonderful what you and Joe cooked up in the short time I gave you." He chuckled. "No pun intended. I'm just getting party day jitters now, that's all. Don't pay attention to anything I say for the next, oh, ten hours. After that I should be fully relaxed and more able to give you the proper thanks you both deserve."

I smiled.

The bell over the door jingled and the first customer of the day walked in: Eric. Of course.

Chapter 12

"Your grandma's got a boyfriend? Oh that is so cute!" Rosie picked up a chunk of ice that had been lying in our path through the woods.

I frowned at Rosie's reaction. "He's not her boyfriend. And it's not cute."

"Oh, just admit it, Jane. It's adorable." She passed the ice chunk to me.

I scrunched my nose and dropped the chunk to the side of the path. Knowing Rosie would continue to press the point until I relented, I said, "Kind of, I guess."

Rosie grinned in triumph, but said nothing more.

I stomped out a pile of snow. "Mostly it's just

weird. I mean—she and Grandpa were together for fifty years."

She nodded, encouraging me to continue.

"It seems wrong that she might be able to just—" I paused, "that she can forget about Grandpa for this new guy. Well, old guy."

Rosie looked surprised at my wording.

"Oh gosh, I didn't mean it like that. I just mean they've been friends for a really long time. It's not like he's someone random she met on the street."

She nodded again. Rosie was being quiet today. If I had been less focused on what I saw as my own problems, I might have asked why, but I was glad for a chance to vent.

"Mr. Jensen was married before, too, and it seems wrong that both of them could just forget their spouse like that. It's only been a year or two since Grandpa died, though for Mr. Jensen it's been longer. I think Mrs. Jensen died in her thirties. But," I frowned, and sighed, "I don't know."

Rosie stopped walking and leaned against one of the trees. She kicked at the ground, as if trying to dislodge the snow and ice that had formed a protective shell around the dirt.

I crossed my arms, which proved to be a slightly more difficult task than I had expected since the layers I wore marred my flexibility, and sat down in a particularly high snow pile. *Why would Grandma do this? How could anyone compare to Grandpa Blake? This just doesn't make sense.*

Rosie, intent on clearing the ground surrounding her of all traces of winter, didn't look up. "It is hard to see that kind of thing sometimes."

"I don't want to see it *at all!*"

Rosie gave up her unachievable task and sunk into a sitting position by the tree. She picked up a stray stick and started breaking it into several pieces. "Sometimes you aren't given a choice," she said softly, and I detected a hint of bitterness. "It's not your life that it's affecting most, even if it does affect you a lot."

I got off my perch and sat on the ground beside her, my brow furrowing in concern. "What's wrong?"

She didn't answer, and kept breaking the stick until the pieces were too small to break again.

I put a hand on hers to get her attention. "Rosie?"

Finally, she looked up; tears were in her eyes.

"Rosie, talk to me."

She attempted to brush her tears away with the back of her mitten, but succeeded only in adding little pieces of snow to her cheeks. "It's just," her voice shook and she swallowed hard, "I know how difficult it can be. Especially when you know you should just be happy for them. But you can't be, because it's tearing you apart that they're able to move on," her voice cracked, "before you are."

I put an arm around her. She was describing exactly the way I was feeling, and seemed to be speaking from experience. It was harder to hear it coming from her than it had been in my own mind, probably because she seemed to be hurting just as much.

Rosie continued. "They're the ones who are supposed to have had such a close relationship with the person." She looked up at me. "My mom now isn't my real mother. She died when I was ten. Dad remarried two years ago. I know what it's like. It had been four years, when he remarried, but even now I still miss my mom."

"I'm so sorry," I said. I knew the words wouldn't—couldn't—help, but I could think of nothing else to do or say. My grandpa was the closest relative I had lost, and as hard as that was, I knew that had to be nothing compared to losing your mother.

"It's not always about moving on, though," Rosie said.

I looked curiously at her, wondering what she meant.

"I don't think my dad will ever forget about my mom. But he loves my new mom, too. Somehow, he can do both. Maybe it's the same for your grandma. And you know," she said, her spirits returning to their usual cheerful state, "Mr. Jensen is a really nice guy."

I nodded a little; even I couldn't deny that.

"I never met your grandpa, but Mr. Jensen sometimes comes to visit people here." Rosie picked up another stick and started carving hearts and swirls into the snow she hadn't already destroyed. "He's funny and sweet."

"Yeah, I guess." I watched the patterns she was creating and waited for her to continue.

"I've been wanting him to find someone new. He lost Etty so quickly—not that I was alive at the time, but I've been told about it. I've always felt he deserved to be happy again." She bit her lip. "If your grandma can do that for him, and vice versa, I am going to find it very difficult to stick by you in determining that he and she should not be together."

I picked up a handful of snow and molded it into a ball as she continued.

"I know a good friend would announce the match perfectly vile and disgusting, but I just can't do that." She shook her head, apologetically. "You have every right to be upset with me for failing in my friendship duties to you."

I smiled a little.

"I do love a good romance though," Rosie said, grinning. "And your grandma and Mr. Jensen seem the perfect pair for one. I don't much enjoy young people's romances," she scrunched her nose. "They fizzle and die so quickly. Until they're saying the wedding vows—and sometimes even after, unfortunately—you're never sure if they're going to last."

"Yeah," I nodded, frowning.

"But with older people, you know they've lived more and have more experience and are wiser and it just seems so much more likely that what they have is something lasting and beautiful. You know?"

I nodded.

"We should talk about something else," Rosie declared.

"Okay. What?" I asked, amused.

"Books! I like books. When did you learn to read?"

I threw the snowball I'd been perfecting at her and she squealed.

"You meanie!"

I giggled. "I think I was four. You?"

Rosie started forming her own snowball, so I did too.

"I couldn't read until I was at least five. I might have been six. I had decided that there were just too many other things to keep me occupied and I didn't want to waste time with all those letters and words. That's what I told my mom." She tossed the snowball at me and I ducked.

"How did she respond?" I asked, launching my own ball of snow in her direction. I missed.

Rosie looked a little triumphant about my poor aim, and continued her story. "She laughed and told me I would change my mind someday, when someone wrote something down and I wanted to know what it said."

She threw another snowball at me and hit me on the shoulder.

"And you know, she was absolutely right. Bev learned to read and write long before I did, and he would write me notes and try to be secretive about them. They were nothing important, just things like 'We played soccer without you today.' But he said he was going to keep writing them and I wouldn't be able to know what they said until I could read them on my own."

I stood up to find some fresh snow.

Rosie followed. "That's when I decided that reading might not be all that bad after all. I was under the impression that it was a secret code only a handful of people could crack—don't ask me why I thought that, since words are everywhere." She shook her head, smiling. "Anyone but me would realize it's something pretty much everyone knows about. But in spite of obvious signs to the contrary, I did think that, and I was determined to be a member of the special club."

I hit her with another snowball.

She stuck her tongue out at me and tossed one in my direction. "Do you want to hear this or not?"

"I'm listening," I said, grinning.

"Sure you are." She waited a moment, but then decided I actually was listening, and continued. "So I learned to read. Imagine how disappointed I was to find out that what all those letters said was really not all that exciting after all!"

I giggled. "I always liked reading. It *is* a sort of code, you know; not everyone in the world can read English."

"Oh, I know. I do love reading. Who's your favorite author? I don't like a lot of the more modern books. I think a lot of the good ideas for books were taken years ago. Maybe now people should just stop writing and accept the fact that nothing new can be created." Rosie giggled. "Oh I sound so mean."

I smiled and chucked another snowball at her. "You'd better not let my grandma hear you. She's a writer."

Rosie smiled apologetically. "I'm sure there are some really good new books that I just haven't found yet. I'm not really looking either, so unless someone tells me about them I probably never *will* find them." She shrugged. "But I just love the classics. Dickens is wonderful. Gotta say Mark Twain is my favorite though. Especially because of his name."

"What about his name?" I asked.

"Oh, just the fact that he decided his real name—Samuel Clemens—was too dull or something so he changed it. I think that's awesome."

"It's awesome that he changed his name?" I sat on the snow pile again and Rosie joined me.

"Well, I mean, your name is such an intrinsic part of you. I have always been called Rosie and it would be so weird to suddenly decide that I want to be called something that sounds nothing at all like Rosie. But that's exactly what he did!" She thought for a moment, and then giggled. "Well, with Samuel, I mean—not with Rosie. If he'd been called Rosie I am sure nobody would blame him for changing it."

I laughed.

"That takes guts though, don't you think? To change your name from something that really isn't a bad name at all, just because you decided you wanted a different one. I don't think I would be able to do that. And it just shows his sense of humor, too, wouldn't you say? Have you read much of his work?"

"I've read Tom Sawyer," I said. "He's amusing."

"So who is your all time favorite author? And if you name a modern one I am going to stop being friends with you." Rosie winked. "Okay, actually I am going to have to apologize for insulting them. And I will probably have to read something by them to see if you're just crazy or if there actually is a good modern author out there."

I smiled. "I like Louisa May Alcott. I've been realizing lately that Jane Austen isn't too bad, either. Since Grandma Blake came, she's convinced me to read *Northanger Abbey*. It's growing on me. At first it was hard to get used to the way everyone in her novels talks, but I kind of like it now. They're all so prim and proper."

Rosie nodded. "I think if I was a bit more of a romantic person I could really enjoy Austen."

I laughed. "Now you're just contradicting yourself. Earlier you said you *liked* romance."

"But the romance in Austen's novels is between young people, isn't it?"

"Yes," I agreed, "but your only complaint with romance between young people is that you don't know if it's going to last, and in Austen's novels you *do* know it's lasting."

"Wow, spoiler alert." Rosie smiled.

I elbowed her playfully.

"So you said your grandma writes. Have you ever read anything by her?"

I shook my head. "I would like to, sometime. Grandma used to refuse to talk about the past, and she included her writing in that. Apparently Mr. Jensen has convinced her the past has some good in it, so maybe now she'll be more willing to let me read something."

"She doesn't write anymore?"

"I don't think she does," I said. "She might when I'm not around, but she's never mentioned it."

"Well of course not! Silly Jane. If she wrote something when you weren't around, by the time you *were* around, it would be, well, in the past. And she doesn't talk about that."

I smiled.

"Speaking of the past, how is your history column going?"

"Great, now that Grandma's here and is feeding me stories." I grinned. I was glad to be learning so much about her and Grandpa Blake.

"Oh, good." Rosie stood up and started following the path through the woods again. "I remember one of your articles was about the galas they used to have each week. I said I wanted to make that a tradition again, but haven't done anything with it. I've decided you're going to help me."

"Oh I am?" I raised an eyebrow.

Rosie nodded resolutely. "Oh, Jane, look!" She stopped walking and pointed.

All I saw was a squirrel; hardly something that would excite a Minnesotan.

"Do you see it?"

"Um. I see a squirrel. Is that 'it?'"

"No, you dork. Squirrels are as plentiful and nearly as annoying as mosquitoes here. You really think I would get this excited over one of them?"

"Well I don't see anything else here to get excited about," I said with a shrug.

Rosie took my arm and brought me to where she'd been pointing. Etched in a stump was a heart and the letters E and M.

"I've always been curious who those initials belong to," Rosie said. "The only M I know of is Michael, and he married a Laura and then Carol. I suppose he could have been sweet on someone whose name started with E before he met Laura. It's too bad he's not around to ask anymore. And Grandma Carol's not originally from here, so she wouldn't know."

"Mr. Larsen's name is Eric," I said. "Well, I suppose you already knew that, since you're his niece. I just found out."

"Yeah," Rosie said, "but he insists he never cared for anyone whose name started with M. I guess I should question if I should believe that, though. He claims that he never cared for anyone at all, and I'm sure I don't believe that for an instant. But I do know he never dated anyone. I never could figure out why."

"Must have scared them off with his charming personality," I said sarcastically.

Rosie giggled. "Well, I do think he's a good guy, if you take the time to get to know him. Like I said when you first met: he has a good heart. It's just hidden under a lot of scruff."

"Yeah," I agreed, "Grandma says he's a good friend of hers—which is a compliment she doesn't give to most people."

"I guess no one took the time to get to know him until after they had already met someone else. You know, if your grandma didn't already have Mr. Jensen, I would be tempted to do some matchmaking here. Who knows? Maybe things won't work out between them. You *did* say they're not officially dating, and you only have suspicions." She waggled her eyebrows.

"Don't you dare!"

Rosie laughed.

From where our walk had brought us, the edge of the woods close to the school, it wasn't far to our houses. Rosie made me promise to come visit the next day and help her plan the gala.

Grandma Blake smiled when I walked in. "As I was unpacking I realized I had completely forgotten to pass out your pre-Christmas presents. The others have gotten theirs now. Would you like yours?"

"I wasn't expecting anything," I said, pleasantly surprised.

Grandma smiled. "I was just sorting through my old things and thought you might like these." She handed me a large gift bag. "If you don't care for them or don't have a place to wear them, don't worry about it. Like I said; they're old."

I pulled the tissue paper out and looked in the bag. It was filled with skirts—black, pink, white, and all with cute little decals on them.

"That style was popular when I was your age," Grandma said. "I know it's not anymore, but I thought you might like them for their vintage style."

I grinned. "They're beautiful! Thank you!" I hugged her and hurried to change into one of the poodle skirts. "It fits great—and I know exactly what to wear it for."

It had given me an idea for the gala Rosie was intent on holding.

In the 1950s, galas were a part of everyday life. Some of you may remember a past article I wrote about them. Each week townspeople would gather in the school gym and dance and eat. Some came just to watch and talk, others came to dance. Everyone enjoyed it.

Somewhere through the years, these galas stopped happening. Now, aside from individuals hosting parties, or plays held at the school, the entire town rarely gathers together. As someone who has only lived here a few months, I know there are people I haven't had the pleasure of meeting yet.

We would like to change that. Starting next Friday, the 18th of December, Rosie Tyler and I (Jane Blake) shall be hosting the first gala in many years. Per tradition, it will be in the school gym, and will begin at 7pm. Please wear 1950s clothing and bring food to share.

Chapter 13

Wednesday, November 4, 1953
Ella Mitchell

"Hey baby," Eric said, sliding onto one of The Diner's stools. "Get me some coffee, would ya? So I hear there's free food today. What're my options?"

"Hot dog and your choice of pop," Uncle Bruce said.

"Yeah? Not bad, Uncle Bruce. Just the coffee for now, though."

I handed him the cup and Joe told him the amount.

Eric gave Joe a look. "How many times you figure I been in here, Joe? How many coffees you think I have ordered from here? If I don't know how much a coffee from here costs yet, I am going to fail at life."

Joe chuckled and accepted the money Eric handed him.

"So dollface," he said, pulling out a pack of cigarettes before glancing at Uncle Bruce and putting it back into his pocket, unopened. "I hear you're giving up on me?"

I looked at him warily.

"You're dating this guy." Eric clarified, nodding at Joe.

Joe slipped his hand through mine and smiled at me. "Hard to believe, I know."

I smiled back at Joe. "Yes, I am," I responded to Eric, grateful for the strength Joe's hand offered.

"So tell me one thing, baby. What's he got that I don't got?"

"You mean besides proper grammar?" Uncle Bruce muttered.

I giggled a little.

"Well? I want to know so that when I find some other girl to try to woo I know what I did wrong here and I do it right next time."

I felt bad for whoever became his next victim, and hoped it wouldn't be Margaret. She seemed the obvious choice for anyone to fall for, and I knew Eric wasn't completely immune to her charm. He always asked her to dance at least once during the Friday night galas.

Margaret had many good qualities, but strength of will was not one of them. She was sweet and cared altogether too much about the feelings of others. If Eric or any other young man decided they liked her, she wouldn't have the heart to say no. Her own feelings would play no part in her decision.

She would continue to agree to anything they asked of her, even up to a marriage proposal. She would probably end up marrying them out of pity! And that was not the life I had envisioned for my beautiful, talented and charming favorite friend.

Margaret was Backus' own Charlotte Lucas, in that her choice in a spouse would likely not be made out of love for the man. I was determined to keep any Mr. Collins type characters as far from her as I could.

Eric was still waiting for my answer. I didn't really know what to tell him. There was a lot about Joe that made him superior to Eric, but it was difficult to pick out the good qualities about Joe and not at the same time make Eric feel he was the scum of the earth.

What it boiled down to was personality. I loved Joe's personality; I hated Eric's. How do you tell someone that their entire...everything...was what rubbed you wrong? The answer to his question, "What's Joe got that I don't got?" was, well, "Everything."

But of course I couldn't say that. Instead I said, "Well, for one thing, he doesn't call me baby, or dolly. He calls me Ella, because that's my name, and most people prefer to be called by their actual name. But really, people just don't work that way. Even if you had acted differently, I probably still would have chosen Joe. I'm sorry, Eric, that's just how it is."

Eric shrugged and took a drink of his coffee. "Doesn't bug me none, just curious is all."

The bell jingled again and we all were grateful for a second customer. Well, I was, anyway. Soon the place was filled. Eric went home and more people arrived. Margaret stopped by and hopped behind the counter with a 'give me a job and I will do it' look of determination.

I hugged her in greeting. "Margaret!"

She hugged me back. "Oh Ella, you and I don't spend nearly enough time together anymore. I have decided to change that. If Joe will spare you—yes, I have heard the news—of course I have, how silly. I live with the guy. Plus, this is Backus. Well, I used to live with him! Now he has his own place and have you seen it? It's darling, isn't it? Still bare but you and I will fix that soon, won't we, Ella?"

I smiled. "If he wants it fixed by us I suppose we can," I said.

Joe shrugged and handed me a hot dog to pass along to one of the customers. "Whatever you ladies think would be best for my house, feel free to do. I trust your judgment."

"Ooh..." Margaret said, grinning. She was most likely contemplating painting his house pink and adding flowers, just to make him regret giving us free reign.

"Hey now," Joe said. "I know that look. I hereby amend my statement to—you ladies should feel free to do anything *within reason*. And that means things that won't embarrass the new kid in town."

"Aw, way to take away our fun, Joe," Margaret said. "Besides, you can hardly be called the new kid anymore."

"You know someone newer?"

"Yes, actually," Margaret grinned at the chance to prove him wrong. "Cindy has been here less than a month."

"Babies don't count; sorry, Maggie."

Margaret pouted a little.

Joe chuckled and handed me another plate. "You wanna be on pop duty, Margaret? We're giving free refills on that. Only one hot dog per person though— this is a much bigger turnout than I had been expecting and even as it is, with everyone taking only one, I'm not convinced we'll have enough to last the rest of the day."

"Pop duty sounds fun," she said.

"Great. Uncle Bruce is taking menu orders—of which there are a surprisingly large amount—and Ella is keeping track of who ordered what and who hasn't gotten their food yet and who has already had a hot dog. She was doing the pop too."

"But I appreciate the respite from that part of my job," I finished for him, and smiled. "I'm really glad you're here, Margaret. I wasn't sure if you would stop by today."

"Free food? You'd better believe I'd be by." She giggled.

"I just mean, I thought you were going to be out of town today."

She shook her head. "I was, but I changed my mind."

I made a mental note to ask her why later. She was supposed to be auditioning with an out-of-town dance company. Although I would have missed her, it was an excellent opportunity for someone who loved dancing as much as she did.

Uncle Bruce announced that a game of charades would be starting soon if people would organize and move to one half of The Diner.

The game was a success. No one was terribly good at it, but we all laughed a lot and had fun taking turns acting and guessing. The Diner was so crowded that multiple people were accidentally whacked in the process of getting their team to guess, but since no one was actually hurt, that just made it even more hilarious.

After the game ended and people either returned to the counter or headed for the door, Joe asked for everyone's attention. He told them his idea to have an adult and teen play, and mentioned that he would be holding auditions at Uncle Bruce's house on Saturday.

Joe and Uncle Bruce didn't feel either of them could be unbiased judges of the talent of the people of Backus. Joe, since he was still fairly new but had gotten to know a few of us quite well and would be inclined to show favoritism to the people he had become closest to; Uncle Bruce because no matter what evidence he was presented with to prove otherwise, he would always be convinced that

Margaret was the very best at anything she tried. Since I wanted to audition too, Margaret and I couldn't be the judge, either. Instead, we asked Mrs. Randall's close friend Millie to be in charge of the auditions.

Although anyone in Backus would have a bias of some sort, we had discussed it and decided Millie would be able to look objectively at the would-be actors.

She agreed immediately, and was glad for the excitement. She had directed one of the children's plays before—never again, she'd vowed—and when she was younger she had acted in a couple plays in neighboring towns. She offered to help us with the play itself if we wanted her expertise after the auditions.

The people in The Diner seemed to think the play was a great idea, and several promised to come to the auditions. Something might actually come out of this kookie idea Joe had. I wanted to be encouraging to him regardless, but my skepticism always managed to take over my good intentions; since the skepticism was the more practical of the two options, that's what I naturally veered toward.

Later we played *Never Have I Ever,* and the day ended sooner than I had expected. Margaret helped us clean up, and Uncle Bruce said the day had brought in more menu orders than hot dog orders: great news.

Eric had never returned for his hot dog like he had promised to. I wondered what was going on with him. Now that he finally seemed to be giving up on pursuing me, I felt bad for not having treated him better. As a Christian I was supposed to show love and kindness to the rest of the world, yet I had treated Eric with nothing but disdain.

I vowed to do better in the future, and to treat him the way I would wish to be treated. After all, underneath his gruff, I-don't-care-what-the-world-thinks, exterior, I was pretty sure Eric was just a frail human like the rest of us. It was time I start treating him like what he truly was, and not like what he wanted the rest of the world *think* he was.

Margaret grabbed my hand. "Joe," she said matter-of-factly, "I am hereby kidnapping your girlfriend for the rest of the night and there is nothing in the world that you can do about it. I'm terribly sorry," she said, though she didn't sound apologetic. "Tell her you hope she has a fun time, give her your goodbyes, and disappear for the rest of the evening."

I giggled.

"I'm feeling very jealous that you have been spending much more time with my close friend than I have been able to lately. Hurry up with your goodbyes! I've been waiting for this for a long time and am reasonably impatient. Chop, chop!"

Joe chuckled and gave me a hug. "Can I walk you to wherever it is you'll be going?"

"No you cannot," Margaret said, crossing her arms. "Did you not just hear what I said? You walk Ella everywhere she goes. I don't like it and this is my turn to walk her to where I want to walk her. Now, disappear!" She waved her hand as though the word would magically turn him into a cloud of smoke.

"I'm worried for your safety, is all," Joe said, smiling charmingly.

Margaret responded with a playful shove. "You're ridiculous. This is my time with my friend, and I will not have you messing it up by being all chivalrous and romantic on Ella. I don't care if the two of you *are* the cutest couple ever."

I smiled, blushing a little.

Joe let out an overly dramatic sigh. "Okay Margaret, you can have it your way this one time. But from now on I think you should realize that boyfriend time comes before friend time."

I stared at him, a slight frown on my face.

He winked.

Margaret grinned, triumphant, and led me out of The Diner.

"What's the plan?" I asked as we started walking away.

"The plan is," she said, "to have a brilliant time free of all the men in our lives. Just like old times. I miss those times, don't you?"

I nodded.

"I would love to go to our special place, but for some reason our ancestors decided that moving to Minnesota—basically the coldest state in America—would be a very good idea, and right now our special spot is frozen over." She frowned momentarily. "I don't think going there would make for a fun evening at all." She shook her head, then grinned and continued, "So Dad has agreed to hang out with Joe tonight—and don't let Joe fool you, he was in on this too, the sweetheart—so we have the house all to ourselves."

"It sounds lovely. I should stop home first and let mom know I won't be back until later, though."

"She knows."

"What, did the whole town know your plan?" I asked.

Margaret giggled. "Pretty much. Hey, where was your mom today? It seemed like most of the town was there tonight, and I saw your dad, Michael, and Linda, but I didn't ever see her. Did I just miss her on one of my trips back to the pop storeroom?"

"She didn't approve of this. She said it was all a publicity stunt and she refused to encourage such a ridiculous idea by attending it, even with the promise of free food and pop." I shrugged. "I'm actually surprised Linda was allowed to come. The last I had heard, mom was going to make her stay home, and was strongly encouraging Dad and Michael to stay home as well."

Margaret made a face.

I shook my head. "I don't know what she found so offensive about it. I guess it was the commercialism it could have become. I thought it ended up just being a great time for the town to get together and hang out, play games, eat good food, and enjoy each other's company."

"I agree," Margaret said, and giggled. "Your mom is just being silly."

I nodded.

We reached Margaret and Uncle Bruce's house.

"Ella," she said. "I hereby declare this a parent-free zone, as well as a boy-free zone. I will not talk about my daddy, and you will not talk about your mother. I do want you to talk about Joe, though, so it won't be completely boy-free. Just a little bit boy-free. Basically, it's boy-free when I want it to be. Ain't it a bite I can't have that kind of control *all* the time?" She giggled. "You are probably very glad that I don't!"

I giggled too.

"I'm going to put on some coffee," she said. "And you are going to sit down and do nothing except spill all the important beans about what is going on between you and my wonderfully nutty but somehow charming cousin Joe."

I blushed.

Margaret smiled. "You're so cute. I can't tell you how much I love the fact that you and Joe are going out. I always told him you—" She blushed and stopped talking.

"What?"

"Nothing. Want a cigarette?"

"Nothing, my foot." I eyed her curiously. "What did you tell Joe about me?"

Margaret handed me a cigarette in spite of my lack of response, and took one for her. "Well, I talk about all my friends to my out-of-state relatives," she said. "So, you know, I just told him things about you every so often."

"Okay." I wondered if there was more to it than that, but didn't press her.

Margaret smiled and finished making the coffee. I snuffed my cigarette out, having smoked the first few puffs already. Margaret kept hers, and we went to her room in the basement.

"So you haven't told me about Joe yet, you've only just blushed. Which is cute, but it tells me absolutely nothing." She giggled. "How was your date? What did you do? You went to see a show didn't you? How was that? You must have liked it, since it gave you the idea to form your own show—which by the way I am super excited about! I've always wanted to be in a show, ever since I was in one of those awful ones when I was a kid," she smiled. "Anyway, this is your time to talk—so talk!"

"I'll make a deal with you, Margaret," I said slowly. "If you tell me why you skipped your audition today and came to The Diner instead, then I will give you some details about what is going on with Joe and me." I frowned, remembering what she had given up that day. "That audition was a huge opportunity for you, and I thought it was what you wanted more than anything in the world! And we all know you would have gotten in. So explain that to me, or there will be no details."

Margaret frowned, letting out a smoky breath. "I," she hesitated, "I don't know. I started on my way, and then I looked around here, at all the houses and all the people, and thought about how very much I would miss everyone if I left," she paused again, "and I just couldn't do it. I couldn't leave you all for that long, without knowing when I would be back in town. And, I, um," She blushed.

"What, Margaret?"

She looked away. "I kind of like somebody here."

"Serious? Who?"

She blushed more, and used snuffing out her cigarette as an excuse not to respond.

"Margaret. The whole *town* knows who I like. It's only fair you tell me who you like."

"Nicholas," she said quietly. "I know he's always been pretty much yours and I should find someone whose heart is actually free. And I know I always told you that things could never work between the two of you, and I'm sorry for that. I don't want you to think I said that because I liked him myself, because I didn't. Not until recently. I've been noticing things about him that I really admire."

I shook my head, assuring her I held nothing against her. "You were right though. It really never would have worked between him and me, because he had different desires in a wife than I could fulfill, and I had different desires for my life that he would not be able to accept. But you—" I smiled, "all you've ever wanted, besides to be a dancer, is to stay at home and raise your kids. Which do you want more? The dancing or the ankle-biters?"

Without any hesitation, she said, "I want children."

"Then I don't think you should feel badly at all about this crush. Especially because Nicholas was never mine. I wanted him to be, and my imagination told me he was, but we were never anything more than good friends."

"Are you sure?"

"I'm positive," I said. "Remember the night he asked to talk to me? When we did, he let me down gently. And by the way, you don't have to apologize for what your heart does. I'm a perfect example that your heart does things when you don't want it to. God simply molds it to feel the way that it really ought to when the right guy comes along. And there's no way to know if he is the right guy until the pieces all fall into place."

"Do you think Joe is the right guy for you?" Margaret asked, looking earnestly at me.

I thought about it. "I don't actually know yet. I think when the time comes for me to decide whether to give him my entire heart or keep it for someone else, I'll be certain of what I should do. But I know that I do like him, and I know that he likes me back." I smiled at the peace those words brought. "Right now, that's enough."

Monday, November 23rd, 1953

"I have a proposition for you," I said, involuntarily wincing at my own words.

Laura, who had been in charge of the *Backus Brochure* for the past two years, leaned against the doorjamb, incredulous. "I'm listening." She was used to me coming by with corrections for the paper. She knew I wasn't afraid to say when I thought it was printing garbage, and by this point she had begun tuning me out when I did.

"Let me write for the *Brochure*," I said.

Laura's eyebrows went up. "You have had nothing but criticism for the *Brochure* since it first began. Why would you want to write for a newspaper you hate? And why would we *let* you?"

"Fair enough," I said, turning to leave. *That was easy. Now I can tell Joe I did my best, and I don't have to write for that trashy paper.*

"Wait," Laura said.

I slowly turned to her, wary.

"Why the change of heart?"

"I haven't changed anything," I said; time to be honest with her. "Joe just pointed out to me that as much as I criticize the paper, I've never actually done anything to change it. He dared me to try to."

Laura smiled. "I think Joe is a good influence on you."

"Yeah, he is." I smiled back, thinking about all the ways I had changed since I met him. "Anyway," I said, coming back to reality, "now I can tell him I tried."

"You can tell him you succeeded," Laura said.

Oh no.

"I'll give you a chance."

I frowned. "What." It wasn't a question; it was a plea for her to change her mind.

She didn't.

"You can write for us. Maybe you can teach us some things. Maybe we can teach you some things. It's one thing we've never tried before. You know, it could be good."

Or it could be horrible. I'm going to kill Joe.

"Our next meeting is a week from Thursday," Laura continued. "I'll see you there!" She closed the door, leaving me dumbfounded on her doorstep.

Joe stepped up to me. "Do you have news for me?"

I looked at him, frowning. "I don't like you."

"I take it things went well." He had a small smile on his face, knowing he shouldn't be happy when I was cranky, but unable to stop himself.

"You knew," I said, narrowing my eyes at him. "You knew she was going to put me on writing staff, didn't you?"

"She put you on staff?"

I crossed my arms. "You owe me."

Joe looked innocent. "All I did was encourage you to do something about your discontent with things as they were. It was you who offered to be a writer for them." He smirked. "Did you really think she wouldn't let you?"

"I don't know," I trailed off. I guess I had expected her to weigh her personal dislike of my constant corrections as greater than any writing skill I might have.

Well, it didn't matter. I was stuck as an author now.

Unfortunately, changing the newspaper from the inside worked no better than simply complaining about it from the outside had.

Even my own articles weren't as full of facts as I wanted them to be. I would write them free of gossip, but somehow by the time they were edited and printed somebody managed to stick in at least one unverified piece of information.

After enduring nearly three months of this, I told Laura, in terms I could have made gentler, that I couldn't write for the *Brochure* anymore. "If you want to keep publishing what you are," I said, shoving the latest issue into her hands, "You should call it the *Backus Blab*. At least then you couldn't be accused of false advertising!"

Laura, scowling, closed the door.

Chapter 14

Friday, December 19, 2008
Jane Blake

In her usual enthusiastic fashion, Rosie loved the idea of making the gala 50s themed. We spent the entire week before the gala decorating the gym and preparing the menu. The menu was my job, since Rosie claimed if she was allowed to cook for everyone we would all go home sick. I loved cooking, though, so didn't mind the task.

We had asked people to bring food, but I knew they would be bringing modern dishes, and I at least wanted *something* from the era. Milkshakes and burgers seemed too cliché, but when I asked my grandma for other ideas, she said they were one of the few things that were cliché for good reason.

The day of the gala, there were no more preparations to be done on my end. Dad and I had pre-cooked the hamburgers so they would only need a few minutes in the oven to reheat; something we'd learned from Grandpa. The milkshakes I would make as needed.

Rosie would be borrowing one of my new poodle skirts, I would wear another, and Maggie, Katty, Mom and Grandma would wear the others. The guys, except Aiden, had begrudgingly agreed to wear suits for the night.

Rosie wanted to check the gym for last-minute touches. She was a nervous ball of energy and needed a chore to calm her down before the gala began. It was the first party since before she was born that involved the entire town, and she naturally wanted it to go well. Rosie said if people liked it, she was going to make it a weekly tradition like it had been in the 50s.

She insisted she didn't need any extra help, so I had the morning to do as I wished. I decided to visit Kyle. Since Rosie still didn't want to see him, I didn't press the point when she was around, but looked forward to spending time with him when she wasn't. I wanted him to meet Grandma Blake, too. His Grandma Carol had moved to Backus after mine had already moved away, so they hadn't had the chance to meet each other yet.

"You mentioned a little about this fella," Grandma said on the way to The Diner. "But not nearly as much as I would like to know. You seem to talk more about Bevin than about him." She smiled knowingly.

I blushed; embarrassed she could see through me so quickly. "Well what would you like to know about Kyle?" I asked.

"Anything that you find interesting."

I thought for a moment. There was a lot I found interesting about Kyle. "When I first met him he was sitting on a snow bank, playing his guitar and singing something in Latin."

Grandma laughed. "I like him already."

"He's a good guy. He and his grandma shared their food with us over Thanksgiving. I think Mom told you about that. And he really takes care of his grandma; you can tell he loves her. But there are mysteries about him, too. His parents aren't around, but he won't say what happened to them. And he and Rosie don't get along, but neither will tell me why."

Grandma had begun to get to know Rosie pretty well by now. As much as Rosie talked, that didn't take long. "You mean there's somebody Rosie *doesn't* get along with? Wow."

"I know. Mr. Larson, who even you say is a sourpuss, she says is a 'hidden darling,'" I shook my head at the thought, "but Kyle is pretty much the scum of the earth."

"You know Rosie better than I do, but from the little time I've been able to get to know her, I'd say it must take something big to get her to feel that way about somebody."

I nodded. "It would. But at the same time, I can't imagine Kyle doing anything like that. I want to think well of both of them," I frowned. "I'm not sure how without knowing the full story. I don't like being put in the middle of it, either. I know that whatever is going on is just between the two of them; but at the same time, I can only spend time with them one-on-one because of it. So it does affect me, too."

"Yeah," Grandma said. "I wish I could help you. But it *is* up to them to make up. All we can do is encourage them to do so, and try to be understanding when they insist they can't."

I knew Grandma was right, but it was still hard to accept.

Grandma stopped outside The Diner, and a look of sadness came to her face.

I glanced at her, concerned.

She replaced the look with a smile. "This place sure has changed since I was here. But it's enough the same that it reminds me of how life used to be." She smiled a little wider. "Uncle Bruce and Joe would keep customers in there for at least an hour, just talking. They were genuinely interested in the people in Backus. Even Joe was, and he didn't come here until he was in his twenties. Everyone loved those two; but they especially loved Uncle Bruce." She shook her head; amused at something I didn't know about. "He was a little quirky at times; always inventing new things—and usually not successfully. But he had the kindest heart." She took a deep breath. "Time to see if it's still got the charm it had when he was here." She pulled open the door and we went inside.

Kyle looked up from the order he was jotting down, and smiled at me. He finished talking to the customer and walked over. Turning first to Grandma, he held out his hand. "Hello, ma'am, I'm Kyle Richardson."

A look of recognition crossed Grandma's face for a moment, but I seemed to be the only one to notice it.

Kyle continued. "You must be Jane's Grandma Blake."

"Yes," Grandma said, smiling. "You can call me Mrs. Blake, for now."

"It's wonderful to meet you, Mrs. Blake."

Grandma sat down at one of the stools and looked around.

"I bet you recognize this place from before the addition," Kyle said, handing us each a menu.

"I do," Grandma said. "Used to be, these stools were the only seating option in here. And we never had menus, because people could just look up behind the counter for it. That is, if they even needed to. Mostly the people who came in knew exactly what they wanted." She smiled. "Usually it was coffee."

Kyle chuckled. He turned to me. "Jane, it's been a while since I've seen you. I read your article about the gala."

"Are you coming?" I asked.

He made a face. "A night of dancing isn't really my thing."

"Right," Grandma said, teasingly. "You're more the song-writing, Latin speaking type."

Kyle and I both blushed.

"So Jane talks about me but you didn't think she'd talk about you?" Grandma smiled. "If it makes you feel any better, I had to press her for information, and she still didn't tell me much. So you're a mystery to me, and I'm hoping that seeing you here in person will resolve some of those mysterious parts."

I missed Kyle's response, because a black-and-white picture distracted me. "Is that 'Uncle Bruce'?" I asked, pointing to a fatherly figure in the photo.

Grandma looked at it. "That's him." She sighed a little nostalgically.

I got up and looked more closely at it. The names were underneath the employee's pictures.

This picture was taken in 1967, of Uncle Bruce Knudson and Margaret Jensen, original owners of The Diner.

"She was his wife."

I looked again at the photo. "Didn't you say Joe worked here?"

"He did, but by the late sixties he had moved away from Backus. This was only a temporary job for him. His real love was business."

"So he moved to pursue that?"

"Oh, no. He moved because the lady he was in love with asked him to." She winked.

Kyle laughed, shaking his head in amusement. "What men won't do when love takes over."

Grandma turned to him, a mischievous smile on her face. "I take it love hasn't taken over for you yet."

"No ma'am; I'm immune." Kyle looked triumphant.

Grandma laughed. "Yeah," she said, incredulous. "Just wait a few years."

Too bad I'm not immune. Well, I certainly didn't *love* Bev; but my crush on him grew every time we talked.

We ordered our food, and Kyle went back to work. A little while later Tayla brought us our order. She was a girl in her mid-twenties who worked in Uncle Bruce's Diner as a part-time second job while she waited for her home business, an internet company offering consulting services, to bring in money.

When we finished eating, Grandma went back home and I went to check on Rosie.

She and Bev were in the gym, rearranging decorations; all at Rosie's direction, of course.

"I seem to remember telling you I didn't need help," Rosie said, hugging me in spite of my disobedience.

"And yet here Bev is, helping," I said. "Besides, *I* seem to remember telling you the gym looked perfect as it was—so we're even." I laughed and hugged Bevin in greeting.

I had learned that the entire Larsen family, including twelve-year-old Rymi, loved hugs. Even though we saw each other nearly every day, Rosie was never satisfied until she had a hug hello and another when we parted. Bev was less vocal about it, but he liked them too.

I glanced around the gym, which now had streamers on the floor, tables askew, and the CD player unplugged until Rosie decided on a new place for it to rest.

"Seriously, this place was just fine. Bev, why did you let her talk you into helping mess up a good thing? Have some backbone, man!"

Bevin chuckled. "Clearly you haven't seen Rosie in her nervous excitement state. You do what she says or you lose your life."

Rosie giggled. "Sorry, Bev. But now that we've started we can't very well leave it like this. And since you're here, Jane, can we recruit you?"

"I came with only an intent to help," I assured her, and began picking streamers up off the floor.

Soon the gym looked beautiful, and Bev and I successfully convinced Rosie not to change even a little part of it again. Because she still needed something to occupy her until the gala began, she and Bev took me on a tour of the school.

I stopped in one of the hallways, in front of a showcase of past student awards and photos.

"Recognize anything?"

I pointed to one of the pictures. "I'm pretty sure that's my Grandma Blake."

They read the name under the photo. Rosie pointed to one of the awards. "Looks like your grandma was involved with basketball. Like, a lot."

I looked at the award she was referring to; it had my grandma's full name on it. "I didn't think she liked any sports," I said. "And certainly not enough to earn a trophy for it." I looked at the award again. "Wow. Basketball Champion."

Rosie giggled. "That's one impressive grandma you've got, Jane!"

"A secretive one, too, if she never told you about her sports career," Bev said.

"Well, until recently she didn't like to talk about her past."

"Okay, but still," Rosie said, an idea now firmly planted in her mind. "That's a weird thing to not want to talk about, even if it *is* in the past. Unless something about it upset her."

"My sister, the premature sleuth."

"I think you mean amateur," I giggled.

"No, I mean premature. In Rosie's mind, the tiniest piece of something slightly off is a huge case to be solved."

Rosie stuck her tongue out at Bevin. "Come on; you can't pretend you don't find it strange that she never once mentioned she even played, when she was the school champion!"

I shrugged. "Like I said, it's only recently she's been telling me things, so there's a lot to catch up on. I'm sure she would have told me some basketball stories eventually."

Rosie made a face, disgusted at our resistance to her detective plans. "Why don't you ever join me in my mystery-solving, Jane? I'm used to Bev being a poop, but you? I had expected better."

I frowned. "I found out who the ring belonged to, didn't I?"

"Do I have to explain again why just that is not enough?"

"No, I suppose not. Okay, Rosie; from now on I will try harder to be more involved in your mystery solving. But in this case, I don't think there is anything to it."

"Well, we'll just see who's right."

They showed me the rest of the school; pretty normal, as far as I could tell. I had been homeschooled my whole life, so aside from a couple plays and concerts I had attended in support of friends, I didn't have much to compare it to.

After the tour, Rosie and Bev helped me transfer all the food to the school, we changed into our costumes, and soon people began arriving for the gala.

Rosie was thrilled. I think we all had a secret fear that even after putting in all this work, no one would show up. Instead, nearly the entire town came, most even in costume. In a town no bigger than five blocks long, there wasn't much else new and exciting to do, so it shouldn't have been surprising that so many people came, but it still was.

I looked around at all the people, searching for familiar faces. Bev was next to me, quietly handing out burgers to those who wanted them; Rosie was less quietly chatting with anyone who would listen, and generally making everyone feel welcome. Jazz music was playing from the CD player, and a handful of people, including Grandma and Mr. Jensen, were swing dancing. Rosie was right, I had to admit; they *were* cute together.

If I had ever learned to dance, I would have grabbed some unlucky friend and joined them when my milkshake-making duty ended. I was compelled instead to join the many people who were satisfied to spend the evening eating and chatting.

I glanced around the room again and sighed. Bev looked at me, curious. He had heard the sigh, over all the noise in the gym? He *was* standing right next to me, but it was still surprising.

"You okay, Jane? Want to take a break? I've been watching and think I know the recipe now. Most people who want them already have hamburgers, so I don't really have much to do anymore."

"If you don't mind, I'd like to go outside for a few minutes," I said.

"Sure, no problem." He took the ice cream scoop from me and turned to get the next milkshake order.

"I won't be long," I promised. "Thank you." I went to the front of the school. It was disappointing that Kyle hadn't come; but it was even more disappointing that I was letting it affect me. I should be able to have fun with the people who *were* there, instead of wanting to be with the one who wasn't.

It wasn't a crush, that much I knew. Those were different; and there was too much I didn't know about him still for me to be willing to think of him in a romantic way. Something told me it just wouldn't work out. Besides, I had fallen for Bev the first time I saw him, and that wasn't going to change any time soon.

Still, I felt a desire to help Kyle. If he would just come be a part of things like this, I thought, maybe he wouldn't seem so lonesome.

I knew that when I was around him he could smile and be talkative, and when he was at The Diner, he was compelled to talk and be a good host. But I'd seen the way he was when Rosie was around, and I had seen him sitting on his front steps looking listless a few times as I walked past with Rosie. Spending the majority of his time around only his grandma couldn't be making him feel a part of the community, even if he did run the only restaurant in the town.

Rosie had accepted me as one of her special friends from the moment I'd come to Backus. Kyle had been here much longer than I had, yet, in large part because of Rosie, he still felt like an outsider. Why couldn't she treat him the way she did me?

A late-arriving couple walked up to the school and waved in greeting as they went inside.

Grandma Blake came out just as the door was closing on the couple. "What's going on, Jane? The song ended and you weren't at your post. Bevin said you'd gone outside, and he seemed worried." She put an arm around me. "Talk to me, darling."

"Are you lonely, Grandma Blake?" I asked.

She smiled. "Only sometimes. I miss your grandpa awfully," she looked up and away from me, remembering, "but I know he would want me to be happy now, and I am."

I nodded. "You were both still so much in love," I said. "I've been thinking about that lately. After so much time, you both still cared for each other. It's mind blowing."

Grandma Blake laughed a little. "Not mind blowing, sweetheart. Love is more a choice than

192

anything else. I didn't always feel loving toward your grandpa, but I did always love him."

I nodded.

"What's been triggering these thoughts and wonderings, love?"

I sighed. "Bev. And a little bit, Kyle."

She looked a little concerned at the second name, but said, "Ah... Both handsome fellows."

"I—I didn't really notice," I stammered. Was my face red? Probably. I squirmed uncomfortably. "I like Bev, but I don't want to. You always said it was better to wait, and I know it is, and I plan to."

She nodded, and seemed proud.

"And with Kyle, it's just," my voice trailed off, unsure how to continue.

"Just what, Jane?"

"Well, it's just I feel this strong pull toward him. Not a romantic one, but, protective, I guess." I bit my lip, wanting to be clear. "I want to see him happy; I want to see his life work out for him."

Grandma Blake smiled. "Oh, my little Jane...I do love your heart."

I blushed.

"You have such a big heart for people you barely even know—and even bigger for those that you do. It's a God thing, you know."

I looked at her, surprised.

"I was never as tenderhearted as you are. My first reaction to people has always been suspicion and dislike."

I nodded. "But what am I supposed to *do*?" I asked.

"Just treat people with the sisterly love that you feel toward them—which I know that you do already."

"It doesn't feel like enough sometimes. I want to actually do things to help. But some people are so hesitant to accept any help from anyone." I frowned.

The few times I had attempted to help Kyle and Grandma Carol, they'd pushed me away.

Grandma Blake chuckled. "Stubborn people are rather annoying sometimes," she commented.

I giggled. "Just a little," I agreed. "They're hard to know how to handle."

"Patiently. It's not easy. In general, stubborn people are impatient," she smiled, "and as one of them myself, I should know," she said. "Patience works miracles. We are impressed by it when we see it, and it enchants us into submission." She winked.

I laughed. "I'm not very patient myself."

"Sure you are, love." Grandma hugged me and went back inside. She made me agree to follow soon. As she stood, she whispered, "I think Bevin is a very nice young man. Let's wait and see how that plays out."

I blushed. A few minutes later, I took a deep breath and turned to go in.

"Aw, you didn't have to wait out here for me."

I turned around. "Kyle! I didn't expect you to come!"

He chuckled. "I'm sorry I'm late. It was my night to close up The Diner, and then I had to get ready. Is this 50s enough?" He stepped back to show me his outfit: a pinstripe suit, complete with a matching fedora.

I grinned. "Perfect. Where did you get it?"

"It was my Grandpa Michael's," he said. "Grandma Carol pulled it out when she learned about the gala. It doesn't fit quite right, but it works. Grandma said to tell everyone, especially her 'Jane dear,' hello from her. She wasn't feeling up to coming out tonight."

I smiled. "Well, let's get inside and get you some food, and maybe some dancing if you want. Most people are just talking. I've gotta take over making the milkshakes again. Bev's doing it for me right now, but I shouldn't have stayed out here as long as

I did. I just needed to get away from the crowd for a while."

We walked back inside the gym. Bev looked up, and quickly looked away. Did he dislike Kyle, too? I'd never noticed that before, but as I thought about it I realized that, because of Rosie, I'd never really been around the two of them together.

I directed Kyle to the burgers and other food; which he declined, insisting he had eaten before he came. A couple guys waved him over so, satisfied he was entertained, I went back to Bev.

"I'm so sorry for being gone so long," I said, reaching for the ice cream scoop.

He didn't relinquish the spoon. "Don't worry about it," he said, though his icy tone didn't match his words.

I bit my lip. "Bev?"

"I'm fine here. You go have fun."

I frowned. "Are you angry with me?"

"No," he said quickly, and this time his gentle tone put me at ease. "We're almost done anyway, so you might as well not have to clean up a second time. You can just go dance or talk or something."

"Okay," I said. "Thanks, Bev." I hugged him.

He smiled a little and waved me away.

Kyle pulled me over when he saw I was free and said, "Wanna dance?"

"I don't know how," I admitted.

"Oh, it's easy. Grandma and Grandpa used to do it all the time, and they taught me how."

"Wait," I said, suddenly turning to him. "What did you say your grandpa's name was?"

"Michael," he said, confused by my excited curiosity.

"Michael Mitchell?"

He nodded.

"Kyle, you and I are cousins!" I grinned. "Or second cousins, or something; but in any case, we're related!"

Kyle looked at me, still confused. "We are?"

I nodded. "Michael Mitchell was my great uncle." *No wonder Grandma had seemed relieved when she learned I didn't have romantic feelings for Kyle. And why she had pushed Bev on me as a much better alternative.*

Kyle grinned. "In that case, cousin, want to dance?"

"I still don't know how," I said, as though I was worried he thought our discovery of a common ancestor would change that fact.

"Just follow along; you'll get the hang of it."

I agreed, and the next few songs he spent trying to teach my uncoordinated feet to behave. My high heels started making my feet sore after a little while, so we stopped. I glanced at the dessert table; Bev was gone.

Chapter 15

"Ella are you ready yet? You've been making Joe wait for an hour already!" Linda complained, folding her arms and rocking back on her heels.

"I have not," I said indignantly. "I'm not ready, and you trying to rush me isn't going to help. Why are you in such a hurry to get rid of me?"

"Mom said once you leave I can see if some of my friends can come over. She didn't want them here when Joe came, in case we got crazy." Linda made a face, and shook her head. "If you are going to marry the guy, don't you think he should be aware of what he's getting into? My husband is going to know everything about my family."

"You are too young to be thinking about a husband already, Linda." I clipped part of my hair up, and scrunched my nose at the result. "Besides," I said, turning to her, "I never said I was going to marry Joe."

Linda frowned. "If you aren't going to marry him, why are you dating?"

It was a fair question, and I had been wondering it myself. We had been dating for over a month now, we had gone through Thanksgiving together, and I still didn't know how I felt about him. I knew I liked him. I knew there were parts of his personality I admired. I didn't know when those feelings were supposed to turn into love. Or, maybe, love wasn't a feeling at all.

Finally I dropped my hair and decided to leave it down. There was no controlling it today. Besides, Joe had told me he liked my hair down. Maybe that was some indication of my feelings. I wanted to do things I knew Joe would like. Was that love, though, or just me being a silly schoolgirl? I guessed it was the latter and brushed it off.

"*Now* are you ready?" Linda asked, tapping her foot impatiently.

I nodded. "Yes, I am."

"Finally!" She pushed me out of the bathroom and down the steps. "Go. Have fun. Don't worry about coming home too late." She grinned. "The longer you stay out the longer my friends can stay."

I giggled. "See you later, Linda."

Joe grinned when I came down the steps. "You look beautiful, El Bell." He hugged me.

I smiled. "So where are we going today?"

"Will you be disappointed if I tell you it's a tiny little restaurant?" He looked nervous.

"I'm very disappointed," I said, frowning a little.

Joe's brow furrowed in concern until I giggled. "It sounds lovely."

"Oh good." He let out a low breath in relief. "I was hoping it would sound, um, lovely." He chuckled a little awkwardly and opened the car door for me. "It's a couple towns over."

We made it there within a half hour and were given a table right away. Joe was right when he said it was small; it looked no bigger than The Diner. There was no long counter, but there were three tables set up inside, and I was surprised they had managed to fit even that many.

The food was good and the staff, consisting of only two people: the cook and the waiter, was friendly and attentive. We decided we loved the place and would definitely be back.

"Where were you this weekend?" I asked, as we sipped our coffee after eating. "I thought you would be working."

Joe shrugged. "I was just visiting some friends. Didn't Uncle Bruce tell you?"

I set my mug down, confused. "You've made friends outside of Backus?"

Joe chuckled. "I didn't realize my ability to make friends was *that* surprising."

I playfully shoved him. "When do you ever get out of Backus, to make the friends in the first place?"

"Every other weekend," he said. "I take it I haven't been missed much."

"No, you," I started, stumbling over the words, "I mean, I had wondered," I blushed, and stopped talking as a mischievous grin came to Joe's face.

Joe chuckled. "You're so cute when you get flustered." He winked.

We had a good evening and headed home. Monday would start our play practices. It had taken a while, but we were finally organized, auditions had taken place, and we were ready to begin. In spite of our insistence that we would be satisfied with minor roles, our supposedly unbiased judge, Millie, decided that Joe, Margaret and I would play the main roles.

"Nicholas, however," she shook her head, "I'm sorry dear, but you simply can't act."

Nicholas laughed a little, and looked embarrassed.

"Unfortunately, there are more small parts than actors here, so we shall have to tolerate his acting nonetheless." She winked.

Eric had auditioned as well, and he was a pretty good actor. I wasn't looking forward to spending that much time around him, but it would be a good exercise in treating him well; something I really needed to work on.

Monday came and Joe walked me to his house.

"Joe, I could have walked to your house just fine alone," I said, nevertheless accepting the arm he offered. "People will be arriving soon," I scolded him. "You should have stayed to greet them." I wouldn't admit it audibly, but I was still happy he had come. I loved that he would willingly walk with me anywhere I might need to go.

When we walked up his driveway, people had already arrived. They smiled at us, though they were a little cranky about having to wait. Decembers in Minnesota are often comparable in temperature to Antarctica.

Joe soothed them by offering hot chocolate, coffee, or tea. Soon the entire cast had arrived, and Millie came by to oversee everything. We started with scene one and did a read-through of the entire script. Joe gave everyone a pen or pencil, and asked them to write in the margins of their script if they had any ideas for how a line should be spoken or where the characters should move.

We read through it in a little over an hour and then began walking through, again from the beginning. Joe moved us various places, and finally we were able to come up with a good way for all of us to move in the first, well, five minutes of the first scene.

This was going to take much longer than any of us had anticipated.

Soon some people had to leave, so we decided to end for the day. We agreed to meet back again the next evening.

The next week was a jumble of working at The Diner, play practice at night, and of course the regular Friday night gala as a break from all our hard work. Saturday was another full day of rehearsal for those who were able to make it, and Sunday we would break completely. By the end of that first week we were all tired. Even I, the playwright, was ready to toss the script in the fire and never have to look at it again.

At the end of the second week Joe asked us all to try to have our lines completely memorized by Wednesday the next week. I knew most of mine already but wasn't confident with them. Thankfully I had Joe to help. Since we were playing opposite each other—he was the detective, Bingley, and I was the woman who had lost the key, Catherine—we could practice most of the scenes with just the two of us. Sometimes we needed Margaret and Tom, the other lead actors playing Jane and Edward, to join us as well.

It was great to see Tom do his part. Since he was shy, I had never heard him speak much. Normally he would stay to the rear of a room, or simply wouldn't come at all. When he was acting, though, he was confident.

Wednesday came and I felt mostly ready with the lines. Joe promised he wouldn't make a big deal of it if people weren't entirely prepared.

Joe was very good at organizing us all and spotting ways to make the play better. He paid attention to the smallest things, like which foot someone began to walk on. Some of it was frustrating because we all wanted to just move on to the next scene, but it would make for a noticeably higher quality show.

Thursday, March 25th, 1954

"Starting from scene one," Joe instructed, guiding people into place.

Margaret and I made some last-minute changes to the set, and hurried into our positions; the dress rehearsals had finally begun. Those in charge of the school had agreed to let us use their property for the final practices, and for as many performances as we wished to put on. In return we would say a "thank you" to the school, and to those people specifically, at the end of each performance.

"Ella and Tom, be ready to enter; Margaret, please take your place on stage." Joe glanced up from his script as furniture from various houses was brought in. "Sally, please slide the coffee table a little to the left. Yes; perfect." Soon everything was arranged to his liking and the costumes were passed around.

Joe insisted that they were necessary, and I had to admit I did feel more like my character once I was in my costume.

Everyone in Backus, it seemed, wanted to be a part of this. They helped with costumes, offered their furniture, and some even brought food, coffee, and snacks for the actors and the behind-the-scenes crew to munch on while we worked.

We stepped into place and waited for Joe's cue to begin the scene.

Joe walked behind stage and nodded at Margaret to begin. Margaret played Jane, the best friend of my character; not difficult, since she was that to me offstage as well.

Jane sits on the couch, calmly sipping at her tea, while also nursing a cigarette. She fumbles awkwardly with her cup and saucer then puts them down. Minutes pass. She takes a drag of her cigarette, and then snuffs it, scrunching her nose. Jane attempts a song, and then sinks into the couch, arms crossed. Her foot starts to tap. Catherine enters, in tears. Jane looks up, concerned, and hurries to her friend's side.

"It's gone," Catherine wails, "gone!"

"Oh, you mean my singing?" A comical grin comes to Jane's face. "I can fix that." She opens her mouth to begin a new song.

"No!" Catherine screeches, rushing to put a hand over her friend's mouth. "Please don't. I don't think I could handle any more tragedy today." Catherine flops dramatically onto the couch, then instantly perks up as she sees Jane's still half-full cup of tea, which she subsequently drinks.

Uncle Bruce sat in the audience, smiling and sometimes laughing, even though by that point he had heard every funny line a hundred times. When we saw how long switching the furniture on stage would take, we decided not to change the set throughout the play, so the setting looked exactly the same for every scene. It wasn't ideal, but we incorporated it into the script and, thanks to some added lines Tom and Joe suggested, made for some humorous moments.

Catherine tells Jane her key was stolen, and the two of them exit as Edward enters. He glances at them with a slight frown as they pass.

"I suppose eventually I'll get used to strange people being in my house," he says. He then resolutely shakes his head. "No I won't."

Detective Bingley enters. He looks confused, peers behind the stage, and scratches his head. "I thought this was Jane's house," he says.

"She thought so too," Edward responds, scowling at the empty teacup on the coffee table. "It's mine."

"Must be scene 4 that I'm thinking of," Detective Bingley says, shrugging, "which also means I must want something with you in this scene, or else I entered early."

That elicited more chuckles from Uncle Bruce. He thought the whole play was one big tickle.

I was pleased with how my script, which seemed so dull on paper, had come to life. One good thing about having heard the lines so often was that we were no longer tempted to burst into giggles every time a funny line was spoken. We were able to act oblivious to the fact that they were amusing in the least; just the way the characters ought to act about the lines.

For some reason since I had met Joe, I had become a persistent giggler. I had always been annoyed by those kinds of people! Things were just *funny* now, and I couldn't help but giggle at them.

The night of the first performance arrived and everyone ran around getting make-up on, pulling on costumes, realizing they had put on the wrong costume, and otherwise acting crazy and impossible to deal with.

I sat backstage with Margaret, doing ridiculous vocal exercises Millie had taught us, and trying to remind myself we were only putting this on for friends and family. I had nothing to be nervous about. Still, my heart beat quickly and it was hard to sit still.

Joe knocked on the girl's dressing room door and asked if we were all ready for the first scene. I looked around at the other girls, and answered in the affirmative. He went on stage to introduce the play.

As he finished, we took our places, and the play began. The performance went much more quickly than I thought it would, and soon I was no longer nervous.

"Ready for the final scene?" Margaret whispered, stepping up to the edge of the curtain backstage and waiting to walk on.

I nodded, grinning.

At our cue, a slight knocking, we walked onstage, where Tom and Joe were already in place.

"Miss Catherine," Detective Bingley turns to address her. He steps back a pace when he sees Jane is beside her. "Yes, well," he stumbles over his words, "I have found your missing key."

Catherine steps forward, eagerly. "Where was it?"

Detective Bingley begins pacing across the room. He turns to Jane and points an accusative finger at her. Catherine also turns to Jane, bewildered.

"You?"

Jane shakes her head, as confused as Catherine about the revelation.

"No," Detective Bingley says, motioning Jane out of the way. "Him." He points to Edward, who had been standing behind Jane.

"You?" Catherine repeats, her tone growing more surprised.

"Me," Edward says, penitently handing over the key.

Catherine accepts it, still confused. "You were pretending to help us this entire time. You knew it wasn't valuable... All it opens is my little jewelry box, and all that has is my grandma's necklace. You know how important that necklace is to me."

"Let him explain," Detective Bingley says, his voice gentle.

Catherine crosses her arms. "Why, Edward?"

Edward explains that he had heard a man named Archibald, who had mistaken the counterfeit jewels in the necklace as real, would steal the necklace. To preempt the robbery while protecting Catherine from 'Baldy,' (who had done far worse than steal), Edward stole it himself. He then worked with Detective Bingley to find the original thief. They had, and 'Baldy' is now in prison for other crimes.

There are hugs distributed throughout the group, with general wishes of goodwill, and Detective Bingley and Jane begin to plan a celebratory bash, until Catherine holds up a hand and says, "Everybody stop!" She frowns and searches the ground around her. "I've lost the key."

The amount of laughter I had heard while we were performing convinced me that we had done well. It was a really great feeling to think of all that we had accomplished with this.

We finished changing out of our costumes and washed the stage makeup off. I looked around for Margaret, to compliment the way she had portrayed Jane, but she was no longer in the dressing room. In fact, I didn't see her until the entire cast was walking from the school to Uncle Bruce's house. He insisted on feeding us a celebratory dinner.

Joe took my hand as we walked. I smiled up at him, loving the feel of his hand in mine. Even after more than four months together I hadn't gotten used to that, and my heart beat a little bit faster.

He smiled back. "Well my dear El Bell, I say that was a great success and we should do something like it again."

I nodded. "We should, but not for many, many months. If I never put stage make-up on again it won't be long enough for me. You did an incredible job directing it, Joe. I'm proud of you."

Joe smiled and leaned in to kiss my cheek.

I blushed and pushed him away a little, worrying what the other people walking with us might think of his public display of affection. Joe chuckled at my self-consciousness and kissed my cheek anyway. I rolled my eyes but smiled a little and looked shyly up at him.

He smiled and squeezed my hand giddily.

We all flooded into Uncle Bruce's and he immediately began bringing out food. He'd spent the evening preparing us a feast. None of us were terribly hungry since we had all eaten before the play began, but the food looked so good that we couldn't resist trying it all.

There were normal Diner foods like hot dogs and hamburgers and lots and lots of French fries, and milkshakes and of course pop, but there were also other things, like pasta, lasagna and hot turkey sandwiches, and any kind of pie imaginable, cookies, bars and all sorts of delicious flavors of ice cream that Uncle Bruce had invented himself.

He would have leftovers for a very long time, but he didn't seem to mind. He loved how impressed we were at the amount of food he'd made. Mostly I think he just loved that we were all in one place and enjoying ourselves with him. He was an extrovert, even more than Joe.

Though I was outgoing and loved being with people, I had introspective tendencies as well; sometimes I just liked being by myself. There would never be a time when Uncle Bruce would choose to stay at home rather than go out and be with the people of Backus. I had to admire him for that. He was almost always kind and friendly, even to people who weren't very likable, such as Eric.

Eric had actually been easy to work with. He really *had* given up trying to pursue me, and since there was no longer that awkward aspect, I could consider him a friend now—though not a good one. He was a pretty nice guy.

Well, maybe nice was the wrong word. My opinion of him hadn't *completely* changed. I was simply able to see him as a person now, instead of as something that annoyed me. It was a welcome change.

Joe hopped from table to table, making sure people had anything they could desire, and talking with them, telling them what a wonderful job they had done, and giving them specific details he liked about each of their performances. How he remembered all that, and how he could have noticed when he himself was acting too, was impressive.

People began to leave, though the evening was far from over. Joe asked if I would go on another date with him the next evening. Of course I agreed to it. Every time we talked I learned something new about him, and everything I learned I absolutely loved.

He was kind and attentive to others, he wasn't focused on himself, he was a hard worker, a good leader, and his faith was strong. I loved it all.

But did I love *him*? That was a question I still couldn't answer. If he had asked me to marry him right then, I wouldn't have said yes. So why *was* I still spending time and energy on someone that I knew I wouldn't be able to marry?

Well, because someday, maybe I wouldn't be able to say no.

Margaret grabbed my hand and pulled me to the front door. She had a huge grin on her face and seemed to be restraining an urge to squeal.

We got outside and she turned to me.

Before I could ask what was making her so giddy, she told me: "Nicholas just asked me to date him! Ella, I'm so excited and happy! I know you cared for him." Her eyes searched my face, and she was clearly trying to mask her excitement. "Oh Ella, please tell me you're okay with this?"

I pulled her into a hug. "I'm *thrilled* with it! You two will be so good together."

Margaret's grin returned.

"Nicholas actually told me he'd be doing this," I said, leading her to the small bench in their yard. "He talked to your dad months ago. I was wondering what was taking him so long." I rubbed my hands together to ward off the cold. "Guess he was waiting for the right moment. Did he find it?"

She giggled. "He was so cute. After the show ended he pulled me behind the stage away from everyone else, and took my hands in his, and asked if I would go with him to dinner tomorrow." She rubbed her arms. "And when I said yes, he kissed me! Ella, I'm on cloud 9!"

I smiled and hugged her. "I'm so happy for you both."

"What was your first kiss like, Ella?"

I bit my lip and sat on my hands.

Margaret looked concerned. "Was it awful?"

I shook my head. "It, um," I shifted a little uncomfortably, "it hasn't happened yet."

"Oh!" Margaret said, putting a hand over her mouth as if she wished she'd kept quiet.

I smiled. "Yeah. Way to make me feel bad." I winked, though it really did bug me now that it was brought to my attention. I continued, more myself than for her. "Nicholas has known you much longer, though. He's had more time for his feelings to grow than Joe has with me."

"Oh, hush," Margaret smiled. "If Nicholas cares for me half as much as Joe loves you, I'll consider myself lucky."

I looked at her, surprised. "He loves me?"

"You're joking, right?" Margaret looked at me, to assure herself I was; but I wasn't, and she could see it. "You're serious. Yes, Ella, he's real gone. He's loved you for a while now. I suppose I should have let him be the one to say so. I assumed you knew; the rest of us know. He isn't good at hiding his feelings."

I nodded a little. "His openness is one of the things I admire about him," I said. "I knew he cared about me, I just," I paused, "I didn't know how much."

Margaret shivered a little. "Don't tell him I told you? He was probably waiting for a good time. I don't want to ruin it."

"You haven't," I said, smiling. If Joe did tell me he loved me, I would be as surprised as if she hadn't said a word; I didn't exactly believe her.

Margaret stood. "Let's go back in."

"You go," I said, looking up at the nearly full moon. "I'm going to stay out here for a little bit."

"Ella, it's freezing!"

I shrugged. "I'm Minnesotan, Maggie. I'm used to it."

She hesitated.

"I'll only be a few minutes," I assured her. "If I'm out here longer you can send a search party with hot coffee."

She giggled. "Righto." She went back inside.

I pulled my knees up onto the bench and hugged them. There were so many thoughts going through my head: so many questions. *Joe loves me? If that's true, why hasn't he kissed me yet? I mean, besides the cheek and forehead kisses that even family members could give one another. I'd assumed it was because, like me, he wasn't sure what we had was going to last.*

The door opened. *She sent a search party already?* I turned around.

"Hey El Bell." Joe sat on the bench next to me and folded his hands in his lap. "Are you okay?"

I smiled a little. "Yeah. It's just nice out here."

Joe chuckled. "You're a horrible liar, Ella. It's cold and windy out here." He pulled his suit jacket off and put it around my shoulders. "The sky is beautiful, but that's all the outdoors has going for it tonight. Why don't you tell me what's on your mind?"

I blushed, and was glad it was too dark for him to notice. "I'm fine."

"Okay, El Bell. Ready to come back inside?"

I set my feet back on the ground. "Yeah."

Joe helped me up. "I'll be heading to the city tomorrow to run some errands."

"Want me to come with?"

He shook his head. "It's just some things I have to take care of. I'll see you tomorrow night, though; your mother invited me to dinner."

I nodded.

Joe opened the door for me. As I stepped past him into Uncle Bruce's house, he gently took my hand. I stopped and looked at him. He smiled and kissed the top of my head.

I looked curiously at him, expecting him to say something more.

He didn't. He simply turned and closed the door behind us.

Chapter 16

In the late 1940s, a man people affectionately called Uncle Bruce built and began serving food in what he simply called The Diner.

This probably isn't surprising to you. Uncle Bruce's Diner is still around today, and pictures of Uncle Bruce and past diner employees line the walls. What you may not know is what kind of person this man truly was.

I wrote what Grandma Blake had told me about him. Satisfied with the result, I shut my laptop and headed to Rosie's. I hadn't seen her since the gala; I'd been busy with last-minute preparations for Christmas. Since she hadn't stopped by I imagined she was doing the same.

Bev let me in. He was smiling, but it seemed forced. "Hey Jane." The happy tone he usually greeted me with was gone.

"Hey Bev." I hesitated. "Are you all right?"

He nodded, but the sadness in his features and tone remained. "I take it you're here to see Rosie?"

"Yeah." I bit my lip. "Is she okay?"

"She's fine," he said, shifting slightly. "But she's upset. I'm not sure if she'll be willing to talk to you."

"What happened? Did somebody hurt her?"

He didn't respond, and glanced toward her room.

I frowned. "Did *I* do something?"

Still he didn't answer.

"Please, Bev; be honest with me. Rosie's one of my closest friends. If I've done something to hurt her, I want to fix it."

"You haven't done anything," he said quickly. "Not on purpose. But she thinks you did. She's being silly."

"Is she in her room?"

"Yes, but—"

I stepped past Bevin and went to Rosie's room, entering without knocking.

She didn't look up from her notebook.

"Rosie," I said.

"I'm busy."

I frowned and walked farther in. "Used to be, you were never too busy for friends."

She continued to write. "I told Bev not to let you in."

"What I do isn't up to Bevin or you."

"Clearly."

I crossed my arms. "Rosalia Tyler, you are going to talk to me if I have to spend Christmas with you to make you do it." I took the notebook out of her hand, forcing her to look at me.

She looked up, and it was then I noticed her tear-stained cheeks and fresh tears threatening to escape.

I sat on the edge of her bed and said much more gently, "Please, Rosie. I'm so sorry. I didn't mean to hurt you. Tell me what I've done, so I can make it better."

She yanked the notebook out of my hand and turned her back to me.

"Rosie."

Without looking at me, she said, "Don't you know it makes it so much worse that you're oblivious to everything?"

I frowned.

Rosie put her head in her hands and continued, her voice now slightly muffled. "It's bad enough you spend time with that guy when you know I dislike him."

"Kyle?" I asked quietly.

"Yes, Kyle!" she snapped.

"You told me you didn't care if I befriended him, as long as you weren't included."

"Yeah, well, I lied; I care a lot." She turned to me, anger in her features. "And as if spending time with him wasn't enough, you added this."

I sat on the bed next to her. "What?"

"Don't play dumb," she said. "It doesn't suit you."

"Rosie, please just tell me."

"You really don't know?"

I shook my head. "I really don't."

Rosie crossed her arms. "You can just go on being oblivious then."

"Rosie—"

"If you say my name one more time, I'm going to have it legally changed," she growled.

In spite of the emotion in the room, I had to smile a little at her ridiculous threat.

"It isn't just me you hurt; it's Bev, too." She frowned. "Of course he'll never let you see it. He's far too much a gentleman for that. I might be able to forgive you for hurting me. But hurting him," she shook her head, "that I can't forgive."

I started putting the pieces together. "I hurt him by dancing with Kyle instead of helping him make the milkshakes."

"You hurt Bev by barely speaking to him and being distracted all night; and once Kyle showed up, you were completely focused on him." Rosie turned to face me, eyes narrowed in anger. "Bev was worried about you all night, Jane, and he was doing everything he knew how, to try to make you feel better."

I bit my lip, but knowing she wasn't finished, nodded for her to continue.

She started picking at the corner of her notebook. "You're just oblivious! You're always oblivious, to everything but yourself. And then to find out you were listless because of another *guy*? It crushed him." She ripped a little of her notebook and stopped picking at it. "Bev is such a good guy, if you'd only told him from the start that it was Kyle you were pining after, he would have gone to get him for you." She looked directly at me. "If you had any thought for anyone but yourself, you would have seen that."

I blinked repeatedly, and quickly brushed away a tear that had somehow made it through my barrier. In a shaky voice, I said, "This is between me and Bevin, then. You stay out of it."

Rosie turned around again, her back to me. "I wouldn't get involved if it didn't affect me, too. I thought you knew me better," she mumbled.

"I thought so too," I said. "But the Rosie I knew wouldn't judge me without first hearing my side. And she wouldn't hold something against me without explaining it and giving me a chance to make it right." I stood up. "When that Rosie comes back, I want to talk to her." I left the room.

Bev stood up and dropped his book on the couch, losing his place, when I came into the room. "Jane?"

I looked at him.

"Don't let her get to you. She's emotional, and doesn't mean what she's saying." He hugged me. I fought my hardest to keep the tears away as he released me.

"Bevin?"

"Yes, Jane?"

I bit my lip. "Are you upset with me?"

He smiled, and this time it was genuine. "No. Do I look like it?"

I shook my head.

"Don't you think we're good enough friends that I would tell you if I was?" he asked.

"I hope so," I said quietly.

"I would tell you," he promised. "Like I said; don't listen to Rosie's emotional talk."

He hugged me again, and I left. Now alone, I let the tears fall freely. I wasn't ready to return home, so I went to the cemetery and sat on my bench there. After a few minutes, through blurry eyes, I saw a shadow come closer to me.

"Well that's certainly not the cheery beautiful face I'm used to being greeted with." My cousin, AnnaMarie, brushed away snow and sat next to me. She was three years older than me, but we had been close friends since we were young. Though we seldom talked except when our families got together, she was one of the few people I could tell anything to. I knew I could count on her for wise advice, and she knew she could count on me if she ever needed someone to vent to or celebrate with.

I managed a smile and hugged her. "I didn't think you'd be here until tomorrow," I said. "If I'd known you were coming today I would have stayed home and waited for you."

"Looks to me like you should have stayed home anyway," she said, offering me a travel-sized box of tissues. "Who has hurt my Jane? Give me a name, and I'll beat them up. Is it a boy? Tell me it's not. I'm not ready for you to start having boy trouble."

"It's not a boy," I assured her, wiping my tears. "It's a friend. We're having a misunderstanding, and she won't tell me what it's really about. She's frustrated that I can't figure it out on my own, but I can't try to make it right if she doesn't tell me why she's upset in the first place."

AnnaMarie put an arm around me. "Sounds like she needs some time to think and calm down. And after she's done that she'll remember how blessed she is to have you as a friend, and you'll be able to work things out." She rubbed my shoulder comfortingly.

"Thanks," I said, starting to believe her.

She shivered a little.

"We can go inside," I said. "I forget you're not used to Minnesota weather now that you've moved away for college."

AnnaMarie laughed. "I don't think I was used to it even when I lived here. Frankly I don't think anybody could be. Florida is much preferable. Well, except that it's missing my favorite cousin."

I smiled. "I'm so glad you're here."

"Yeah, me too; now get me inside and make me some of that amazing hot chocolate, or I'm liable to turn into a Popsicle." She winked.

I giggled.

She grinned, victorious. "I got you to laugh. One more daily goal I can mark as done. Thanks for always making my daily goals so easy to accomplish, even on days that are rough for you."

We went across the street to my house, and Aunt Mical and Uncle Davey greeted me with hugs and asked how I liked living in Backus. Uncle Davey said he remembered a little about it from when he'd been young, and missed the atmosphere.

Aunt Mical absolutely refused to move to such a small town, and also wanted to stay close to her sister, Mira. I'd met Mira a couple times and knew her as a quiet but happy woman. Her love story, like my grandparent's, was one I wouldn't mind mimicking eventually.

Aunt Mical and Uncle Davey's, though, wasn't one anyone would hope for. It had turned out well in the end, though.

I promised everyone some freshly made hot chocolate, and AnnaMarie helped me in the kitchen. Either my face had cleared enough that traces of my tears were no longer visible, or my relatives knew me enough not to mention it. Whatever the reason, I was grateful to not have to explain.

As we sat in the living room sipping our hot cocoa, Grandma Blake and Mr. Jensen finally admitted they were dating, and had been for a few months. They hadn't wanted to say anything until the entire family was together. Of course, we'd all had suspicions and knew that if they *weren't* officially dating, they were at least acting like it. Mr. Jensen would take Grandma's hand when he thought the rest of us weren't looking, and Grandma's smile grew brighter whenever she looked at Mr. Jensen, or even just mentioned his name.

I was glad they had postponed the announcement, though. It had given me time to get used to the idea, and I could honestly tell them I was happy for them both. Seeing the way Mr. Jensen treated Grandma: always with respect and tender care, and seeing how happy they both were when they were together, had convinced me they were meant to be together.

I had been thinking selfishly when I first objected to the match; Rosie had helped me see that. I vowed to try harder to keep my natural tendency to be self-centered at bay.

Aunt Mical and Uncle Davey were given Katty and Maggie's room, and the girls stayed in the living room. AnnaMarie spent the night in the basement with me. She caught me up on how her second year of college was going, told me about her new friends, and talked about the guy who she was praying about.

She insisted she wanted to wait for God's timing, and wasn't willing to prematurely give the guy her heart, but she knew she cared for him, though she wouldn't call it love yet, and he had been showing signs he reciprocated the feelings.

AnnaMarie had a peace that no matter how the situation turned out, it would be wonderful because she knew she would be following in God's steps.

"I'm a little jealous of the assurance you have," I said. "I certainly don't feel that."

"I don't usually *feel* it either," AnnaMarie admitted, "but I always know it. I pray daily for God's guidance, and even when there are no clear signs of what He'd like, I can usually tell what choice He would want." She smiled. "As long as I'm doing what I can to follow God, how can I have anything *but* a peace that things will turn out the way He wants?"

"I guess that makes sense," I said.

"Though," she said, smirking, "sometimes what He wants doesn't match up with what I want. But that's okay, too. His plan is better anyway."

I smiled. I told her about Bevin and Rosie and Kyle, and about the newspaper and the staff, and about the handful of other people my age I had gotten to know.

By the time we got to sleep, it was early morning Christmas Day.

After breakfast, we passed around presents, and the remainder of the day was spent in conversation and team games.

Near the end of the day, Mr. Jensen pulled a scrapbook from his bag. "I don't know how interested you all are in your grandma's past, but I thought you might like to see a bit of it," he said.

"Oh Nicholas, put that thing away," Grandma Blake said, a little flustered. "Where did you ever find it?"

Mr. Jensen colored. "I stole it from your house," he admitted. "Turns out your husband was a bit more fond of the past than you are. He labeled this book, 'My Treasured Memories,' and he saved articles, photos, letters, pieces of hair," he trailed off.

"Gross." Katty made a face.

Mr. Jensen chuckled. "Okay, I'm joking about that last bit. But just about anything that ever mentioned your grandma is in here." He turned to Grandma. "They look interested. Shall we put it to a vote?"

"Oh fine," Grandma said, pouting a little. "You win."

Mr. Jensen grinned and together we began flipping through the scrapbook and listening to Mr. Jensen's and Grandma's occasional anecdotes.

We went through it much more quickly than I would have liked, so when everyone began to head for bed and Mr. Jensen went back to Mr. Larsen's house, I asked if I could keep it. Grandma relented when I pointed out that it might give me ideas for articles.

The next day, everyone returned home. Two days was not nearly enough time with AnnaMarie, and even the two weeks I'd spent with Grandma Blake seemed far too short.

I started looking through the scrapbook again, this time pausing to read the articles, letters, and love-filled captions under the photos. There were love letters to and from Grandma and Grandpa, articles that mentioned Grandma, a handful of articles Grandma had written, and many photos. Each caption under the photos of Grandma said something along the lines of, 'My Beautiful Wife,' 'My Precious Darling,' or 'Life's Greatest Blessing.'

Someday, I'll find a guy like Grandpa. They still exist, don't they?

I smiled at the pictures as I recognized some of the poodle skirts Grandma had given me. There was one with music notes, one with a cat, one with a record; but none had the typical poodle. I wondered if that had been on purpose.

There was a knock on the door, so I reluctantly set aside the scrapbook to answer it.

Rosie stood on my front steps, looking cold and penitent. "I'm so sorry, Jane."

I hurried her indoors and directed her to a seat in front of the fire.

"Bev helped me see how ridiculous I was being to you, and I'm so sorry," Rosie said, accepting the coffee I gave her.

"It's okay," I said, smiling. "You were frustrated."

She nodded. "I *am* still mad at you, though."

I bit my lip, mentally preparing myself for whatever she had to say.

"You mean you aren't going to ask why?"

I smiled a little. "I know you well enough to know you'll tell me whether I ask or not."

Rosie giggled.

Well, at least she's happy enough to take a joke.

"Okay, here it is. I'm mad at you because you were at my house, and you hugged Bev, but I didn't get a hug hello *or* goodbye!"

I smiled, largely in relief.

"No Jane," she said, shaking her head, "it's not funny. I expect you to make amends."

I laughed and pulled her into a hug. "In my defense, you didn't seem very receptive to hugs at the time."

"Yeah, I know." She hugged me back. "So let's talk this out like the mature young ladies we pretend to be."

Finally willing to talk about the long-standing animosity between her and Kyle, Rosie explained that before I came to Backus, the two of them had been very good friends. Then Rosie realized she was starting to get a crush on him. He encouraged the crush by flirting with her, and it grew until she was certain that when they were old enough, he would ask her out.

"That was before Tasha came to visit her grandparents for a summer," Rosie shook her head at the memory. "I could tell Bevin had a crush on her. I couldn't tell what Tasha's feelings were, but you know Bev. I can't imagine anyone *not* liking him."

I blushed, wondering if she knew my own feelings toward him.

Rosie continued, oblivious. "Then Kyle started spending time around Tasha. First we spent time as a group, the four of us, and there wasn't a problem. But then Tasha and Kyle began spending time without me and Bev, and they began flirting."

Since Bevin's feelings for Tasha were so obvious to her, Rosie couldn't imagine Kyle being unable to see them too, and she saw his flirtations as betrayal. And of course, she felt the pain of rejection as Kyle's attentions moved away from her.

Tasha went home at the end of the summer and nothing ever came of anyone's feelings, but Rosie couldn't look at Kyle the same after that. She hated to admit that feelings for him still came every so often, and she was afraid that if they spent more time together, the feelings would come back in full, and her heart would be broken yet again.

"I'd thought I was immune to that, until I saw you with him at the gala, and the feelings came back. I was jealous and hurt, though I know I had no right to be."

I assured her I had no romantic feelings for Kyle; she smiled at that news.

She told me she would let Bev explain his part in it when he felt the time was right.

"I want to make something clear, though," Rosie said. "Bev is the most level-headed guy I know. He balances me out in that area." She laughed a little. "He wasn't upset throughout any of this. Not at Kyle, not at Tasha, and not at you. He says that no one is to blame. I can't see it that way yet, but maybe someday I will."

I could guess what her suspicions with Bevin were: she thought he liked me. I doubted he really did. Bev saw me as a good friend, nothing more.

That was okay for now. I wasn't ready for a guy. The thought, though, however unlikely, that Bev might reciprocate the feelings I'd been hiding for him did make me a little giddy. It was time for me to let my practical side take over and make me grounded again.

Chapter 17

Saturday, May 8, 1954
Ella Mitchell

"You going to tell me what this is about yet?" I asked, crossing my arms and remaining standing beside Joe's car. He had told me he had a surprise a few towns away. I let him have his fun and drag me there, but now I wanted answers.

I received none: only a grin in response.

I frowned.

"Oh, just stop being a stubborn ninny and come play with me," Joe said, reaching for my hand.

I raised an eyebrow, but took his hand. Joe could be just as stubborn as I was sometimes, and some things weren't worth arguing about.

We began walking, when a three- or four-year-old

boy sped past us on a rusty tricycle. He skidded to a stop and backpedaled until he reached us again. "Who's the baby?"

Joe smiled at the boy. *They know each other?* "David, what is it we call women?" he asked gently.

The boy hung his head. "Sorry," he mumbled, and then perked up. "Who's the *lady*?"

Joe introduced us. "David, I was hoping you could spend some time with Ella and me. How would you like to go swimming?"

David smiled widely. "That'd be swell! I just gotta ask Frank." He ran inside a large school-like building.

I turned to Joe, and gave him a questioning look.

He noticed, but simply smiled and said nothing.

I scowled.

"Uh oh. What did I do this time?"

"Who is David?" I asked.

Joe grinned, knowing his response would annoy me, but unable to resist. "The boy you just met."

I narrowed my eyes at him.

He chuckled. "Sorry. He's an orphan. I met him on my way to Minneapolis to sign the papers on my house. I've been coming here to spend time with him and the other orphans every weekend I can." He smiled, as if recalling happy memories.

Why didn't you include me in that part of your life, Joe? I want to share those memories with you.

David returned, having gotten Frank's approval, and we went to the beach. David was a lively, cheerful little boy, and his laughter was contagious. He had dimples in his cheeks, and thick light brown hair that could use a pair of scissors and a hairbrush.

Joe ran down the beach with him, catching him, tipping him upside down, and spinning him around. I joined in some, but watching them enjoy each other was more fun than participating, so I spent most of the time relaxed on a towel. Not caring that he drenched the bottom half of his pants in the process, Joe dunked David in the water. David popped back up, squealing in laughter.

I smiled, and waved at them when they looked in my direction. *Joe is going to make an amazing father someday.* I hoped David would find a good home soon. He deserved a loving mother and father.

Friday, February 11th, 1955

Joe and I had been dating for over a year. Occasionally we would go back to the little restaurant we had discovered; that was still our favorite place. He now took me with whenever he would go visit David, and I had fallen in love with the little boy. My heart broke for him that he still hadn't been adopted, while many of his friends had. If only people would spend some time around him, they would love him as I did.

Focusing at the task at hand, I pulled on my favorite poodle skirt and put my hair in a clip, then went outside to wait for Joe to arrive.

He drove up in his light blue Ford Thunderbird. The car meant he planned to take me someplace out of town, again. Well, not tonight.

I stayed seated on the steps and Joe got out and walked to me. He grinned and held out a hand to help me up. I stood up, but didn't take his offered arm.

"Something wrong?" he asked.

"No, nothing," I said. "It's just," I bit my lip, "I don't want to go out tonight."

Joe looked concerned. "Why not?"

"Well, because we almost always leave Backus on our dates, and even when we don't, we go to The Diner." I sighed and slipped my hand in his. "I'm perfectly satisfied spending a quiet night around here. We could go for a walk, sit at the park, or have dinner at home."

"I do like the sound of those. But why, Ella?"

"You're always spending money on me, and you don't need to."

Joe chuckled. "That's silly, El Bell. You're worth any penny I spend."

I blushed.

"We can stay home tonight. And any other night you want to. But Ella, please," he looked me in the eyes and continued in his gentle tone, "don't ask me not to spend money on you. I'm going to do it no matter what, and I don't want to feel I'm disobeying you whenever I do."

I giggled. It was nice to feel pampered...and loved.

Yes, loved. I had felt it for quite some time, and now Joe had begun to tell me that he loved me. I hadn't been expecting it, in spite of Margaret's revelation, and even now that he had been saying it every so often it always caught me off guard.

I didn't know how to respond to him when he said it. I couldn't tell him I loved him too. Even after knowing him for a year and a half, I still didn't know, and I couldn't lie to him even to spare his feelings.

We spent that night walking through the woods around Backus. We ended up in Margaret's and my special spot, close to the school. Joe stepped closer to one of the trees. "Looks like there's been some vandalism here," he commented, pointing to the carved-out heart Margaret and I had made a couple summers before. "You wouldn't happen to be the E in this E & M equation?"

I smiled. "Yeah, I'm the E."

"Can I hope the M is *not* for Matthew?" Joe asked.

"You can hope that if you want," I said, unable to resist teasing him. He did it to me enough; he deserved it.

"I don't remember you ever saying you were sweet on him, but I suppose it's possible."

"It is."

Joe raised a knowing eyebrow at me. "Possible but not likely."

I smiled. "You know me too well," I said. "The M is for Margaret. This is our spot; we found it years ago and come here whenever we have some time and the temperature's not below freezing." I started ushering him back into the woods. "Knowing how jealous Maggie can get, I don't think it's wise for you to stay here. She doesn't like strangers in our spot."

"Whoa, when did I become a stranger again?" Joe asked, looking slightly appalled.

I giggled. "To this particular spot, you must always remain a stranger."

"And why is that?" he asked, a mischievous smirk coming to his face.

"Because I sort of like you better alive."

Joe chuckled. "But only sort of." He kissed my cheek. "Righto, I will do my best to resist the anger of Maggie."

We headed back to my house, and he made us all some hot chocolate.

"Joe," Linda said, bouncing in her seat in excitement, yet somehow managing not to spill her drink. "Did you hear about the basketball championships?"

"What town do you think this is, LeeLee?"

Linda giggled. "Well then you also know I'll be competing. Will you come?"

"And see my favorite basketball star as she becomes the towns' new champion? You really think I would miss that?"

She grinned.

Linda's team won, and Linda was awarded Most Valued Player. A trophy was made for her, but there had been a miscommunication with the engraver, and my name showed up on it instead of Linda's.

"You don't even play sports!" Linda frowned.

"I know...I'm sorry, Linda. I'm sure they can correct it."

Linda put a finger on her bottom lip, thinking. A smile came to her face and she shook her head. "Let's keep it this way."

I tilted my head at her, confused. "Why?"

She giggled. "Because it's so improbable! Everyone knows that of the two of us, I'm the sporty one. This is funny! Ella the basketball star." Linda grinned.

I smiled. "Yeah. You're the star, and no silly trophy can give or take that away from you."

"I hope they put this up in the school trophy case." She giggled.

Monday, February 14th, 1955

Aside from Sweetest Day, which is a day in October to celebrate friendships, Valentine's Day was Joe's favorite holiday. Last Valentine's, he had bought me two dozen roses, given me a candlelit meal, and danced with me in the moonlight until it got too cold and we had to come back indoors.

Most girls would feel like a princess under that treatment. For me, it was too cliché. I appreciated the thoughts behind it all, but I was determined to show Joe that I preferred less flashy displays of affection.

I opened the door before Joe had a chance to knock, and went with him to his car. He told me I looked beautiful and I blushed, as always.

"Where are we going today?" I asked.

"We're going to visit David," he said. "So I suppose it doesn't really count as a date."

I was thrilled at this news.

We pulled into the parking lot and he opened my car door for me. He held out his hand and I accepted it. As we walked in, immediately ten or fifteen kids, all under the age of ten, jumped up and hugged us. "Joe and Ella!" they squealed.

Joe smiled and returned their hugs, and then looked around, wondering the same thing I was. "Where is David?"

"He's sick," Betty, a girl of six, answered. "He's in the sick room and we aren't allowed to see him 'cause he might make us sick too."

Joe's smile changed to a concerned frown. "Where is the sick room?" he asked.

They pointed and Joe and I, followed by the rest of the kids, went in that direction. Frank noticed us walk past.

"Hi," he said, and glanced at the ankle-biters with a smile. "I see you've already been greeted."

"I was just going to check on David," Joe said. "Betty tells me that he's sick."

Frank nodded. "He is, and it's pretty bad, Joe. I don't know if you should go in there. To be safe, we're assuming he's contagious."

Joe went in anyway. He sat next to David's bed and took his little hand in his. I went inside too, but stayed by the doorway, watching.

Though I had always known Joe had a sweet and patient spirit, I had never seen him treat someone so gently and tenderly before. He whispered a soft prayer for David and dabbed the sweat off his small brow.

David stirred a little and woke up. Seeing Joe brought a weak smile to his lips. "Hi," he said feebly. He glanced toward me and the smile grew slightly.

Joe smiled in return. "Hey buddy. How are you doing?"

David shrugged a little, as best he could while lying down, then turned away and coughed. It was a feeble cough that didn't appear to do much good. It seemed to only make him more miserable.

I glanced at Joe, intending only to see how he was reacting, but something else caught my eye. There was something about him that was different; it made my heart skip a beat.

He had his head bent and was praying. I had seen him pray before, but it had never affected me the way it did today. I couldn't look away from him. I would have loved spending the rest of my life watching him the way that I was in that moment.

It wasn't about the way he looked. I had always known he was handsome, and I had seen him in this position many times. Today, though, there was something about it that had never been there before. Maybe I was the one who had changed.

Joe looked up, having finished his prayer, and smiled gently. He looked peaceful, somehow.

David stopped coughing and motioned for Joe to lean forward so he could tell him a secret. I stepped away to give them room. Joe turned bright pink at whatever David said, but a wider smile came to his face and he nodded and whispered something in response.

We stayed at the orphanage another hour and Joe played games with the other kids, brought things to David to keep him comfortable, and offered Frank some suggestions of how best to take care of the sick boy. Joe said he didn't think the sickness was serious, it seemed just like a regular flu, so to watch him and if it got worse to talk to the doctors. He promised that if David needed to be put in the hospital, he would pay for it.

And somewhere in the middle of the joyful chaos of the children I realized what had been so different.

I had finally realized just how deeply I loved this man.

Neither of us spoke for most of the trip on the way back home. Finally I broke the silence. "You think David will be all right?" I asked.

He nodded.

"What did he say to you?"

Joe glanced at me, and then turned his attention back to the road.

I bit my lip, and looked out my window. I should know better than to ask him to reveal the secrets of a little boy.

"He told me he saw love in your eyes," Joe said.

I looked down at my hands, and then looked at him. "And what did you say to him?"

He stopped the car, pulled the key out, and turned to me. "I told him I saw it too."

I blushed.

Joe didn't start the car again. "I also told him it was what I had been waiting for."

I turned to him, confused. "Waiting to do what?"

"I never told you why I came here," Joe said. "To Backus, I mean. I think," he hesitated, looked at me, and began again. "I think you should know. I warn you; it's embarrassing for me."

"You told me there was nothing left for you in your original town," I said, not sure why that would embarrass him.

"Yes, and that's true; there isn't. But I could have made my home anywhere. I could have stayed there, or I could have gone to another town I have family in."

I nodded, urging him to continue.

"Well first things first. My parents lived in Afton with me. They died in a fire a few months before I came here. I had been gone that night. I went to a bash they had told me to stay home from. If I had been home," he trailed off.

I put a hand on his, which was sitting on the gearshift.

He took a deep breath and continued. "I've always felt I could have helped them if I had been there."

"Or," I said softly, "you could have been killed right alongside them."

"That's another possibility," he said. "I've learned not to keep thinking about the way things might have been, though. Things are the way that they are for a reason, even when you can't see what that reason is; even when nothing makes sense."

I nodded.

"The fire consumed the entire house...including the letters I received from Margaret." He turned his hand up and interlaced his fingers with mine. "I'm not sure if you knew this, but we wrote back and forth for years. She knows all my secrets. You want to learn anything about me at all, ask Margaret; she'll probably know the answer."

I nodded again.

"Well, one thing those letters contained were descriptions of you. You were her best friend; naturally she told me all about you. She wrote about what the two of you did together, and how much she enjoyed spending time with you and how much she admired you. You know. Anything you would say about someone that you were close to."

"Yeah."

Joe blushed a little. "At first I just read her descriptions of you the way that she meant them: as a friend my cousin got along well with. Eventually, though, I realized that you were someone I really wanted to meet. And the more she told me, the stronger that feeling became."

He paused.

"Yes?" I said, hoping the simple word would be enough for him to continue.

It was. "When I said we had been writing for years," Joe said, "I don't think that fully encompasses just how long those letters dated back. We started writing when I was ten years old."

He hesitated again. I looked at him, and squeezed his hand a little, urging him to continue.

"That was when I first met Margaret," he said, "when I was ten. And that is also when I first saw you."

"I don't remember meeting you then," I said.

"You didn't. I was a shy little boy and couldn't bring myself to talk to you. But I saw you, and I wanted to talk." He shrugged. "Just to see what you were like. I was ten, and I hadn't yet figured out that girls could be better than just people who were easy to make fun of."

I giggled.

"Years later, when Margaret was describing you in her letters, I realized that girl was you. There could be no other girl with the beautiful blonde curls she described, and as the girl in the cemetery had."

"You saw me at the cemetery?"

He nodded. "You were there writing. You looked so calm and peaceful that the memory of it has stuck with me all this time. You do love the cemetery, don't you?"

"It's where I go to think. Hardly anyone disturbs me there, except you sometimes." I winked. "It's the ideal place to go when I want to write, or just think and pray. I love it."

Joe smiled. "So, Ella," he hesitated again. "What I'm saying is, *you* are the reason that I came to Backus."

I stared at him.

"And that is exactly why I didn't tell you this before." He chuckled a little awkwardly, probably trying to change the mood.

I smiled. "You are so strange sometimes, Joe," I said.

He smiled. "I am...but you love me anyway."

"Yes, I do," I said.

Now he stared at me.

I said it plainly: "I love you, Joseph Blake."

Joe grinned and got out of the car. It was only when he opened my door that I realized he had parked in front of the cemetery.

He led me to the middle of the graveyard and took both my hands in his. Looking me right in the eyes, with the grin still in place but intensity in his eyes I had never seen before, he said, "Say it again?"

I giggled. "I love you, Joe." I looked at him, smiling at the way his eyes lit up again, even having heard it only a moment before.

In an instant, he was on one knee, holding a small box out in front of me. "Ella Christiana Mitchell, I love you with my whole heart and have been falling more in love with you for quite some time. I don't want to spend another moment apart from you. Will you marry me?"

I stared at him, grinned, and nodded to say what my voice was currently failing to. "Yes, Joe; oh yes!" I said finally.

He grinned and slipped the ring, a beautiful silver band with flowers made of pearls and sapphires decorating the center of it, onto my finger.

"Joe," I hesitated, but his gentle look urged me to continue, "I need you to promise me something."

"Anything. Except the moon; that could be hard to accomplish."

I giggled a little.

Joe turned serious. "What is it, Ella?"

"Promise me," I said, blushing a little, "promise you'll be with me for at least fifty years." My insecurities were coming through; I wanted an assurance this would last.

He looked a little surprised at my request, but smiled and said, "I won't leave you, Ella." He stood, keeping hold of my hand, and I stood too. Leaning close and wrapping his free arm around my back, he pulled me into a kiss.

I felt my legs grow weak as I kissed him in return.

Chapter 18

Saturday, January 17, 2009
Jane Blake

Bev, Rosie and I sat on the floor in the Tyler's living room, looking through the scrapbook again. By this point I had read the articles and letters and seen the photos several times, but I would probably never get tired of it.

I hadn't seen a lot of the sweet, romantic side of my grandpa before. He and Grandma held hands often, and kissed when they thought we kids wouldn't notice, but mostly I had seen Grandpa Blake as a big tease. His favorite thing to do was make people laugh, and he was good at it.

After seeing this other side of him, I loved him all the more. Grandma had been so blessed; and she knew it.

Rosie pointed to one of the articles. "Hey, did you notice this?" she asked.

I looked at the article she was pointing to. It was about a play my grandparents had put on and starred in. Mr. Jensen and his wife Etty had been in it, too.

The article claimed that the play was the beginning of Jensen and Etty's relationship, but Grandma had warned me not to believe the majority of what was printed in the paper. Besides, the wording in the article didn't lend itself to believability:

> **All this author knows is that Nicholas and Margaret were not dating before the play began, and now they are. Could it be there was more romance happening behind the stage than on it?**

"I read that one," I said. "What about it?"

"What about it?" Rosie mimicked incredulously. "It's your chance to read something your grandma wrote!"

I looked at her, confused. "Grandma Blake didn't write that article," I said. "There are others she wrote in there, but that's not one of them."

"Oh, I know," Rosie said, shaking her head in impatience. "That's not what I'm talking about. You know she couldn't have been passionate about writing those articles—she wrote them because she wanted to give the *Backus Brochure* some credibility."

Bev slipped the scrapbook off Rosie's lap and read the article, to attempt to figure out what Rosie was trying to say.

I ran a hand through my hair. "I don't think I understand," I said.

Rosie groaned loudly.

Mrs. Tyler peeked her head out of the computer room, where she'd been reading a book. "You okay in there?" Seeing that no one was hurt or upset to tears, she returned to her book without waiting for a response.

"Just peachy," Rosie said. "Jane and Bev seem to be purposely misunderstanding me, that's all." She frowned in our direction.

"That must be frustrating," Mrs. Tyler said, though her tone was distracted.

Bev passed the scrapbook to me and pointed to one of the phrases in the article. "Bet this is what she's all excited about."

> **The play was called "These Treasured Memories" and was written by our very own Ella Mitchell.**

"That was your grandma's name before she married your grandpa, wasn't it?"

I nodded.

"The script must be around somewhere," Rosie said. "How cool would it be to read that? Would you mind if Bev and I read it? If you find out where it's hiding, that is."

"Sure," I said, "I mean—I don't care. I just don't know where to even look for it."

"If it was used for the play," Bevin said, sitting up straighter, "there had to have been several copies of it made. Right?"

Rosie nodded energetically. "So we're sure to find at least one!"

"But where?" I asked.

"The school library," Rosie declared. "I bet they have a copy. And if there isn't one, we could ask Mr. Larsen if he still has his. According to the article, he was in it, too."

Convinced that we had formed a good plan, we set out to find the missing scripts. We found them much more quickly than I had expected, in the school library. Three copies of *These Treasured Memories* were placed with various other scripts, including some by Shakespeare and Oscar Wilde.

"I wonder if your grandma knows her writing shares a shelf with literature greats!" Rosie giggled. "I told you your grandma is impressive."

All of the scripts were riddled with writing in the margins.

"Jane?" Bev pointed to one of them.

I picked it up, smiling, and fingered the handwritten name at the top: Joe Blake. It was Grandpa's copy.

We took that and another of the scripts, leaving one in case someone else had the urge to read it, and went back to Rosie and Bevin's house to read and act it out.

We hadn't quite reached the Tyler's house when I heard footsteps pounding on the sidewalk. We turned to find Kyle running toward us. He was out of breath, from more than just the short run it had taken him to get to us, and was shaking.

"Kyle? What is it?" I asked.

Rosie, concerned, tried to direct him to a nearby front step, to give him a chance to relax a little and explain what was wrong. He shook his head at her gesture, and held up a hand as he took a few deep breaths, indicating he was in a hurry and had something to say.

"Grandma—" he finally managed, "something's wrong."

I started walking toward Kyle's house and the others followed, as Kyle continued.

"I," he took a deep breath, "I called 911."

Our pace changed from a walk, to a jog, and ultimately to an urgent run toward his house. Kyle let us in, and Rosie went directly to Grandma Carol. *Did we lose Bev on the way here?*

Grandma Carol was lying on the couch, wrapped in blankets, and coughing up a dark liquid that must have been blood. She seemed to be having difficulty breathing.

Rosie knelt beside her, to see how to make her more comfortable until the EMTs arrived. She turned to Kyle. "I need you to be calm right now. Your grandma needs you to be calm."

Kyle nodded, though he kept shuddering. I wanted to comfort him somehow, but could force myself to do nothing but watch.

Rosie continued. "Have you noticed any other symptoms? How long has this been going on?"

He hesitated. "She complained of chest pain this past week." He frowned. "She always changed the subject right after, so I didn't think," he trailed off.

"That's fine," Rosie said gently. "I'm not pointing fingers. I just want to know what to tell the EMTs when they arrive. Is there anything else that might be important?"

"I don't know," he said, flustered. "I don't think so. I mean, she's been tired. But she's in her 80s," he trailed off again.

Rosie nodded. "And when did the coughing start?"

"She's had a small cough for the past couple weeks. But it wasn't anything," he paused. "But it got bad today."

Bev entered the room from the kitchen and handed Kyle a cup of tea, ordering him to drink it. "Breathe," he said.

I stood numbly by and watched the siblings work together to calm Kyle and keep his grandma comfortable. I could do nothing but attempt a prayer.

Soon, sirens were heard, and the EMTs rushed inside. We stayed out of their way as they gave Grandma Carol an oxygen mask and moved her to the back of the ambulance. Rosie gave them the important info. Kyle was allowed to ride in the front, to be there when she was brought in, and on hand if she needed comfort.

Rosie, Bev, and I watched them go, lights flashing.

"It's times like this I wish I'd gotten my license," Rosie sighed.

The hospital was 30 miles away, in Park Rapids: much too far to walk.

"I have mine," I said.

"You do?"

I nodded, walking quickly toward my house, and glad of the ability to help. "Got it before I moved here. Meet me at my garage."

We told our parents what had happened and where we were going, and soon we were on our way to the hospital.

The lady at the front desk directed us to the waiting room, where she said Kyle would probably be. I spotted him as we entered.

He didn't notice us walk in, and in fact didn't notice until we sat next to him and patted his shoulder.

Kyle gave a little jump. "Jane?"

I smiled a little. "Hey Kyle."

He looked at Bevin and Rosie.

"You didn't really think we'd let you stay here alone, did you? We thought you could use some friends." I hesitated, biting my lip. "How is Grandma Carol?"

He shrugged. "They don't know a whole lot, and that worries me. I thought doctors were trained to discover what the problems were." He looked down at his hands.

I gave him a side hug. "We've been praying for her the whole way here. My parents are praying too."

Kyle nodded.

"God would listen to you, too, if you wanted to pray," I said gently.

He shook his head.

242

Bev sat on the other side of him and Rosie sat next to me.

"Thank you," Kyle said, looking at each of us. "Thank you for coming. I didn't know how much, but I do need friends right now."

We smiled a little. Rosie jumped up and found a puzzle in one of the waiting room cupboards. She emptied the box onto a table and motioned for the rest of us to join her in putting it together. I had never realized how good Rosie would be in a stressful situation. She and Bevin both had more strength and calm than I could have hoped for, and knew exactly what was needed.

After a while, Kyle left to see if there was anything more the doctors could tell him, and Bev went with for emotional support.

Rosie watched them go. She frowned. "Poor Kyle. Grandma Carol has basically been a mother to him since his own parents left. I don't want to see him lose her, too." She sighed. "Things like this either force you to trust in God's strength, or turn you away from Him. And his faith is already so shaky, or nonexistent."

I nodded. "You lost your mom," I said slowly. "How did you handle it?"

Rosie frowned. "There is a reason I don't talk about that part of my life much," she said. "I was at my worst. I wish I could say my faith grew stronger, but it didn't. Bev's did. Bevin has an inner strength that is to be envied."

I nodded; I had seen glimpses of it today.

"He took the news of mom's death just as hard as the rest of us, but he relied on God for comfort." She frowned, shaking her head. "I couldn't do that. I was angry with God for allowing her to die. I was angry with Him for leaving us without a mother."

I put an arm around her shoulders.

"When my step-mother came into the picture," she continued, "I was angry with Him for letting Dad find someone to replace Mom. Bev tried to help me, but I pushed him away, too. I said I wanted to be alone, but you know me," she said, smirking a little. "I'm a people person. I needed people then more than I ever had before." She rubbed her arm. "Telling everyone to give me space only made things worse. It gave me more time to wallow in self pity and focus on my anger."

"You're not still angry though;" I said, "you're one of the happiest people I know. What changed?"

"Mostly," she said, "*I* changed." She shook her head as though disgusted at her old self. "God helped me see how self-centered I was being. His patience with me during that time let me see that none of it, after all, was His fault. Yes, He allowed it," she paused, fingering one of the puzzle pieces, "but I would much rather have a God who allows bad things to happen than one who controls every action we take. Besides, the whole point of earth is that it is a fallen place, and that's why we need God. And, you know, I am slightly jealous of mom now. She gets to be in heaven with God so much sooner than the rest of us." She smiled a little. "And I know she's happy."

Bevin and Kyle returned, bringing with them four hot cups of coffee, but no news.

A little while later, a nurse came to bring Kyle to see Grandma Carol. She asked that the rest of us remain behind, saying she only needed Kyle to confirm some things and let his grandma know what would be happening in the next few days.

As Kyle left, a young lady, probably a little older than me, walked into the waiting room and sat down. She started picking at her nails. I glanced at Rosie.

Rosie had noticed her too. I bit my lip, wishing that talking to strangers came easier for me than it did. Now would be the perfect time to do it.

Another nurse came in and spoke to the girl in hushed tones too quiet for us to hear completely. I heard something about cancer and not catching it. It was enough to know that this was not welcome news. The girl had already been on the verge of tears. Soon, the nurse left the room but the girl remained in her seat, staring at her hands.

Rosie stood and walked to her. "Hi," she said, gently. "I'm Rosie—and that's my friend, Jane, and my brother Bevin."

The girl nodded in acknowledgment, but said nothing.

"I just hate hospitals, don't you? I know they're supposed to help people, but did you ever notice that there are more sick people in a hospital than there are anywhere else in the world?"

The girl smiled.

Rosie sat down next to her without waiting for permission. "I avoided hospitals for a really long time after the last time I came in here. This might be the first time I've been in a hospital since then." Her tone grew gentler and she looked with compassion at the girl as she continued. "My mom died in a place like this. I kind of held it against the hospital itself for a while, but I know it wasn't their fault. It was simply an incurable disease. Who are you here for?"

"My mom," the girl said quietly, the first words any of us had heard her speak. She hadn't even spoken to the nurse; she just nodded like she understood, but wished she didn't.

"Is she going to be all right?" Rosie asked, knowing the answer likely wasn't good.

The girl shrugged. "I don't know. I mean, the nurse doesn't know. It doesn't look good, and the surgery they have to do is risky," she trailed off.

Rosie put an arm around the girl.

The girl leaned into Rosie and took a deep breath. "They said she has cancer. That's not even what she was in there for. They have to get rid of it, but it's dangerous." She paused.

Bev and I stepped closer and joined Rosie in the seats next to the girl. I put a hand gently on her shoulder.

She looked at us gratefully, and continued. "They don't know if they'll be able to get it all and if they don't, it's the end, and—" her voice cracked and the tears she'd been fighting came through, "it just can't be the end yet. I'm not ready for that."

Rosie pulled her into a hug. "Would you like me to pray for her?"

She gave a slight nod.

We all closed our eyes and Rosie started praying.

The prayer ended and the girl looked up at us with tear-glistened eyes. She didn't say thank you with her voice, but her eyes spoke with more clarity than any words could have. "I'm Carly," she said at last, and wiped away her tears with the back of her hand.

Rosie asked if she would like to join us in putting the puzzle together, and Carly said she would.

Soon, Kyle returned to the room, worry still etched in his features. "Grandma Carol is doing well, considering," he said. "The doctors found the problem," he trailed off, and glanced at Carly, noticing her for the first time.

"She's a friend," Rosie said.

He nodded and continued, his voice faltering a little. "She has lung cancer."

My heart sank. Grandpa Blake had died from that. *Please God—don't take Grandma Carol. Don't take the only person Kyle has left.*

Kyle sighed. "It was hard enough when Grandpa Michael died, and I wasn't very close to him."

"What are the doctors doing for your grandma, Kyle?" Rosie asked.

"They seem optimistic," he said. "Tomorrow they're going to perform surgery and attempt to remove the cancer. If that doesn't work, they might try chemotherapy."

It was getting late, so we had to go back home. I offered Kyle a ride, but he refused.

"How do you plan to get home?" Bev asked.

Kyle just shrugged. "I guess I'll just stay here. They don't mind if you spend the night."

Rosie looked around at the waiting room. "These chairs are not made for sleeping in," she commented.

"Yeah," he sighed, "but I probably won't be doing a whole lot of sleeping anyway."

We hugged him and promised to return the next morning.

When I got home, Mom told me Grandma Blake had called. I glanced at the clock. 8pm. Not too late to call her back.

"Jane!" Grandma said. "I've been missing your cooking each night."

I smiled. "You called just to tell me that?"

"No; I always have ulterior motives in my phone calls. I'm not your grandpa, after all."

I giggled. "What's the ulterior motive this time?"

"First, how are Kyle and his grandma doing?"

"Okay, I guess." I took a deep breath. "She has lung cancer, but they think they can remove it."

Grandma Blake was quiet for a while.

"Grandma?"

"Next time I'm going to give you my good news *before* I ask for your bad news."

I chuckled a little. "What's the good news?"

"Nicholas has asked me to marry him!" She couldn't keep the excitement out of her voice.

"Oh, Grandma! What did you say?"

"What do you *think* I said?"

Her excitement was contagious. I giggled. "Does this mean I have to start calling you Grandma Jensen? I'm not sure I could do that."

"Absolutely not!" She seemed offended by the very idea. "I would never give up Joe's name."

I smiled. "When is the wedding?"

"Next month."

"So soon?" I opened my cell phone calendar to mark the date.

"It won't be a big one," Grandma said. "No extra fancy clothes or anything. But we'd like you to be there."

"And see my grandma marry a wonderful man who will keep her happy and show her love *almost* as well as Grandpa did?" I smiled. "You think I would miss it?"

Grandma Blake giggled.

"Hey Grandma," I said. "Kyle's related to us."

She was quiet for a moment, and then said, "Yes; I know."

"Well why didn't you say anything?"

"At first I wasn't certain he was Michael's grandson. Then I knew, but he didn't seem to. I had intended to talk to his grandma and tell you when she told him, but clearly that didn't happen."

"So Grandma Carol is Uncle Michael's second wife?"

"Yes. Kyle was ten when Michael and Carol were married, and had been living with Carol for about a year. Kyle's dad walked out one day and never came back. His mom tried to be strong, but eventually, she too left: on a fool's errand to find the runaway father. She hasn't been back since. Michael was a good father figure for Kyle, but they only knew each other for a few years before he died. That left Kyle to be raised by Carol—but of course, Carol isn't doing well herself. I think Kyle does more care of her than she does of him."

The surgery the next day went well. Rosie, Bev and I formed a circle and prayed for Kyle's Grandma Carol, and also for Carly and her mom.

The doctor told us we could see her. They believed the surgery had been successful. Still, it wasn't *all* good news. Grandma Carol had another disease that was incurable: Alzheimer's. We should have seen the signs earlier.

We gave Kyle hugs of support and followed him to Grandma Carol's room.

She was a little drowsy and unresponsive at first, but eventually grew as talkative as we were used to.

"Kyle, boy, how is that bratty neighbor kid?"

"Freddie?"

"Yes, Freddie." She scrunched her nose and shook her head. "I tossed a grape at him."

"A grape?" I asked.

"It would have been an apple, but Kyle has officially declared apples off limits to me. Can you believe that? No wonder I am in the hospital. My own grandson is keeping me away from the one thing that has been guaranteed to keep doctors away!"

We giggled.

Grandma Carol continued. "I threw the grape at him because he was traipsing across my lawn and killing all my dandelions, and I didn't much appreciate that. Well, he didn't much appreciate the grape." She shook her head and made a face at the memory. "The wimp, it didn't even touch him. He just didn't like that something was thrown in the direction of his exceedingly large head."

Yes, Grandma Carol was back to her normal self.

Chapter 19

Mitchell - Blake *Monday, May 14th, 1956*

Ella Mitchell
Joseph Blake

Ella Mitchell and Joseph Blake are planning a May 18th wedding in the woods behind their new home (better known as Old Granny Mara's place).

> The bride-to-be is the daughter of Adam
> and Jane Mitchell, residents of Backus,
> MN. The prospective bridegroom is the
> son of William and Helen Blake (both
> deceased), of Afton, NY.
>
> Ella and Joe have both been working in
> our town diner for years now; Ella
> began while still in high school, and
> Joe started when he moved here in 1953.
> When asked about their plans for the
> future, the couple had this to say: "No
> comment."
>
> Who will be next? This author suspects
> young lovebirds Nicholas and Margaret
> will have news to share in a very short
> while.

Friday, May 18, 1956
Ella Mitchell

After more than a year of preparation, the day of
the wedding had arrived.

Margaret helped me into the dress she had made:
beautifully designed, with fabric flowers decorating
the rounded neckline, a lacy overlay and a knee-
length skirt that would be perfect for the swing
dancing that would follow the ceremony. The short
sleeves, made of a soft translucent fabric, draped
gracefully over my shoulders.

"You're gorgeous, Ella," Margaret smoothed the
skirt of my dress. "I know I pester Joe for stealing
you so often, but I really am happy for you both."

I busied myself by softening my curls. My hair
was threatening to turn frizzy.

"Seriously," Margaret continued, trying to gain my attention. "You have grown so much these past few years, and so has Joe, and I know it's because of the time you've spent together."

I nodded.

"If it was anyone else, Ella, I couldn't let you do it. Either of you. You know me, I'm jealous of any time spent away from me."

A smile crept across my face. "You know you're not nearly as jealous as you pretend to be, Maggie."

"No? I suppose not. I do miss the time we used to have, though, and I'm sincere when I say I couldn't give that up for anyone but Joe. If anyone could deserve you, it's him."

I shook my head. "It isn't about either of us deserving the other. It can't be—or I would be in big trouble."

Margaret opened her mouth to object, but I continued.

"Joe is..."

Mother and Linda entered with the veil and makeup.

"Ready?" Mother asked, then put a hand to her mouth. "Oh Ella, your hair." She frowned and set the veil on the table. "Let's just pin this up," she started moving my hair around.

"Mother, please. Joe likes it down—that's how I want it."

"It's frizzy, and it's in your eyes."

I shook my head. "I'm not worried about it. If he can't love me with frizzy hair, our relationship is in serious trouble."

Mother smiled a little. "Okay. You're right."

I turned to her, surprised.

"I just want everything to be perfect for you today," she said. "But you are my beautiful daughter, you look wonderful, and I'm not going to mar your happiness by being picky." She put a hand on my cheek and kissed my forehead, then gently, laughing, rubbed off the lipstick mark she'd created.

I smiled and hugged her. This was a side I had rarely seen. I supposed I'd always known she cared for me, but actually seeing that wasn't something I was used to. Part of me wanted to be bitter and question why she couldn't have shown that same affection all through the years... but I had to simply accept that she hadn't. Accept it, and enjoy this small moment.

Mother put my veil in place and arranged my loose curls around it as Linda applied lipstick.

"You certainly don't need any extra blush today," Linda said, grinning.

Margaret fixed my dress where the hug had rumpled it.

Between the three of them, I felt like a princess with overly fussy ladies-in-waiting; not a role I had ever hoped to play.

I hadn't seen Joe yet, and I was anxious to. Tradition of course dictated that we would not see each other until the moment I was walking toward him through the church—which in this case, was actually the outdoors. I fidgeted, pushed a curl behind my ear, and wiped off some of the makeup.

Linda frowned, pulled the curl out again and dabbed on more makeup where I'd removed it. "Stop ruining our beautiful work, Ella."

I rolled my eyes, and smoothed out the dress, glancing in the mirror and biting my lip. "Margaret, do you have a cigarette with you?"

"No," she shook her head, "sorry, Ella."

I sighed, and pushed the curl behind my ear once more.

"You don't need that foul thing anyway," Mother said, as she stubbornly returned the curl to its visible place in front of my ear. "Those cigarettes of yours make me cough so much. Sometimes I wonder if Nicholas is the only smart one among you. I always liked that boy...he never cared to even try smoking."

I shrugged. Uncle Bruce was the only one who really objected to cigarettes, and all he said is that inhaling smoke couldn't be healthy. He had nothing to back up that claim. They did make us cough sometimes, but that was normal, and you got used to it.

Margaret put an arm around me. "My cousin is so blessed to have you."

I shook my head. "I'm the one who's blessed."

Margaret smiled. "You both are. And as long as you don't forget that, you will continue to be."

I raised an eyebrow at her. "You think God stops giving good things to people when they forget they've been blessed?"

"No, silly; but people stop recognizing what He does give."

That made sense. *Knowing Joe, I'm sure he'll keep his focus on the good things we've been given, and he can help me do the same. He already has.*

"Ella."

Mother's no-nonsense voice demanded my attention.

"You have nothing to be nervous about."

I nodded, but wasn't convinced.

"Joe is a genuine, good guy, and he's clearly in love with you—and you with him. I couldn't ask for better for my oldest daughter." Mother smiled. "But that's enough mushy nonsense. Everyone's waiting for you."

Mother directed me out the door.

Margaret gave my hand an encouraging squeeze. "Go make my cousin the happiest guy in the world," she whispered before she took her place beside Nicholas.

The outdoor wedding we had decided on was simple but beautiful; we didn't need something big and fancy. People sat in folding chairs, facing where

Joe was standing with a backdrop of the woods behind him.

I slipped my arm through my father's. He kissed my cheek and told me I looked beautiful. I turned and hugged him.

The music began: my cue to step forward from behind the nearby house that was keeping me hidden. Dad smoothed my dress and veil—which actually messed it up more, but I didn't mind.

"There's still time to back out," he whispered, with a wink.

I scrunched my nose at the playfully meant suggestion, and smiled.

He patted my hand and together we walked to the front.

Joe grinned when he saw me. Everyone turned and watched as my father and I stepped closer to him, and Dad released me into Joe's waiting hands.

Our vows now spoken, Davey, who we would officially adopt once the wedding ended, held out the rings to us.

Joe took mine, a twisted gold and silver band with an arrangement of diamonds around it, and gently placed it on my finger. I did the same with his.

Davey held his little arms up to us, and we both hugged him before he went back to his seat in the audience.

It began to rain as Joe and I were declared husband and wife, and we shared a kiss as a slightly wet married couple.

The entire town ran to the school gym for the reception.

I had never seen the gym look that beautiful before. Margaret had somehow made time between sewing my dress and teaching dance at the school to lead the decorating. The result was gorgeous.

They had draped sheer white fabric all around; there was a huge punch bowl, the beautiful tiered cake Uncle Bruce had created—cliché but somehow unique in its swirling design—and plenty of food, also provided by Uncle Bruce.

Soon the gym was filled, and people began to eat, talk, and of course dance.

We filled out the paperwork to make both the wedding and the adoption official.

Wednesday, March 3rd, 1965

Joe packed the rest of our food in the last remaining box: a small one with a handful of other knickknacks that had been missed in the rest of our packing. "Are you certain you want to do this?" he asked. "We can put everything back and stay here if you're not."

"I'm sure," I said. "I'm very sure. I'm over 30, Joe. I wanted to be out of here before I was even 20." *I need to get away from the memories this place brings.*

Joe picked up the box and handed it to Davey, now fourteen, to bring to the car.

"Besides," I continued, "we can't keep living off your inheritance, and as much as I love Uncle Bruce and know he's being as generous as he can afford to be, he's not paying you enough to support us."

Robbie came into the kitchen, clutching his plastic dinosaur. I took his hand and we walked outside. "You're a good businessman, Joe," I continued. "People are drawn to you. You said you had begun to get involved in that in New York. You can do it again."

Joe looked around the now-empty house and took my hand. He kissed me and smiled. "You always were the practical one. Ready for the next part in our journey?"

I nodded, smiling.

We had hoped that Nicholas, Linda, and even Eric, who we had grown closer to in the past few years, would consider joining us in the twin cities. Nicholas had as many painful memories as Joe and I did. It would have been good for him to go someplace where he wouldn't constantly be reminded of all he had lost.

I could no longer be in places that reminded me of the friend I had lost...my dear Margaret. Her death had been sudden; jolting. Even more than two years after it happened, tears came on an almost daily basis. I knew it had to be even worse for Nicholas, who had enjoyed less than five years as her husband before the illness hit, but he refused to leave Uncle Bruce.

Linda also chose to stay in Backus, for her own...romantic reasons.

Eric simply didn't want to leave Backus. His sister Sally had married, and he had a young niece whose life he wanted to be a part of. Romance, he said, wasn't something he cared to have.

We said final goodbyes and promised visits; after all, we would only be three hours away. Joe started the moving truck, and we were on our way to our new home.

That night, we hauled the final boxes in, and stepped outside once more to admire the new, larger house. Without warning, Joe lifted me up and, grinning, carried me through the front door.

I giggled.

He kissed me as he set me down again. "Always wanted to do that," he said. "I don't care if it *is* cliché."

I smiled and hugged him. "I love you, Joe."

"Say it again?"

I giggled at the way those words always lit him up, no matter how often I repeated them. I kissed him. "I love you."

He kissed me a third time. "I love you too, my beautiful El Bell."

"Yuck," Robbie said, watching from the door of his new room.

Davey stood beside him, and nodded in agreement. "Too much love going on in this house right now."

Joe chuckled and motioned them over. "I love my Davey and Robbie, too," he said as we bent to their level and pulled them into hugs.

"We're going to be happy here," Joe said confidently.

"If we're lucky," I said.

"Luck has a very small job in life," he said, smiling, "aside from turning smart people into fools. Life is a series of choices, love, and very special people."

Chapter 20

Sunday, June 14, 2009
Jane Blake

My grandma will never forget the first time she met her eventual husband, Joe Blake. She had been writing in the cemetery when he interrupted her. (Don't judge; it's my favorite place too.) In 1953, the bench hadn't been put into place yet, so Grandma Blake (you may know her as Ella) sat instead on the ground, leaning against one of the headstones.

Grandpa Joe, in his typical quirky fashion, chose to make the situation as uncomfortable as he could.

"So, um...this is awkward, but...that's my grandma you're sitting on." But he said it with a smile.

To say my grandma was embarrassed would be an understatement.

In spite of this strange beginning, my grandparents had a love story I have always hoped my own would emulate. It wasn't until recently, however, that I began to learn exactly how it had come about. It wasn't the fairytale I had envisioned.

When my grandma first met Joe, she was hoping he would move back where he had come from: Afton, NY. She made no secret of that fact, but grandpa was determined. He stayed in Backus, and soon fell in love with the town and the people, including my stubborn and sometimes frustrating grandma, Ella.

Feelings of friendship turned to more, and Joe pursued her in spite of every indication she didn't share his love. His persistence paid off; when he asked Ella on a date, she happily accepted.

As they began going out, misunderstandings and disagreements arose. Most people would have given up. They would have declared that if their love was really meant to be, it wouldn't be so difficult. I doubt my grandpa ever heard that true love didn't require work, and if someone had told him so, he would have laughed in their face.

My grandparents' love story didn't begin like a fairy tale, and it didn't finish with a happy ending. Grandpa died too soon for any of us, when all his years of smoking translated into lung cancer.

Their relationship was far from perfect, but its imperfections are part of what makes it beautiful. What hero hasn't had obstacles to overcome? They wouldn't be heroes if they were never given something to fight for. And what princess or even average girl doesn't want to be reminded they're worth it?

As I learned more about my grandparents' lives, I only grew more determined to wait for the man who would treat me the way Joe treated Ella. I will wait for the man who will not back out when things get rough or I get cranky; the man who will fight through it because, in his eyes, I'm worth it.

My grandma once said of the people here in Backus, "We have nothing but our memories." I would like to challenge

that. Memories are part of what shape
us, but they're not all we have. We
have a beautiful future, too, just
waiting for us to embrace it.

About the Author

Jansina has been writing ever since she could do more than make meaningless scribbles with a crayon. Her first serious writing career was at the age of 13, a newspaper column called *Jansina's Journal*. It ran for 6 years. Also at age 13, a college professor recognized her talent in writing and requested she tutor; something she has done ever since.

Her goal is to create realistic Christian fiction for young adults that will both entertain and inspire. This is her first published novel, though she has over one hundred published articles, short stories and poems in various newspapers and magazines (including the *Saint Paul Pioneer Press* and *Brio*).

She is a native of Minnesota, and a few years ago discovered Backus, a little-known town of 300. Although she may never live there herself, she lives vicariously through her characters. Jansina is in the process of writing two additional novels, and several short stories—all with the setting loosely based on that little town. Many of the characters in *Forgotten Memories* play larger parts in those stories.

When not writing, Jansina works in marketing, and also copy edits others' books, scholarly papers, and articles. In her spare time she enjoys Irish and swing dancing, singing, and rereading Austen's novels. She doesn't spend much time in cemeteries.

10368213R00171

Made in the USA
Charleston, SC
29 November 2011